PRAISE FOR B

The Liar's Guide to the Night Sky

"*The Liar's Guide to the Night Sky* is Shrum's best book to date; a survival tale lit with sparks. A winter thriller that combines witty dialogue with a slow-burning romance, Liar's Guide is the book every teen needs in their life this year. Shrum's plot hurtles forward unceasingly, and even the coldest readers will find their hearts lit by the romance between Hallie and Jonah." —Colleen Oakes, author of *The Black Coats*

"This clear-eyed examination of trust, sex, and family dynamics is enhanced by vivid, lucid prose and a thrilling plot." —*Publishers Weekly*

"An adventure that will keep readers wondering what will happen next. . . . While romance is a major factor of this novel, Shrum's frank, yet gentle, exploration of self-discovery on the side of a mountain make this stand out." —*School Library Journal*

Kissing Ezra Holtz (and Other Things I Did for Science)

"Realistic and will resonate with many teens. Give this to readers who love witty, humorous love stories mixed with STEM." —*Booklist*

"Predictable hate-becomes-love romance is given new life by an inclusive cast. . . . Worth picking up." —*Kirkus Reviews*

The Art of French Kissing

"Fun, flirty, foodie, and filled with way more heat than your average kitchen, *The Art of French Kissing* has all the ingredients for a perfect summer romance!" —Dahlia Adler, author of *Behind the Scenes*

"I ate up this hate-to-love-and-back-again romance! If you love *Top Chef* but wish more of the show was focused on the romance and rivalries behind the scenes, you'll eagerly devour *The Art of French Kissing*. Like the best sweet and savory pastries, Carter and Reid deliver both sugar and spice." —Amy Spalding, author of *The Summer of Jordi Perez (and the Best Burger in Los Angeles)*

"This meet-cute romance stands out thanks to the nuanced characters and subtle treatment of bigger issues such as race, gender, and money (Carter's family flirts with poverty). . . . A thoughtful and delicious romance." —*Kirkus Reviews*

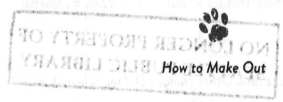

How to Make Out

"An addictive mix of heart, humor, and hot. *How to Make Out* is the perfect lesson in how to fall in love with YA romance." —Gina Ciocca, author of *Last Year's Mistake*

"How to write a seriously addictive book? Mission accomplished. Smart, hilarious, and un-put-down-able, *How* to *Make Out* will capture readers' hearts." —Laurie Elizabeth Flynn, author of *Firsts*

"Full of humor, heart, and some serious chemistry, *How to Make Out* is a fun and romantic read with dynamic characters I won't soon forget." —Chantele Sedgwick, author of *Love, Lucas*

"This is a story with an obvious lesson to it, but the lesson is delivered in an entertaining manner and will be an easy sell to teen girls." —*VOYA Magazine*

"This laugh-out-loud coming-of-age novel engages readers immediately and never lets go . . ." —*School Library Journal*

REBEL BOYS

& RESCUE

DOGS

OR THINGS THAT KISS
WITH TEETH

ALSO BY BRIANNA R. SHRUM

Never, Never
How to Make Out
The Art of French Kissing
Kissing Ezra Holtz (and Other Things I Did for Science)
The Liar's Guide to the Night Sky

REBEL BOYS
& RESCUE
DOGS

OR THINGS THAT KISS
WITH TEETH

BRIANNA R. SHRUM

Sky Pony Press
New York

Sky Pony Press books may be purchased in bulk at special discounts for sales promotion, corporate gifts, fund-raising, or educational purposes. Special editions can also be created to specifications. For details, contact the Special Sales Department, Sky Pony Press, 307 West 36th Street, 11th Floor, New York, NY 10018 or info@skyhorsepublishing.com.

Sky Pony® is a registered trademark of Skyhorse Publishing, Inc.®, a Delaware corporation.

Visit our website at www.skyponypress.com.

10 9 8 7 6 5 4 3 2 1

Library of Congress Cataloging-in-Publication Data is available on file.

Cover design by Daniel Brount
Cover photo credit: Shutterstock
Edited by: Nicole Frail

Print ISBN: 978-1-5107-5782-0
Ebook ISBN: 978-1-5107-5783-7

Printed in the United States of America

For everyone except TERFS, Joanne

CHAPTER ONE

ON A MESS-OF-STRESS SCALE from one to ten, I'm somewhere between shredding my DIY manicure with my teeth and *I regret to inform you, Miss, but you've spilled the contents of a burrito down your shirt.*

I'm not kidding.

I've been working through this monstrous pile of documents for forty-five minutes with beans drying on my boobs.

I have bean breasts.

I don't care.

Well, I care a little.

I care enough to grimace each time I shift and feel the gritty squelch of thirty to one hundred bean carcasses making their way enthusiastically to second base.

I grit my teeth.

I can do this.

I've been here for four hours (three and change *before* the burrito disaster), and hell if I'm stopping now for something as petty as my own personal comfort.

I'm never like this, I swear. I can't believe my nail polish is flecking, that my shirt is probably stained, for gosh sake. Where people could potentially see. My hair is coming out of my bun and keeps falling in my eyes, and this is the biggest whirlwind of chaos I have been since the tenth grade when some jerk smoking in the gym (smoking! In the gym!) triggered the fire suppression system and drenched the room three hours before the homecoming dance I was on the planning committee for.

The point is, the school security cameras and probable dust mites in this room . . . are not seeing me at my best.

I blink at the bright orange atrocity before me, willing my eyes to interpret the lines written on it as something approaching English. But nothing can get me past the color. This is a professional application! Who turns in a *scholarship application* on *tangerine paper?*

I'll tell you who: someone who's not expecting to get it.

I roll my eyes and toss it in the trash to be shredded with a hundred other applications. If I can't read it, you didn't earn it.

And this scholarship? It's one you've got to *earn.*

It's a huge deal, the Wilkeson Scholarship. There's a bunch of rounds of service and academia and papers and everything, and at the end of it, one standout student gets twenty grand to jumpstart the service-oriented career of their dreams.

It's not even about school; it's about getting enough cash to really *start* something. Something that matters.

I mean, for a lot of the applicants (yours truly included), it's still about school. Nothing makes you stand out to Yale like sliding into school as a freshman with a guaranteed

Alumnus of Note placement on your back. And like . . . starting a charitable organization?

Check.

Done.

You're solid.

I'd kill for this opportunity, and so would a hundred fifty other kids, apparently.

We've already selected the top nine applicants. I was left with the remnant to figure out on my own, and I've chosen two more myself.

A committee member who wasn't me evaluated my application and gave me a spot, which, thank god. I would have been crushed if I hadn't been selected but *then* had to pick someone else. I've just been tasked with the final three.

Now it just comes down to one more.

The lights in the school are shutting down one by one as the janitorial staff finishes its rounds. I can hear the squeak of basketball shoes and the gym door opening and echoing as it slams shut after each group of sweaty athletes vacating the gym.

I'm so tired.

I'm here, blinking at words that are starting to swim together in front of me—just trying to keep my eyes peeled open. Here longer than the freaking student athletes and custodial staff.

I can't do this much longer.

I'll rot my own brain out or die trying.

I need sleep or a stiff drink.

(*Ha. As though I've ever tasted anything stronger than coffee in my entire life.*)

I shake my head.

No. You can do this, Riley.

Ten more apps to power through. Ten more and you're free.

I scrunch up my face and move through them.

There's a couple animal projects, a community garden—that might be nice.

The gym opens and closes in time with my sorting and it feels extra important with all that loud, echoey punctuation. The boys' basketball team cuts past the computer lab in shadows.

I want to be at *home*, god. Not here, assaulted by waves of boy sweat, slumped over a computer desk. But the wifi back at my place is spotty at best, if my brother even paid the bill this month, and I've got to get the final results emailed to Avery tonight.

So yeah. I suffer the squeaky tennis shoes and the sweat.

Someone stops in the doorway and I briefly glance at the application in my hand.

Ha. Oliver West? Oliver I-Forcibly-Commandeer-The-Sound-System-On-Tuesdays-And-Set-Livestock-Loose-In-The-Freshman-Hallway-To-Feel-Joy West? He's never taken anything seriously in his entire life. I don't even need to read his proposal to know it's going in the trash.

I toss it behind me and clear my throat. "Can I help y—"

The prim question dies on my lips.

Leaning in the doorway, one wiry arm propped on the frame, the other in his jeans pocket, crowding me from there, is McKinley High's starting point guard: Oliver.

Haha. Oh god.

His eyes are narrowed, and I don't know if it's the angle or the shadows in this computer lab that make them look so dark.

"Come again?" he says.

His voice is low, lower than it was last year. I haven't really talked to him since he started T, but god, the difference is remarkable.

"Uh," I say. "I just—can I help."

Oliver quirks an eyebrow.

Christ, his bone structure is a nightmare. The kind that all the novels say you'd cut yourself on. Just cut yourself on his cheekbones, nick an artery on the slip down his jaw, and bleed out on the floor. If the look on his face is any indication, I think he'd watch the life pulse out of me for a minute, shoot me a quick *It's been real, Riley*, and leave me to die.

"Can I help you?" I force out.

I follow his gaze to the trash can and heat floods my face.

Quickly and exaggeratedly, like someone who has not just been caught doing something wrong, I swipe another application from the dwindling pile and toss it on top of his.

"You gonna read that?" he says.

"I did."

"Yeah?"

I straighten and cross my left leg over my right. "Yes."

His mouth tips up. "What's it say?"

I stutter for a second. Then I manage to get myself under control. "That," I say, "is privileged information."

He affords the trash can another glance, then he looks back at my face.

He saw, he saw, he saw.

He saw, and he's daring me to admit it.

Or is he daring me to pretend I didn't?

I can't tell. All I know is that his eyes are glinting with challenge.

He doesn't look away from me, doesn't even blink, I don't think. If he does, I miss it. That's got to be murder on the eyes.

I'm withering under his gaze, absolutely collapsing with the weight of it. His eyes and that sure smirk and the smell of deodorant and rubber and—

"You smell like basketball," I say. It is quite against my will.

He blinks. "I'm sorry, I—what?"

I spread my fingers across the application in front of me and blink down at the chipping polish. I breathe—in through my nose, out through my mouth.

I say, as though the observation is entirely reasonable, nay, mundane, in its regularness, "You smell like basketball."

I meet his eyes when I say this.

This turns out to be a bad choice, but it means I can see the exact instant that Oliver West decides I am an idiot.

"I play basketball," he says.

"Yes."

He glances down at the carpet, brow furrowed. Just leaning there. All arms and offensive jaw and stupid, perfect hips. "Listen, I'm supposed to tell you to get out. Custodians are locking up."

"Oh," I say. "Oh, sure. I just—can I get five minutes? I've got some stuff to finish up, and—"

His gaze cuts to the trash can again and glances off me entirely. "Sure," he says.

This time, he spits it.

Shit, he *knows*.

"Thanks," I say, and he leaves. I keep glancing back at the applications in the garbage, like maybe I owe it to him to take a look.

But I don't! Why would I! Nothing in his app or in the pile that's left is going to beat that community garden.

I glance over the last few and I'm done and I feel good about it.

Great about it, even.

I feel fan-freaking-tastic about all my choices and I think they're specifically, deeply ethical, and I'm TIRED and is that such a crime?

No it isn't, and Oliver *West* of all people is not going to make me feel bad about this.

I add my three to the list of finalists—now twelve names long—and shoot it off to Avery, then shut down the computer and leave.

I don't look back to see if Oliver is waiting when I leave the building.

I'm free.

That's what matters.

I've given up so many nights to studying and volunteering and racking up extra-curricular after extra-curricular just so maybe, maybe I can get out of here and go to . . . I don't know. Yale.

It tastes funny in my mouth, even when I don't say it out loud. Like it's impossible. But I've worked for years to get it and it's not impossible.

I clutch the paper clip in my pocket.

It's not. Impossible.

That is what I've killed myself for, sacrificed a social life for, given up sleep and health and a hundred other things for: the hope that it is not impossible.

My phone buzzes on the way to the bus stop and I slide it out of my pocket.

It's my sister in the group chat. She says . . . she says something I, uh, can't believe would go in the family group chat.

I wait for the myriad WTF texts to come through, but they don't. Not before she texts again: *OMG SORRY LOL. That was for the boyfriend <tongue out winky face emoji>*

I stare up at the sky, petitioning the big genderless guy upstairs.

My older sister is sexting the family chat, one of my cousins is encouraging it (and the other cousin is in the group chat but not answering because they're in jail for another few days for something having to do with alcohol?). And my oldest sibling, my very responsible brother, is sophisticatedly on probation for this absolutely bizarre destruction-of-property phase he went through? I don't know—you wouldn't believe the amount of stuff he's destroyed or graffiti'd.

That—*that* group chat, and the look on every single teacher's face when I said I was the littlest Riley, *that* is what I've killed myself fighting.

IT'S NOT IMPOSSIBLE.

Not for me.

My teeth grind together and the bus pulls up.

That stupid group chat lights up.

I don't want to look.

I will feel too tired and dirty and . . . jealous.

Jealous that my sister is tired from whatever ridiculous stuff she's doing with her boyfriend and my brother has all these stories about brick artwork and . . . and . . . here I am. Red-eyed and wiped out in the school parking lot because I stayed out too late sifting through scholarship applications!

I ignore my phone.

I ignore it.

I *ignore* it.

Until I don't.

There's all these inside jokes lighting up my phone, and I'm so angry at all of them and at Oliver West because I screwed him over (yes, that makes me mad at him, I guess), and—

I get a new message as I board the bus and take an empty seat.

It's none of them; it's my best friend.

Alisha: *Come out and play?*

Something nice cracks open behind my ribs. I say, *When have I ever come out and play?*

Alisha: *Tonight. It's in the history books. I've traveled to the future and read them already.*

I blink down at it.

I don't have time.

When do I ever have time? She knows that. It's not in the cards for me.

I slick my hand back over my straight, blonde hair and stare out the window.

Oliver shoots me a look as he passes me in his truck, rolls his eyes, dismissing my very existence.

My phone buzzes. It's not Alisha; it's my mom: *The only one of you I can trust is Brynn!! *cry-laugh emoji, laughy sweaty emoji, cry-laugh emoji**

Something unfamiliar bubbles up in my chest. Something dangerous and angry.

I snort out this furious breath, fully intending to go home.

But when I move the wrong way, those beans, those *stupid beans*, squish into the band of my prettiest bra.

No, bean boobs.

NOT TODAY.

I don't know what comes over me.

But I text Alisha back: *Where are we going?*

CHAPTER TWO

SHE DOESN'T TELL ME, and I don't think I want her to.

I just take the bus route to her house instead of mine and say, "Alisha, I need to borrow a bra."

She slides a glance up and down my torso. "I—no, you know what? I don't actually want to know. Fine. You're lucky my boobs are like a size bigger than yours."

I cock my head. "Why is that lucky?"

Alisha shrugs and I follow her upstairs. "Because," she says, "I *could* be like two sizes smaller and then you and your girls would have to suffocate all night."

The Cooks have this really cool old house on the Catawba rez—it's narrow and tall, three floors plus the attic, which always felt kind of like . . . mysterious to me or something when I was a kid. Something about an *attic*. Especially with these thin, winding stairs leading up to it. Like that meant there was something to explore up there.

It did not.

In the attic was: insulation.

And a little later, after Alisha's parents added two younger siblings to the family, Alisha's room.

The attic in the cool, tall house is not a mystery anymore; it's the place I've spent more time than I could possibly measure, laughing and getting ready for dances and crying my eyes out every time I got dumped by a boy, or worse, a friend.

Alisha ushers me into her room and theatrically flings open her closet. "Do you need clothes, too?" She sizes me up. "You need clothes, too."

I roll my eyes. "Alisha, what I'm wearing is—"

"Beans."

I sputter.

"You're wearing *beans*, Brynn. I see them all over your shirt. I can only imagine that's what's caused this whole dramatic change of bra, and let me tell you something: I'm not bringing a plus-one to a V.I.P. event if she smells like beans."

Suddenly I'm embarrassed—did Oliver notice?

Not that that matters; it's just . . . god, this is embarrassing. Clearly, leaving my academic hole was a mistake.

"Plus," she says. "You're wearing a collared shirt. It's a crisp, collared Oxford. *That* is not what we go to parties in."

I glance down at myself. I think my crisp, collared Oxford is perfectly lovely, thank you very much. Apart from the beans. I look back at her and say, "You know what, I just remembered, I have some big, important stuff to do tonight, and—"

"NO," she says. "Brynn. No. Come with me. Take, like, a literal *single* night off."

I roll my eyes.

"Look," she says. She pulls this perfect, cerulean sweater out of her closet. "I'll let you borrow this."

"Alisha."

"What?" She blinks her bright brown eyes, all lashes and innocence.

"That's my sweater."

"It isn't!"

"That's not even *approaching* your color palette!"

She says, "You racist."

I shove her.

"Make sure you return that," she says.

"I will not."

She sticks her tongue out at me and laughs, then throws me a black bra that closes in the front.

"I know, I know," she says. "But I didn't realize it *closed in the front* when I bought it, and also: I think it'll make you desperately uncomfortable to wear all night."

I groan. I slip out of my clothes and snag a tissue to remove the burrito from my chest. "Nice tits," says Alisha. I curtsy.

Alisha is bisexual. She's taken to saying things like this or telling me she'll marry me one day since she let the news slip, but as I am tragically heterosexual, that is unlikely to happen. She knows and I know and there's nothing actually there between us. Nothing but the perfect friendship that is borne of a zillion years together, linking arms as comrades when you face down the hormonal battleground that is middle school together.

I slip into Alisha's slightly-too-big, accidentally-closes-in-the-front bra and my perfect sweater.

She says, "Spoilsport."

I say, "Please, in *this* slutty bra? You're welcome for the visual."

"Good point." She winks bisexually at me and throws in a finger gun for good measure.

I say, "Are you going to tell me where we're going?"

She pokes a perfectly manicured, short fingernail on top of my nose—boops it, really—and says, "No."

When we bound down the stairs, Alisha's mom is at the kitchen table, sculpting. Most of the women on the rez make money from pottery, even now, and Ms. Cook's work is legitimately exceptional. She's . . . she's just *good*.

I say, "Hey, Ms. Cook!"

Alisha's mom waves us off. "Don't do anything I wouldn't do."

"Please," I say, "I've heard your stories."

She cackles and Alisha says, "Gross, are you flirting with my mom?"

"Alisha," I say. She closes the front door behind us. "You know if I was ever going to fall in love with a girl, it would be you."

"Aw, I'm touched."

We make our way out to her old car and I lean against the driver's side door and pluck the keys from her hand. "Okay. Where are we headed?"

"Nuh-uh," she says. "Give me the keys, bitch; this is mine. I'm driving."

As it turns out, the V.I.P. event is: a huge party at the lake.

It's not even thrown by anyone at my school—it's kids in the neighboring county—but I've heard whispers about this one. Alisha has friends all over the place, so of course she scored an invite. Happy fizz bubbles in my chest at the idea that I'm at a *party* people *whisper about* in a neighboring town—just this tiny spike of elation at something shallow—then I quash it. I don't care about this kind of thing. I care about the kind of recognition that comes from being, like . . . Student Council popular, Smart, High-Achieving Popular, not about trashy lake parties I shouldn't be at. That's my siblings' kind of thing, my cousins' kind of thing. Not mine.

I don't care what any of these people think of me!

Or if they think of me at all!

I don't.

"Alisha!" comes a shout over the crackle of the bonfire.

"Hey!" she calls. She whispers to me, "Ethan O'Hare, student body president at the big school in Tega Cay. Sparkling smile, dimples to die for, and a reputation for sleeping with everything that moves."

I snort.

She was not kidding about the dimples, damn.

"This is Brynn Riley," she says to him.

His eyes light up. "A Baby Riley!"

He's got a blond Superman curl bisecting his forehead and it looks stupid and he's stupid but I'm a tiny little baby bit thrilled that he knows who I am. I say, "How do you know my name?"

"I've been coming to these things since I was a freshman, and my brother went a few years earlier than that. So did your people." He does that slow slide with his eyes from my ankles up to my chest, then finally lands on my face, mouth tilting up. "How much of your sister you got in you?"

I narrow my eyes, a flare of feminist offense and sisterly loyalty burning through my throat and chest. "I don't know what that's supposed to mean."

He snorts and half-rolls his eyes. "Yeah, alright. Figures; I've actually heard about you. You want, like, a water bottle and a game of Jenga, the kids' table is that way." He gestures out toward the woods, and Alisha, who has somehow, in the last fourteen seconds, already managed to procure a beverage I assume is a beer, furrows her brow and dumps the entire contents of her SOLO cup down his shirt.

He leaps back, arms spread, fabric dripping, and screams, "What the fuck!" just as a chorus of "Ohhhhhhh!" rises up from the around the fire.

My eyes are big and round and my jaw's about to hit the floor and I can't believe she just dumped a drink on a guy who looks like *that*, like he runs the party now and like he'll probably run the city in a few years. But she's walking it off like it's nothing.

Of course she is.

"That's real Coke, Ethan," she says. "Gonna wanna wash that shirt before the sugar stains."

She tugs at my elbow and pulls me along, and when we get far away from that sputtering, dripping, swearing mess, she hops around on her toes for a second and shakes her hands out. "Whew. Well. Now that that's out of the way."

"Is that . . ." I throw a look over my shoulder at the ruin we have already left in our wake. "Is that just . . . the way parties go for you these days?"

"Not usually," she says, eyes sparkling. "I should have known you'd cause trouble the second I brought you out."

"Ugh," I say, and she says, "Come on, let's get you a Coke."

Because *Coke* is short for *soda* in the Carolinas, I dig through a cooler someone brought and pop up with a Sprite, my beverage of choice, and decide to just kind of . . . let my hair down.

There's a light breeze coming off the lake, and the heat and crackle from the fire are warming my blood. And something about being here with Alisha makes me feel . . . just a little brave.

She's not part of like, the in-crowd, exactly. She can just float from person to person flawlessly and happily, so most everyone knows her. She's also stupid pretty with shiny black hair cut in layers that fall to her shoulders and the biggest, most mischievous smile I've ever seen. She's magnetic.

She's magnetic in a way I'll never be.

And that's . . . that's fine.

Of course it's fine.

Like I said, that's not the kind of popularity that has come my way. It was never going to be. The thing is, I'm not invisible at my school. People know me and like me and I've really, *really* truly made a name for myself that has nothing to do with my family. They know me for planning dances and being the smart kid and showing up in the school's closed circuit television every week to update the student body on council goings-on and scholarships and budget committee things, and knowing what the hell I'm doing.

It's just that that's a little different than *drawing* people to you like that. And that's what Alisha has. That tiny stab of sadness disappears when I discover that being in her orbit means that people are paying attention to me for nothing that has to do with my GPA.

Not that I want that.

But . . . I don't know. It kind of doesn't suck when Quentin Howard, starting forward at his school and captain of like fourteen thousand academic clubs—as Alisha informs me, and as I knew already since I've actually competed against him in knowledge bowl and mock trial from time to time—sidles up to Alisha, gets roundly rejected, then sees *me*. It doesn't suck when he turns that smooth smile on me, deep brown skin lit up by the crackling fire, and says, "I've seen you around."

"No, you haven't." Come on. He doesn't remember me. Why would he?

"I have!"

I roll my eyes.

"What?" he asks, eyes glittering. "That sound like a line?"

"Yes," I say, eyebrow raising. "Because it *is* a line."

He hits himself in the chest. "That's cold, Riley."

I'm so surprised that I don't even try to disguise it on my face. "I—"

"Mmmhmm," he says. "And you thought I was lyin'."

I laugh and he moves in just a little closer. I can feel the quick lack of space and it sets my heart ten paces quicker. Quentin has always been, like, *deeply* kind, not that it's ever aimed at me. We don't exactly run in the same circles. We're not in the same school, plus he does sports, and that's a whole different level of recognition. The point is, he's not an asshole like star jocks are supposed to be. He's cool, and the fact that he's, well, pretty clearly hitting on me doesn't come off like it did when Ethan did. It just . . . feels nice.

I feel nice.

My toes shift closer to him and I lean in. "So you're on the basketball team, right?"

His mouth quirks and he rolls his eyes. "You don't care about that."

He's right. "Don't I?"

"You care about the smart kid shit. The mock trial and debate and mathleticism."

I laugh and tuck my hair behind my ear, glancing at the ground. "My reputation precedes me. But . . . you're right. The fact that you can handle a derivative that smoothly really does it for me."

His face lights up with laughter and I can't believe I just said the phrase "does it for me" to Quentin Howard.

My phone buzzes in my back pocket.

It's one of them, my family. There's no way in hell I'm answering.

Quentin says, "Hey, can I get you a beer?"

I open my mouth to say no, but then my butt buzzes again, and it's them. I know it's them, talking about some wild exploit or giving me crap for being *good, boring Brynn* and laughing with each other about it and . . .

"Yeah," I say. "Yeah, you can."

Alisha sees me take a bottle and pop the top and raises her eyebrows at me.

I shrug and take the drink, and she shoots me a quick thumbs up when she sees me flirting—*flirting!!*—with one of the hottest guys here.

And it is at that very second, the actual instant that I raise the bottle to my lips and my tongue touches the first drop of beer I've ever tasted in my life (which I hate, by the way. It tastes like crap. *Why* is this worth it?), that red and blue lights flood the beach.

CHAPTER THREE

I PLEAD GUILTY.

Of course I plead guilty; my family has been in and out of this courtroom a thousand times and no judge in this county is going to take a single drop of pity on me. Why would they? I might be a squeaky clean, honor roll, student of the month, but that won't mean a thing to the judge. Not when my last name is Riley.

They picked me up for an MIP—Minor in Possession.

It didn't matter that I wasn't drunk or that half the kids there did this all the time when this was literally the first time I'd ever touched alcohol in my life. It didn't matter that after one sip, I was about the dump the whole thing out.

Should, coulda, woulda.

They *arrested* me. Actually arrested me! I was handcuffed and shoved unceremoniously, in front of everyone at the lake, into the back of a cop car and read my Miranda rights and dropped off in a cell. I wasn't the only one, and like . . . it could have been worse. Could have been *way* worse; it could have been in front of kids from my own school.

But still.

It's been a week and a half, and I can still feel the fury tickling my lip just thinking about it, just putting a name to what happened. The injustice of everything washes over me in waves and I feel my fists curling and uncurling at my sides. My nails digging into my own skin.

I just . . . I can't believe I have an arrest record now.

I'm so furious. At them. At the people who arrested me, at my best friend for inviting me to the party in the first place, at Quentin Howard for giving me the beer, at whoever threw the stupid rager in the first place, at my family for getting me so totally keyed up that I felt like I had to drink just to prove I wasn't some boring goody-two-shoes, at . . . at . . .

I blink down at my mint green Toms, kicking the front legs of my chair with my heels. Again and again and again. If I kick it enough times, I can fall into a rhythm, into this meditative zone where I don't have to think about the fact that I'm kicking this chair in a public defender's waiting area. That I did this, and I got myself here, and I so *deeply* screwed up.

I'm not mad at any of them.

I'm mad at me.

I'm so mad at me that I want to cry, but then I'd be even *madder* at me for ruining this frankly perfect eyeliner job, and I don't think I can take that level of self-betrayal right now.

I want to look put-together when I walk into the lawyer's office.

I want to look like I don't belong here, like I'm worth her time.

I will not—I repeat—I will *not* wreck my eyeliner.

I go from kicking the chair to tap-tap-tapping my fingers against my thigh obsessively to ward off the tears.

I just . . . how? How did I become, overnight, such a colossal fuck-up?

I drop my head into my hands, blonde silk that I'm very proud of falling over my knuckles. Well. We'll always have Paris, or whatever. I'll always have these soft, moisturized tresses.

Not in juvie, you won't, says a horrible ghost voice in my ear.

Panic jolts through me, and then I force myself to breathe.

They're not going to send me to juvie for . . . for a single sip of beer.

That's not the way this works.

Thankfully, Alisha is fine. She got out of there before cops could pin her for anything, and good. Law enforcement doesn't exactly have a great reputation for treating Native kids fairly. To say the least. She's been worried about *me*, but this . . . I just, I know. It could have been so much worse.

"Miss Riley?"

My face shoots up and I look into the eyes of my lord and savior for the next twenty minutes. Her name is Iliana Guitierrez, and she takes no shit. Even if I hadn't met her once before, I'd know. No one with that sharp glint in her eyes, that confident sweep of dramatic purple eyeliner, those wicked, pointed pumps that must be absolute murder on her feet but make her imposing when she walks into the room, rolls over and says, "Tie me to the railroad tracks, cartoon villain."

No.

No, Iliana Guitierrez wields the rope.

I stand and square my shoulders. I brush my hair quickly out of my face and hold out my hand to shake hers.

I want—I *need*—her to understand that I'm not like the rest of the kids she has in here. I'm different. I'm different because I've never done this before and I'll do whatever it takes to get out of this and I'm willing to work. I'm different! My future is precious to me.

I follow her into her tiny office.

I used to think all lawyers made absolute monster money, but she's a public defender and it turns out there's not much green in providing an essential service like the right to a lawyer.

"Are your parents here?"

"My dad's in prison," I say as primly as I can. Like that's a totally regular sentence that rich, non-screw-up kids, say. "My mom couldn't make it."

She nods. "Well, Brynn," she says, shuffling some papers in her manila file, "I've talked to kids like you a thousand times before."

Just like that, I deflate.

"Crystal clear record, and then one crazy night, and boom. It's all down the drain."

"All?" I manage, blinking. Tears sting my eyes. No, *no*, not today. You will not do this.

"Not if I can help it."

There it is—a modicum of hope.

"They've offered you a deal."

"Okay . . . ?"

"It's . . . alright, let me give this to you straight, Brynn. Under normal circumstances, I'd say fight it. An MIP isn't responsible, exactly, but it's not uncommon. Judges let kids off easy for this kind of thing."

"Yes?" I say. My expression is brightening already. I knew it. I knew I was in capable hands.

"But," she says, and there it goes. Deflated again. I can practically hear it when the balloon in my chest pops and makes that pathetic little squeaking noise, and my shoulders drop. Nothing good has ever come after a *but* like that. "Your family, as you're well aware, I'm sure, has a . . . history. And the judge they've assigned your case has tried them all. I know him, I know his style; he's going to throw the book at you, honey."

"I—" Now my throat does catch. Now, I know that I am going to wreck my perfect eyeliner. It is an inevitability. In the same way that the cops coming to arrest me was an inevitability the second they pulled up to the lake.

I start to cry.

Iliana hands me a tissue box; she's done this a thousand times, too.

I am just like everyone else.

My ribcage caves in on itself; I guess I'll just sink into the floor. I guess I'll just die.

"I'm sorry," I say, and I don't even know what I'm apologizing for. The crying, the black smears around my eyes that I'm sure make me look extremely fucken haunted, the crime I committed in the first place?

"Don't be sorry," she says. "Be proactive. This is a good deal, under the circumstances."

I don't even want to look at what she's pushing me to accept. I can't. What if it's juvie? What if I'm going to *jail*? What if I have to leave everything I've ever known for six months and—

Oh.

"It's just . . . community service. That's it?"

"That's it," she says. "You're eligible for what's called a diversion program. In the state of South Carolina, under certain circumstances, you can bypass all the bullshit of the justice system and complete a diversion program instead. You get it done, the judge will dismiss your charges."

"Oh!" I sit up straighter, make myself smile. That's alright. That'll be fine. It will be *completely* fine; I can totally do this. "Well, I want to take it," I say.

She ignores my decision. "Because there was no victim to whom you could pay restitution or with whom you could reach any sort of resolution, the route the court is suggesting is community service, as you noted. And you're looking at thirty hours."

If I were drinking something, I'd spit it out. "*Thirty hours?*"

"Thirty hours."

She is unrattleable.

Thirty hours. Jesus, I doubt I can get more than two hours in on a good day, and who are we kidding? It's gonna be way less than that, realistically. I have school and homework and committees and activities, and I've got the scholarship to compete for, and—

It doesn't matter.

And it doesn't matter.

I don't have a choice, at least not a sensible one.

It's thirty hours of community service to get this stupid mistake off my record forever, and of course I'm going to take it. If I don't get this wiped, forget the scholarship I want; I bet I get my admission to school revoked. I can't have a record.

"Okay," I say quietly.

"Okay?"

"Okay," I say. "I'll take it."

The next few minutes are a blur, and I'm extremely glad she offers to email me a copy of what we just discussed, because I barely hear it.

I'm so exhausted already, and so disappointed in myself, and so embarrassed. I'm so embarrassed to walk in my front door and know that my siblings and my mom are thinking, *Look how the mighty fall.*

I'm embarrassed about what the lawyer thinks of me, and this is her job! It is her job to be compassionate! She's the very opposite of a cop or a judge! But it doesn't matter; my cheeks are hot with shame.

I forget so much of what she says, even as she says it.

And then I'm being ushered out, feeling, even with the objectively really positive outcome, totally shell-shocked.

I look up from the floor, just to orient myself. To find my way to the elevator, and when I get there, I interact to the absolute bare minimum with the scenery. I press the button, I wait for the doors to open, I step inside. Someone gets in with me, I guess. The doors shut. Down from the second floor to the first floor.

Cool.

It doesn't matter.

I just want to go home.

I don't want to go home.

Ugh.

I want to go back in time.

"Uh," I hear, and then this little cough.

I look up, and—shit.

Oh my god. Oh my god, no.

"You," I breathe.

"Me," says Oliver West. He narrows his eyes for an instant, like he's got me, and this, all figured out. Then wipes his face back to neutrality.

He's dressed to the nines, like I am, and usually, a suit means you're up to something sophisticated, something classy. Or at the very least, something for speech and debate.

But when you're leaving a legal office, I dare say it means the opposite.

We are both ruffians.

Ruffians? Why am I even thinking this way? Was I briefly possessed by a ghost from the 1860s?

Oliver just looks at me. He cocks his head and his mouth tips up, one eyebrow raised, teasing me. "So," he says, "come here often?"

I half want to laugh, but I'm exasperated. How dare he see me like this, in a place no one was supposed to? This will all be wiped from my record, but it can't be wiped from his mind. I suppose I have no choice but to kill him.

I'll just add premeditated murder to the list of my crimes.

How dare he see me like this and how dare he smirk at me like that?

And how *very dare* he go around smelling like deodorant that's probably named something like *Frostwind Ax Man*, and therefore smelling like a lumberjack dreamboat? That's right. Dreamboat. I thought it, and I'm not sorry. Oliver West smells like something I want to eat for dinner, and by that I mean take to my room under the guise of studying, rip his tie off immediately, and kiss him so hard it bruises.

I say, instead of that, "No. But I'm sure you do."

He breathes out this single laugh, and that single laugh, that quiet breath, makes me so much more aware of the tiny space we are trapped in together. I can't breathe without breathing his air. His handsome, diamond-jawed, Frostwind Ax Man air.

CHRIST, what a nightmare.

I look away, prim and collected, and I agree silently that we will never speak of this again.

And when the elevator dings, I practically fall right out the doors and *run* to the bus stop.

It turns out there's one place worth fleeing to home from, and that is right here, where Oliver West has nosed too close to one of my secrets just after he saw me wrecking his future career. With beans on my boobs.

I'll stand at this stop for an hour if I have to.

I'm leaving here, and I'm going home.

CHAPTER FOUR

HOME IS A DOUBLE-WIDE on cinderblocks over gravel. That gravel is located in a place called Magnolia Estates, in gold leaf cursive on a sign out front, because if you call a place an estate, it automatically becomes true.

The bus drops me off right out in front of the park along with a couple other folks I wave at, and I make my way a few spaces down and to the left, to the gray trailer with the lavender shutters. Mom is very proud of those lavender shutters. She's also particularly proud of the flowerbeds out front, which do coordinate perfectly well with the color scheme. Says it makes it feel kind of like a house.

Whatever it is, it doesn't feel like home.

I've never felt like I belonged here, and maybe that's snooty or something, but I don't know if it's wrong to want to get out. To not relate at all with your family.

I don't . . . I don't really relate with mine. I don't think I ever will.

You don't want to.

I feel guilty when that thoughts cuts into my mind.

But . . . well . . . I don't.

I don't think I have to.

I hug my jacket around my shoulders and square them, take a deep breath, and push into the house.

It's alive with activity. Patrick is in the little kitchen, doing something with pasta to fancy up a buck-a-person meal, and his girlfriend, Randi, and Evian (like the water) are squealing about something in Evian's old room. Maybe Evian's still sexting and they're laughing about *that*. I don't know, and I don't really care.

I'm so suddenly exhausted.

I'm instantly more so when Patrick calls out from the kitchen in this weird almost-Cockney that I can't really begin to figure out the reason behind: "Is tha' our long lost sister? Returned from the war, guvna?"

I pause.

"Y-yes?"

"Well, BLIMEY!"

"You don't even know what that means."

He scoffs and says, "Well, jolly good, eh, that's a right load of spotted dick now, innit?"

Randi and Evian emerge from the bedroom at his chaos.

"Evian," I whisper. Pleadingly.

She just smirks, and Randi shrugs.

I groan. "Patrick, I'm not in the mood for you being weird. I'm just not."

"C'mon now, luv; I've been in here makin' this cuppa and crikeying all day and—shit! Shit shit shit shit—"

I hear the splash and sizzle before I hear the load of American-accented swearing that comes out, I swear, once a week because Patrick cannot cook without hurting himself. He just absolutely cannot.

"Patrick! Jesus!"

"I'm FINE," he says. His hands are covered with tiny little scars from incidents like this.

"Where's Mom?" I yell over the giggling and the Patrick and the television to no one in particular. "Where's Mom? Someone tell me—"

"She's at work, Brynn, where do you think?"

I blow out an annoyed breath. "It's dinner time."

"She's working a double," says Evian. "Why do you think we're here? Patrick didn't want to leave you to your own devices."

"Oh."

Mom's been working a lot of doubles lately, since Dad failed to make it out on parole once again two months ago. It's fine. It's all fine and I'm fine about it; I can do this on my own.

I don't even know what I mean by *this*, just that . . . that I'm capable and I'm okay.

"Well, I'm just going to change before dinner," I say. I move to pass behind the couch, and Evian and Randi are whispering again. Their faces are pink with laughter. I want to ask them what it's about, to let me in on the joke, but I don't. It's none of my business.

Randi runs a hand through her fire-red hair and looks me up and down. "Someone's fancy, by the way," she says. "Perfume and everything."

Evian's mouth turns up. "That's not fancy; that's a scent called *eau du courte*."

"What?"

"Baby's first day in court."

My lips thin into a line.

"Ooooooh," Randi says. "That *was* today, wasn't it? Shit, I wish you would've told me. Your brother and sister and I would've come to support you."

Randi has: fourteen piercings, twelve tattoos, four gauges, and fire engine red, half-shaved hair. I do not think her presence in any sort of court room or legal office would have helped my case.

I sigh. "It wasn't court. I went to the public defender's office. I'm accepting this deal they have called a diversion program—"

"Oh, the diversion program! Aw, I remember when I got to have my shit diverted." Evian smiles fondly.

My fingertips are curling and scraping inside these fancy-ass pants, and I'm picking at the pocket threads. I'm being driven to nerves again. I can't *wait* to get out of here, and one day, when I have this community service blip taken care of, I will.

I blink back to my irritating reality when she says, "Well, look at you anyway. All grown into a Riley."

Patrick, from the kitchen, starts singing "Family Tradition," and I am just NOT in the MOOD. I am not in the mood and I haven't *been* in the mood and I'm not going to get any *more* in the mood standing here tolerating everyone. I just scoff out loud and huff all the way back to my room.

It's tiny and there's wood paneling everywhere, but it's mine.

It's got my honor roll certificates pasted everywhere, and my friends on the bulletin board, and my fairy lights strung around the old wood pallet I took and Pinterested into a headboard, and my trophies on the dresser, and a door that locks.

And that's all I need.

I strip out of my lawyer clothes and into one of my rattiest, most comfortable T-shirts. It hangs just past my plaid shorts, which makes it a little trashy, I guess, but I'm comfortable. I'm home. I don't have to worry about the length of these shorts or the impression that gives or wearing a bra.

I take off my bra.

Angels sing.

I mean to go out and eat with everyone, but I don't know if I can face them. They're all talking about me, all judging me, probably. I know it. I can feel it; of course they are. I'm sure judging me.

I was the one who never screwed up, the one who was going to college and going to live in a suburb with a big fenced-in yard of lush, green grass, who never met a lawyer outside honors club meet and greets. And now here I am. Just like . . . like every other Riley.

How could I have been so *stupid*?

It's not the end of the world, I tell myself. *The judge is going to strike this from your record after you do what you need to do! It's so fine. It's so, so fine.*

And conscience, I know that. I know. But even if the legal books don't know, I do.

I don't come out for dinner.

I don't really think anyone expected me to.

They like to hang out here in the evenings if Mom's out, don't want me to have to exist as some kind of latchkey kid

Gen X-er, which is nice of them. But sometimes, I'm just not in the mood.

I, rudely, don't say goodbye when Patrick, Evian, and Randi head back to the little apartment they share.

I just stay and mope.

I feel like doing nothing but staying and moping. And what do they care, really? This is old hat to all of them. Randi's not technically family yet, but she's like a Riley at this point. And everything that comes with it. Patrick got arrested eight times and Evian got expelled because she wouldn't stop bringing weed to school and giving blow jobs in the parking lot, and Randi's gotten in for petty theft and drinking underage or public intoxication a few times. Which means this isn't major to any of them; no one remembers what a big deal this is.

I stay in my room, trying not to think about exactly everything I can't stop thinking about, and eventually, my door cracks open. I don't know if it's the cat or the wind or—

"Baby?"

It's my mom.

I sigh and my shoulders fall. I didn't know shoulders could be tense lying in bed, but I guess they can.

"You had a day today," she says.

"No," I say. "*You* had a day. Working doubles at the hospital again?"

"Yeah," she says.

"How can they make you do that? It's not like CNAs get the easy jobs; they can't make you lift people and change bedpans and . . . and . . . all that stuff bending over and standing back up and running around the hospital like that so many hours in a day. It isn't good for you. You know that. They can't make you."

"One, yeah they can. And two, they're not making me. You know it was a blow when your dad didn't make parole, and I've got to take care of this family. I volunteer for this. You know I do."

I breathe through my nose, draw my arms in around myself. I'm upset. I'm mad.

I'm mad that she has to be gone so much, and that I'm so tired that I can't even interact like a human with my family, and I guess I'm mad that she didn't come today.

She couldn't.

I know.

But I'm . . . it's unfair, but I'm mad.

Tears peek out from my eyelashes. "I needed you today, Mama," I say.

I don't say *Mama* anymore. I'm not five years old.

But here I am, seventeen years old, comforted by the familiar weight of my mother sitting on my mattress, gently breathing, and I'm calling her Mama.

"Brynn," she says. She brushes her fingers over my comforter and rests them on my back. Mom used to keep her nails long and painted—pinup red, always pinup red. But that was before she got the job at the hospital, and they make her keep her nails short now. She can still scratch my back, though.

She does.

I am immediately soothed, even though I'm a little resistant to feeling soothed, on principle.

She says, in a quiet voice, "You know I wanted to be there for you. But I—we were understaffed and we have to pay rent in a few days, and . . . what was I supposed to do?"

I sniffle and shrug. I know I'm being so young. I'm being so needy and immature. But I do it anyway. "Be there," I say.

"I'm there for you now."

I'm quiet for a long time. But after a little while, long enough I wonder if she'll be startled that I'm awake at all, I say, "I know you are."

She lets out a long breath, like I've relieved her, and then I feel bad for being a butt about this in the first place. "What did the lawyer say?"

"She said I can do some community service and they'll drop the charges altogether."

"Oh Brynn, baby, that's great." She squeezes my shoulder.

"Yeah," I say. "Yeah, no, it's great."

"Your dad called, by the way."

I shut down so immediately that I can physically feel the walls lock in place.

"Four times."

"Okay."

"He wants to know you're okay, after everything."

I fist my hands in my covers. "Yeah."

It's quiet for a while. Then Mom sighs and says, "You get some sleep."

I don't respond. I'm upset and it's not fair, but I don't know how *not* to be. How to make my mouth say any more words. It really is okay. Today worked out about as well as it could have, and doing this alone was no one's fault but mine. It's okay. I know.

I breathe, still facing my wall.

It's great. It's fine.

But when I fall asleep, my blanket is strangling me.

CHAPTER FIVE

I WOKE UP AT four a.m. because insomnia is a bitch—three mornings in a row.

So, when I get to school on Thursday, I'm . . . disheveled. Well, okay, not *entirely* disheveled; I'm not one of those people who shows up to school wearing pajama pants or something. My hair is done and I've got a light little dusting of makeup going and my skirt does, in fact, match my top, thank you very much. I'm not a *garbage monster*. But I have bags under my eyes. A few fly-aways that I normally would have taken the time to fix. I'm just so *sleepy*.

Thank god Alisha shows up to the buses with an extra travel mug of coffee from home. My mom used to try to tell me not to drink it—it would stunt my growth—but I think I'm about topped out at this point, so sweet caffeine and creamer, here I come. Honestly, it's not nearly the magic elixir that adults swear it is, but it does *something*, and something, at this point, is better than nothing.

"How you doing, babe?" Alisha asks.

I shrug. "Fine. I can't sleep."

She furrows her brow. "Insomnia is my thing. That's not like you."

I shrug and take a long, slow drink. "This was so necessary. Thank you for this, I owe you."

She waves me off.

"I'm just stressed, I think."

We make our way around the quad, taking an extra couple loops. It's brisk outside, but nice enough that neither of us wants to commit to being fully trapped in the school just yet.

"Community service?" she asks.

"Yeah. It just . . . god, it makes me feel like a delinquent."

"Please," she says, "you're not a delinquent because you had one sip of beer at a party."

We pass by smokers' corner, which is technically about five feet off the school's property, and it's where the actual delinquents gather. Oliver West is hanging out there in his honest-to-god leather jacket, and when he catches my eye, he smirks. Like he knows a secret of mine.

I flush and look away. He doesn't. I could have been at that law office for any reason. *Any* reason. He doesn't have a thing on me. Except for the smirk, which is devastatingly hot and *does* hit me right in the gut. I'd be grossed out that he was smoking, except he's not. He's just hanging out there. When Alisha and I leave the area, he *does* exchange cash and who knows what else with a scraggly-looking guy beside him, so I roll my eyes and endeavor to forget the whole thing. Everything about him.

Alisha's right. *I'm* not the delinquent here.

I pass my attention back to her and say, "No, I know. You're right. It's just . . ."

"I know," she says.

She gets it. She knows my relationship with my family is more about my relationship to the reputation they've built for me than it is to the people. But it's followed me since I was a kid, and I don't know how to shake the paranoia.

"You'll be alright," she says. "Seriously. I know *everyone* at that party, and no one there goes to our school. It's gonna be fine." Then she says, "Know where you're gonna volunteer yet?"

The advantage to all that insomnia is that it gave me nothing but time to research. And after researching about a million different potential paths for my court-ordered community service in the past seventy-two hours, I've finally settled on one: Pibbles and Kits. It's this rescue on the North Carolina side of the state line, but I got it cleared with my lawyer already (well, my lawyer's assistant. As it turns out, public defenders don't have the time for anything or anyone. They're inundated). So it's not going to be a problem.

I called the rescue yesterday morning and already got pre-approval to do my service with them as long as I show up to orientation Saturday.

I tell her, and she approves. Then her girlfriend shows up and I see Alisha's shoulders raise to her ears. The girlfriend, though super sweet and cute, stresses her out. I think it's more about Alisha just kind of being over it than anything in particular that Paige has done (except be extremely chipper, which can be a lot), but I'm not going to bring it up until Alisha does. I believe in boundaries.

Alisha kisses Paige on the cheek and I get suddenly whisked off to class by a student councilman chattering about the dance we've got to get planning and can I come after school to get some stuff set up? (I can, and I will.)

So that's the end of that conversation.

I shoot Alisha a helpless wave and she blows me a kiss, and through the window, I glimpse Oliver. Still hanging out at the corner in that stupid jacket when the bell rings. Slacking, as usual. I don't feel bad about his application.

Not at all.

So it's seven a.m. on a Saturday morning and I'm up, bright and early.

I slick my hair back into a ponytail and slip into some cutoffs and the cutest pale yellow tank that I can stand to sacrifice to animal life today. This really shouldn't be bad. I mean, I'm sure I'll get tired of cleaning up poop and all those kinds of thing, but I love animals. Who doesn't?

And Pibbles and Kits isn't just an animal rescue; it's a rescue specifically for pit bulls and Maine Coons. What's not a total delight about that? I don't know much about giant cats, but I've loved pits since I was little. My uncle has three and they're the biggest babies in existence. They're slobbery and bat-eared and sweet, and he treats them like royalty. Even lets them sleep in his bed every night.

You know, pits used to be called "the nanny dog"? Before assholes realized they were loyal enough to do just about anything the person they loved told them to, and big enough to do it with damage. Then they got a hold of pits, chained them up in their back yards, made them fight, and long story short, here we are—everyone hates them.

It's always made me *furious*. I probably should have signed up to volunteer for this earlier, to be honest. But when have I had the time?

I guess I magically have it now, but it's amazing what a person can do when they have no choice.

I wash my face with cold water and off-brand Dial, and I don't bother with makeup. Then I head up the length of the park, gravel crunching under my tennis shoes, toward the bus stop.

It's going to be a massive pain in the ass, getting to this rescue multiple times a week. I obviously can't afford a car, and usually the bus isn't a big deal. I can take it most places I need to go without too much hassle, and if I need to get uptown, I can take it to the train station, then just hop the light rail.

But Pibbles and Kits isn't in Charlotte; it's in the middle of nowhere and a half hour away from me by car. Lyft is way out of budget (which is as close to zero as possible), and Alisha offered to drive me, but I can't let her do that. She's got a life. It's going to take me two and a half hours to get there via public transport. *Two. And a Half. Hours.*

Every time I go.

Brynn! you might say. *Dear lord! Why on Earth would you go do community service somewhere that many hours away when I'm certain there's a rescue—a pit bull rescue, even!—in your area?*

Well, I'd tell you: it's because I just . . . can't risk anyone I know seeing me. I can't go somewhere that isn't a massive inconvenience for me because if anyone from school saw me doing community service, my reputation would be shot.

It's already horrible enough that kids I *don't* know saw me being pushed into the back of a cop car, but at least I can blur that with the fact that ten other kids were picked up at the same time. I can't have everyone at my school finding out that I'm serving a sentence. That I got arrested. It's humiliating.

This gets found out, gets around, and so much for sparkly clean Brynn Riley. One mistake and everyone will throw me in with the rest of my family and its ... torrid history. I'll no longer be Brynn, Who Rose Above.

I'll be: That Riley.

And that is unacceptable. Court-ordered community service? Okay.

Hours and hours and hours killing myself to get there, weeks of giving up sleep and a social life to do it? Fine.

But the smoldering wreckage of my reputation? Absolutely not.

So, I suck in my lower lip and wait it out in the late autumn heat for the bus to show.

It's pretty full this morning, but it always is on weekends. I drop in my fare and shoulder my way to the middle of the bus—the back isn't really where you wanna be if you can help it.

And I settle in for the long, long, *l o n g* haul.

The Carolinas pass by, tree after tree and building after building, and a hundred people get on and a hundred people get off and, somewhere along the way, I guess someone starts yelling about something, but I don't know what it is and I don't care; it's just ... a day on the bus.

I pop my headphones in my ears and turn up the volume.

I should have brought a book, probably.

But all the books I had at home are books I've read a thousand times, and sometimes you're just not in the mood to know the ending.

I'll have to really stock up at the library when this gig kicks into gear, I guess.

Some older guy in a stained white T-shirt slides into the seat next to me. There are four empty seats—count them, four—in the vicinity. But he picks the one with the underage girl.

He slides his gaze over to me and says, "Where you headed?"

The guy's voice is smoke-worn and old and I feel grimy just answering.

"Raleigh," I lie.

"Raleigh?" He throws his arm over the back of my seat. "What are we getting away from?"

My lip curls. I bat my eyelashes. "Mean teachers. In middle school."

He blinks, still gives me a once-over.

"My daddy's a police officer," I say.

He snarls and examines the rest of the bus for seating.

I hate taking public transport. I've done it all my life and I'll keep doing it, but god. I hate it.

I try to ignore the guy and do some schoolwork I'm behind on for all my various extra-curriculars, but I can't. I can't focus until he's gone.

Finally he gets off the bus, and I can breathe. I can focus

without obsessing, without my anxiety asking me if he's still interested? If he'll sit right up next to me again and breathe in my ear? If maybe I really *will* have to go all the way to Raleigh just to keep up the disguise and then he'll follow me or ask for my ID to prove I'm in middle school and then catch me in a lie and—

Anxiety, kids. It's fun! It is great!

Anyway. He's gone, finally. And my brain and overactive limbic system slow and quiet.

When I can feel that the change, the descent from semipanic, is close to permanent, I re-open my notebook. I've got a few more bus changes and another two hours to go.

I while them away with the Red Hot Chili Peppers and Cardi B and whatever the hell else comes up on my shuffle.

By the time we pull up to the final stop, a half a mile down from the rescue, I'm pretty much recovered from Weirdo Bus Guy, and no worse for the wear, but my phone is almost dead. Cool. Great.

I check the time and I'm running fifteen minutes behind.

I spend the next ten minutes wishing I'd chosen some sort of athletics for my extra-curriculars, but I did not, and it shows.

I spend the following five struggling through the exact potential implications if I am too late. Will they drop me altogether? Where else can I volunteer? Okay, a lot of places. But will they report that? Does that put me in contempt of court, or something? Would I have to go to juvie? I think I would, or something. At the very least, it would wreck my chance at wiping my record. The judge was . . . not lenient on me. He's giving me one chance at this. That's it. You only get one shot. Do not miss your chance to blow. Mom's spaghetti or whatever.

Oh god.

I'm going to fail community service.

On my first day.

I was not cut out for a life of crime.

When I get to Pibbles and Kits, I'm red-faced and sweating, and all my muscles are on fire and stretched out within an inch of their life, and I'm absolutely exhausted.

Air shreds my lungs and there's a stitch in my side. I bend over, hands on my knees, and pull in oxygen. I can do this.

I can walk in there and gasp, "I am here for community service that a judge requires me to do, and I am late!" and that is exactly what I do.

I bat back my anxiety, walk right up to the front desk, where a college student with freckles and large chip in her front tooth smiles at me and raises an eyebrow when she looks me up and down. The eyebrow drops quickly; it was involuntary and I guess I can't blame her. I smell like bus and sweat, and I'm sure I look it.

"I'm here for—I'm—I'm—Jesus."

"Well." She cocks her head, mouth tipped up. "You might be looking for the church just up the road?"

I manage to laugh and hold up my index finger while I gather myself. "Sorry. I'm sorry." I take one more steadying gulp of air. "I'm here to volunteer. I'm here for the orientation."

"Ah," she says. "And your name is?"

"Brynn Riley?" I say it like a question, like I don't even know my own name.

She pulls out a clipboard, scans it, then says, "Oh, okay, yes, I see you. You're going to have a couple more forms to fill out for me at the end of training since this is court-ordered."

She smiles politely, but not with her teeth, and my stomach drops into my gut. I can feel the heat from all the blood rushing to my face.

Christ, I can't believe I got caught up in this. I can't believe that I know what this particular shame feels like. The shame that has you actively grabbing for a hundred excuses to make for yourself, for ways to extricate your body from the situation of existing in the room with someone else, because you know—you *know*—they find you intrusive. You are making them nervous, because, probably, you're just a little lesser.

There is nothing like knowing that your very presence in a room is an inconvenience to someone.

She can be as sweet and polite as she wants to be, but I know that's how she feels because it's how I've felt about my own family a hundred times. Might be shitty, but it's true.

I want nothing more than to escape, even though I'll just be escaping this room into another room of judgment.

I mumble, "Yeah, of course."

She tips her chin toward the right, where there's a big door and a picture of a dog silhouette, and says, "They started out in the back, so you'll just head through there and they're straight through."

"Okay," I say. I hate how sheepish and small I sound. "Thanks."

"Nice meeting you." She smiles again, that professional smile, and looks back at whatever she has on that computer screen.

Now that I'm released from her gaze, I take a second to look at the surroundings. They're friendly, cheerful. Bright, happy blues and creams and lavenders. A striped, cushioned bench that goes with everything else. It doesn't look clinical or run-down. This looks like a place where happy animals live, even though I'm sure it's filled with sad stories.

There's pictures on the wall—of huge, happy, very good boys and girls of both the canine and feline varieties, and for the first time all morning, I find myself getting . . . a little excited. Feeling just a little bit of joy. Maybe at least what I do here will make a difference to some animals *and* some people.

And hey, that's something.

I smooth down my tank top and pull at my shorts, run my hand back through my hair to tame it one more time, and then I push through the doors.

The floors are cement, like they always are at shelters, a couple rows of cages for the dogs. It's loud and echoey in here, so every little whimper and huge bark roars in my ears and makes them ring.

The first few pups are really chill, just curled in their beds or wagging happy, stubby little tails and smiling at me, and I'm so tempted to crouch down and start petting, dog by dog, but I don't have the time. I'm already late. And the fact that this isn't exactly of my own free will is going to have me on a tight enough leash (no pun intended) already.

So I resist the urge. I'll get to play with all of them as much as I want, and *more* than I want, later.

I brush past the happy pittie and then about fall on my butt when a . . . less happy guy leaps on the cage and starts barking at me.

My heart is pounding out of my chest, but I'm fine. I'm fine and I'm sure he's fine. He's just big. And loud.

I'm out of breath again, just from the sheer shock of all of that, my lizard brain popping out to protect me, then not letting me go when it needed to.

But I march forward, determined to make it to the freaking training before I get booted and ruin everything.

I studiously ignore all the dogs to my right and left (I'm lying. I fail.; it's impossible) and push out into the back. There are a few pens where dogs are being exercised by perky-looking people in red Pibbles and Kits T-shirts, and to the rear of the plot is a group of people in various kinds of dress. They've got to be mine.

I run to the group (determined to wreck my hair and complexion, apparently), and I'm short and stuck behind several tall people, so I can't see who's talking.

He stops, clearly mid-sentence, and says, "Like I said earlier, be on time. Respect my time, and I'll respect yours."

An embarrassed flush hits my cheeks, but a familiar tingle runs down my spine.

That can't . . . no. No, absolutely not, it can't be.

"Who's this *just now* joining us?" he says.

And I'd know that voice anywhere.

The Red Sea of Tall People in front of me parts and I just stand there like a fish on land gasping for water.

You've got to be kidding me.

"Oh," he says, "Brynn Riley." Oliver West's grin is so bright and shit-eating that I can *feel* the meanness running all the way down to my toes. "You made it."

I don't say anything. I can't.

He shoots me a wink before he moves on with his lecture, like I'm not even there.

And simultaneously like he was waiting for me to arrive before he could really get started.

CHAPTER SIX

WE GO THROUGH THE motions, learning what we'll be doing and when—how often the dogs need their cages cleaned, when they all get walked and fed, when we rotate kitties in the cat room. Red tags on kennels means an animal isn't ready for human interaction and might, for some reason or another, need to be quarantined. Yellow is for animals that need a little caution—aren't ready to be adopted yet but can be handled and taken under consideration but need a few more tests or something. Green is good to go.

There are endless rules and procedures, but I don't mind, for several reasons. One being that, honestly, working weekends with slobbery tongues and fluffy tails is the easiest anyone has ever gotten off with from a judge. The other? Well, I can't stop thinking about Oliver.

We're all sitting in the waiting room now, listening to him go over the last several guidelines he has in mind before we all sign or decide Pibbles and Kits isn't for us, and I just . . . can't quit staring at him.

How did this happen?

Of all the freaking places—I went *two and a half hours* out of my way to volunteer here so this exact thing wouldn't happen, and it did. Of course it did.

I've spent the last hour intermittently listening and getting totally distracted zipping through possibilities in my head. But there's no way out of this. The bell has already been rung. Even if I quit right this second, just walk up to the desk and say, "No thank you. I hate animals, I've realized. I'll go pick up trash on the side of the road," Oliver will have seen me. He will have seen me and led me on a guided community service tour, and, worst of all, he will know—he will *know*—that I'm here because a judge made me be here.

No matter what I do, Oliver West will always know that the single skeleton in my otherwise pristine closet (more like a full-blown body; it hasn't even had time to decay) is that I, student council golden child, am just like every other Riley that ever walked through the doors of McKinley High.

And there is nothing. I. Can do about it.

I'm doing it again, I guess. Wallowing. I've fallen into an *Alice In Wonderland*-style rabbit hole spiral of self-loathing and confusion and acid trippiness, because no way can this be happening in real, regular life.

The talk concludes and everyone starts signing and I'm just sitting here because I don't know how to get up and look him in the eye. Him and his sparkling, arrogant eyes and his stupid, official clipboard.

It isn't until the room empties and he clears his throat that I force myself to look up.

"Riley," he says.

"West," I say.

"Are you in or not?"

He says it curtly, like I'm a nuisance. Like he wants me out of here as much as *I* want me out of here, and I don't really get that. I'm here to do free work for him; how annoying can that possibly be?

"I . . ."

"Brynn." His voice is sharp. He's looking down at me over that long, Roman nose, sharp cheekbones slashing across his face in a way that makes him look even more arrogant, intimidating. It's not his height; he's the same height as I am. But the way he holds himself makes him look about a million feet tall. The voice he's using on me makes me feel like the opposite.

I say, "What?"

"Are you going to sign this? Or find somewhere else to fuck off?"

I blink. "Excuse me?"

"I have work to do."

What the hell? "Are we—I'm sorry, do we have a problem?"

The lady at the front desk isn't even pretending not to listen. This is drama and it's good, and I don't blame her. I'd be eavesdropping, too. Maybe that would give me a clearer picture of what's going on here.

If it's about the other night . . . but no, it can't be. I was paranoid in the moment, but he didn't see—there's no way. And even if he did . . .

Oliver huffs out a laugh and says, *"Do we have a problem?"* He lowers his voice and leans in. "Jesus, Riley, you've got a lot of nerve."

I force myself to stand straight, to look him in the eye. "I'm sorry; I don't know what you're talking about."

His eyes lock on mine. They're so dark and furious and intense, and I refuse to believe that this is all over the damn contest, so whatever it is that I did that's pissed him off, I— god, I don't even know that I regret it.

He glances back over his shoulder and his fingers skim my arm. He doesn't grab me, he just touches me. I can barely breathe.

"Come with me," he says, low and through his teeth, and I don't actually know if I'm freaked out or turned on, but my pulse is about to strangle me. This is his fault. How dare he be both so astoundingly hot and invade my space like this?

His fingers slip off my arm and he turns down a hall we didn't tour earlier. He makes a sharp left into a little office with his last name on the front.

"Damn," I say, though I know it's a deviation. I can't help myself. "You have your own office? You're seventeen."

"It's my dad's. He runs this place. Did your research, I see."

"Oh, come *on*."

"What?" He shrugs and leans back against the desk behind him. "Not like you're big on reading."

I narrow my eyes. "Excuse me? I'll have you know that in my reading challenge this year, I'm a full three books ahead of—"

"Oh my *god*." He rolls his eyes and runs his hand over his forehead, stares at the ceiling, clearly begging for any kind of release from whatever hellscape I've forced him into.

The movement of his hand, his wrist, his arm, forces my eyes in that direction—the direction of his rolled up sleeves and the lean muscle and vein peeking out of them. They're an attack. An attack I shouldn't even be noticing, let alone acknowledging. I rip my gaze back up to his eyes, and he's already staring me in the face.

I wonder if he caught me looking.

Not that it matters; he clearly hates my guts.

And you know what? The feeling is mutual. It is! *You don't take anything seriously and you're just—just—infuriating. All the time. I find you intolerable.*

Or something.

He says, "I'll spell it out for you, Brynn: You screwed me over and we both know it."

I clamp my mouth shut. I blink.

"The application. For the scholarship. I saw you toss it before you'd even read it."

"Seriously?" I say. My face is burning up, from indignation, from shame, from being shut in an office with Oliver West—I don't know. "That's what this is all about? That's why you've been giving me serial killer eyes for the last hour?"

He doesn't say a thing, just keeps staring at me, challenging me.

I can feel the sweat breaking out on my forehead. I'm starting to crack already. My gosh, I would do terribly under interrogation.

I fumble out, "Besides, I did read it. That was my second round through them. Yours wasn't good enough."

He blinks, slowly. I think for an instant that I see the barest hint of a smile on his sharp mouth, but even if I do, it isn't comforting. It's a taunt; it's a challenge. "What's it about?"

"I—what?"

"My grant app. What did I write about? What's the project I said I wanted to enter the running with? You tell me and I'll graciously accept defeat."

My mouth goes dry. I shut my eyes, willing myself to suddenly have been blessed with an eidetic memory. I visualize Oliver's application, I visualize it in the trash, and then—that's it; that's all I've got.

I stand there like a landed fish for a minute, then bluster, "Well, I'm sorry but I can't be expected to remember every single person's application details."

"Ha." His laugh is humorless, just an exhalation. He glances up at the ceiling again, leaning back on his hands, then levels me with a cutting look. "I knew it."

"Oliver, listen."

"No," he says, "you listen. That grant was my one chance to get this thing off the ground. It's the only thing I care about, and you're such a prissy, stuck-up bitch that you decided that your beauty sleep was worth more than the thing I've dreamt about doing for two years. Yeah, Brynn, we've got a problem."

I want to lash out, I want to yell at him, I want to . . . do anything to defend myself. But I can't. What am I supposed to say? He's caught me and we both know it.

I square my shoulders. "I'm sorry."

He blinks again. The guy knows how to use silence. I myself do not know how to abide it.

"I trust this won't affect the service I do here."

"I'm your supervisor," he says.

My shoulders drop in relief. Thank god. He's going to be professional about this; I really do owe him one. "Thanks so much, I—"

"I'm gonna nail you to the fucking wall."

My voice cuts off of its own volition. I manage, "What?"

Oliver leans in, so close I can feel him breathe. He says, "You don't get to screw with my future and just get off. That's not the way it works."

"You can't just—you can't just threaten me."

"It's not a threat; it's a promise."

"A promise of what?"

"You volunteer here, I'm going to make working under me a living hell. I might not even sign off on your hours. And if I do, every hour you work for me is going to be like three. I swear to god. I'm not screwing around."

"You're really . . . you're really angry about this."

"You think?"

I'm shaking everywhere. I'm not afraid of him; he'd never do anything to me physically. I might not be best friends with Oliver West, but I know that.

But it doesn't matter. I'm scared of who he'll talk to. Maybe. I don't know, maybe he'll keep my secret. Maybe.

I'm scared this will all have been a waste and I'll have to start the whole process over again. I'm scared I'll have to just pick a place closer to home. I don't know. I hate everything; I'm so mad at myself. I'm so mad at scientists for not having yet invented time travel.

Shit. Shit, I ruined everything.

"I'm going to make this impossible for you," Oliver says.

Great. Awesome. I'm going to cry. Right here in this office.

"Okay," I say. "You win. I guess you win." I shrug, throw my hands slowly in the air, and let them limply fall to my sides.

I turn and reach for the door handle, and he stops me with an, "Unless."

I sigh. He's toying with me and I hate it and I hate him and I hate myself.

I turn back around to face him. "Unless what?"

He cocks his head, leans back again. "Unless you get me into the competition."

"I can't," I say. "Everyone's already been selected."

"Mmmm," he says. But it's not concession. It's a challenge.

"I don't know what that means. But I'm tired, and I have a two and a half hour bus ride back home, so if you don't mind . . ."

"Give me your spot," he says.

"What?"

He shrugs. "Give me your spot." Like it's the easiest thing in the world.

"I . . . Oliver."

"No," he says. "I've gone over this and over this. I'm not asking too much. You tossed my application away like it was nothing, but yours? Heaven forbid you didn't get in. Didn't get what you wanted. You freaking princess."

I'm seeing red now. "Princess? I'm sorry, have you seen where I live?"

"The trailer park? Big damn whoop. It doesn't mean anything. You get everything you want and you treated me like shit and I'm not taking it. I'm not. Give me your spot."

He yanks a pile of paper from behind him on the desk and thrusts it in my face.

"Read it. You tell me I didn't deserve a fair shake like everybody else."

"Oliver—"

"Read it."

I purse my lips.

I look him in the eye.

I take his stupid application.

And—

Shit.

Shit.

By the end, I'm gritting my teeth and my eyes are burning and my muscles are shaking because . . . he's right.

He's right; he deserves a shot. He deserved one that night, and if I would have pulled my head out of my butt for two seconds, I would have seen that.

I . . .

"I—I'm sorry," I manage.

He won't let me look away from him. His eyes are too arresting. The way he looks at me doesn't really leave room for me to dismiss him. He says, in a gentling voice that's still firm as hell, "I don't need you to be sorry."

The room is so quiet.

All I can hear is us breathing. A couple dogs barking two hallways down. The old-fashioned clock on the wall ticking.

It's so quiet that it rips through the room like a siren when I whisper, "Okay."

Oliver can't disguise the instant shock that ripples through him.

In that second, I can see it—the letdown from the adrenaline. He didn't think I'd do it. Well. Surprise.

I don't have a choice.

"Okay," I say. "I'll do it. I'll—I'll give you my spot."

I don't give myself the room to think about it—to consider what this means for me, everything I'll be giving up. Not in here, not with him.

He doesn't get to have the satisfaction.

I'll break down later.

I pull myself up and lock my jaw. Fine. He wins. But I'm getting something out of this, too. "But you have to give me rides here," I demand. "And back. And treat me fair. Just like you would any other volunteer."

"Deal," he says. It comes out in an ecstatic rush and then he overcorrects, back to forced apathy. "Deal."

He reaches for my hand and I shake his, ignoring the nerves that light up at the scarred touch of his palm against mine.

I'm so mad and sad and humiliated and . . . *betrayed* isn't even the right word. I don't know what it is except *bad*. I feel *bad*.

That's it, that's all she wrote.

I feel bad and tired and I hate Oliver West and I point out the window to his truck and say, "Give me a goddamn ride home."

He says, "As you wish, princess. My shift's over in three hours."

He flashes me his pearly whites and closes the office door.

CHAPTER SEVEN

IT TURNS OUT THAT waiting is not as horrible as I thought it would be. I mean, I'm mad. Of course I'm mad, even though I guess, technically, I have no right to be mad at Oliver. What's he going to do? Just knock off work three hours early to drive my transportationless butt home? But I'm mad anyway—about everything.

Paperwork isn't even processed, so I can't count the next few hours toward my service requirement, and there's no way I'm going to ask Oliver for favors already. He'd eat me alive.

There's a little tattoo shop up the road, a cute ice cream place several miles away, but one: it's several miles away, and two: ice cream is like five bucks a scoop and I don't have that kind of cash. I can't fathom being a person who does.

So I sit around for a while, until the place closes and the girl at the front desk asks me if I want to play with the animals while they get settled in for the night.

I cock my head and take about four seconds to consider before accepting her offer outright.

I let a few of the cats out of their cages and do a sweep of the cat room. And *god* are Maine Coons absolutely GIGANTIC, WHOA. Then I take a couple of the pups on walks in the fenced-in area (not allowed to take them off the property yet, not without all my paperwork processed). It's fun because, gosh, dogs are adorable, and I love them all.

But then I come to a stall marked yellow, with a big, black pit—just an absolute tank of a thing. He looks like every picture of anti-pit propaganda I've ever seen. All muscle and jaw, squat and sharp-toothed, with those clipped ears that make him look like the living embodiment of badass. Of "dangerous."

Except for one thing: he's only got three legs.

Lord, I'm a sucker for a tripod.

He eyes me warily when I approach his kennel and Oliver stops me, hand on my shoulder. "Whoa," he says.

"What?"

"No." He touches my wrist, long fingers insistently pulling it back. "Look at me," he says.

I furrow my brow, glancing back at the dog in the kennel, who is suspicious and scared and puffing out his chest in the corner.

"This?" Oliver says, showing me his forearm and the long, angry line bisecting it at the bone. He tips his chin at the dog. "Frankie."

"Oh," I say. I glance back at the dog—Frankie—and say. "I—what happened?"

Oliver shrugs. "Got too close when I was feeding him and he got jumpy."

"He's not eating now."

"Don't touch him," says Oliver.

I'm so . . . so freaking drawn to Frankie that I'm frustrated at the order. "Well, I—"

"You're not allowed."

The unspoken threat is there, hanging solid in the air between us. I step out of line, he doesn't sign off.

"Fine," I say. "He's—is he really that dangerous?"

Oliver looks at him through the glass, and Frankie's stump tail thumps the ground, just the once. "Nah," he says. Fondness lights up his face. "He's not a bad boy; he just needs some TLC. Isn't that right, buddy?"

I keep watching Frankie even after Oliver moves on, does whatever clean up and dog and cat maintenance he has to do. Then Front Desk, whose name, I discover, is Devika, has me help her out sweeping and doing last minute non-animal crap maintenance (I can't be forced into that until it's all official) and turning off lights and all that.

When I get to the nearly empty parking lot, Oliver isn't there.

Devika tells me he's probably out back. That I can wait for him at his truck. I tell her I will, and she takes my acquiescence as leave to head home.

But I don't want to wait.

I want to see what he's up to.

The second Devika's car disappears, I slide off Oliver's hood and quietly make my way around the back of the rescue.

It's quiet back here, a little lonely, in the muted colors of the early evening. Just a couple lights that must perpetually be on—like the lights at a ballfield. It's all chain link and barren grass and dirt. In the empty dark, it looks more like a place for abandoned animals than a place of rescue. Both are true, but the emptiness makes it feel next to haunted.

I slip up to the gate, careful not to drag my feet through the rocks, to give my position away. I don't even know why I'm sneaking; I'm not doing anything wrong. I'm just . . . looking for my ride.

But what I stumble on feels so private my cheeks flush.

It's nothing inappropriate, even bordering on it. There's nothing going on that should make me blush. It's just that it's . . . it's personal. It's intimate. It's something I don't think I'd be verboten from seeing for any reason; it's just that I wasn't invited.

Oliver West did not invite me into his unfettered joy.

And that is what it is: without constraint.

He has Frankie out in the yard, in the quiet dark. Hopping around the yard like a little puppy, even though he's got to be six or seven.

Oliver has a stick, and it casts shadows on his face, sharp and soft all at once in the floodlights.

"Get it—get it from me! Oh, come on, you big baby, you can do better than that."

Frankie is lunging for the stick, then clamping down and yanking backward, growling and sprinting and leaping and . . . and Oliver can't stop laughing.

They're playing.

Oliver's laugh is always a little smug, a little cocky, a little . . . intentional.

But when he falls to his back, giant monster of a dog

tackling him and slobbering all over his face, he *giggles*. He giggles loud enough that it cuts right through the dark.

He is relaxed.

I . . . I back up, slow so he can't hear my footsteps on the ground.

I don't mind how long I have to wait on the hood of his truck.

CHAPTER EIGHT

THE TEXT COMES ACROSS my screen and I smile.

Alisha: *Wyd*

What I'm doing, at this second, is scrolling through obscure duels in history in order to soothe my rattled nerves. It's like eleven p.m. and tomorrow is school, and I should be asleep. But I can't sleep.

I can't sleep because tomorrow I have to resign from the competition I've been desperate to enter since I was a freshman. From the contest I've spent years thinking about, meticulously planning. I had this whole thing set up—this big idea to help get heat and power and electricity assistance to people below a certain income line. I had this entire plan and a great presentation and . . .

I shut my eyes. Tears sting my eyelids. I can't think about this. I did it to myself.

I also can't sleep because earlier this evening, Patrick and Randi announced that she's pregnant, and they're so *young* and I'm just afraid that that means Mom is gonna have to help out, and I don't know. I don't know, I'm trying not to freak out. But I guess I'm freaking out a little bit.

Usually when I get like this, I find something to do with my hands, to fix. But there's nothing to tinker on right now, because anything in the house's system that needed to be fixed in the last several months, I've worked on already.

So I'm obsessing over the only other thing I care about: history. Weird history, especially.

I write back: *Did you know that back in the 1700s, there was a duel fought over sausage*

Alisha: . . .

Yeah, I respond. *Over like unsafe conditions. And so these two rivals decide to duel. And the guy who is challenged gets to choose the weapon so he chooses SAUSAGES.*

Alisha: *Oh my god. It's worse than I thought.*
Me: *What is*
Alisha: *Your neuroses*
Me: *One of the sausages is infected with trichinosis. So they're supposed to both eat one, and then the loser dies a slow death.*
Alisha: *Stop this. Come over*

I write back: *Okay*

I slip out of the house, because going to Alisha's has got to be a better distraction than this. There's a bus running in the next few minutes. Cool.

Me: *They didn't, by the way.*
Alisha: *what*

I get on the bus. Happily, I'm not far from the rez, so this ride should only take twenty minutes longer than necessary, not an hour.

Me: *die. From the sausage. The challenger retracted.*
Alisha: *well. thank god for that.*

Alisha is in her pajamas when I get there. For me, that means something that's been worn into rags and old, mismatched shorts if I'm fancy. (If I'm not, I bother not with pants at all.) For Alisha, a master thrifter, that means something adorable and matched and absolutely killer on her. This evening, she's sporting a warm yellow tank with little flowers on it and some loose-fitting pants in the same pattern. It would make some people look like an old woman. On Alisha, it's charmingly vintage and it hugs her exactly where it should.

"See," I say, "now *that* is within your color palette."

Alisha twirls. "This old thing?" She winks. "Come have some popcorn."

I hop over to the couch and plop there beside her on the cushion. She's watching something absolutely horrifying, blood spraying across the screen, an ingenue shrieking.

"Jesus, Alisha."

"No," she says. "You tiny baby. Horror makes me feel

alive. Besides, menstrually, you deal with losing like four pints of blood a month."

"Four *pints*? There's no way that's accurate."

"Well," she says, "that's what this lady is losing."

I stick my tongue out and fake gag.

"Also," she says, popping some popcorn into her mouth, "you listen to all that true crime shit. That's way worse because it's real."

I snuggle up under the fuzziest star quilt in the world; her grandmother made it and I've never felt anything cozier. "Only historical crime!"

She rolls her eyes. "Oh yes, that makes it not real, you freak."

I smirk, and we go back to the atrocity on the screen.

Alisha says, through the popcorn and ice water, "Okay, so. Community service. Tell me how that went."

I groan. "OR," I say, "we could talk about anything but that?"

"Fine," she says. "Let us discuss the rez party I went to this weekend."

I press my hand to my chest. "And you didn't invite me?"

She spits out a laugh. "White girl, please. I love you, and you know you could not handle a rez party."

I laugh. "I can't handle any parties."

"I know, baby." She pets my head, mock consolingly.

"Get any action?"

"Nah," she says. "There were like four people there who aren't my cousins."

"Hashtag rez problems."

"Rez. Problems." She toasts me with her ice water and leans back on the couch, throwing her legs over my lap. "Now, ssshhh. This is the good part."

I lean my head against the couch and relax. There's some kind of absolutely heavenly smell coming from the kitchen. Tacos, I think. Her parents are all about the midnight snacks, which is an absolute blessing. I'm cuddled up with one of my favorite people in the world, and Mom's at work so no one cares where I am, and no one cares, and for five seconds, I can just relax. Not worry about what I have to do tomorrow. And who I have to do it for.

She says, "You should see the stuff I've been doing on my trap set, by the way. That's the other big news. I've come up with this riff, and listen, man. Keith Moon would shit. It's incredible."

"Play it for me."

"At eleven p.m.? Mom and Dad will kill me. I'll show you my musical stylings later, though. Promise."

After the killer nearly gets apprehended (the killer who I think, may in fact, be a vampire's ghost? I don't know; I don't even know if that's a thing), I say, to the ceiling, "Well. Randi's pregnant."

"Oh damn," she says. "Congrats, man."

I shrug. "I guess."

She raises an eyebrow at me. "What do you mean, you guess? You hate her or something? Hasn't she been with Patrick for a million years?"

"No. I mean, I love her, it's just . . ."

"Oh," says Alisha. She blinks at the screen for a while. It's very quiet. Just the vampire ghost slash possibly squid thing? On screen. Vampire ghost squiding at everything. Then she says, "Don't take this the wrong way?"

Now my defenses are up. Who has ever said not to take something the wrong way when that thing could *possibly* be taken in a cool and gentle way?

"Okay," I say. I curl my hands in the quilt. My nerves start to jump.

"You're just kind of, like, harsh on your family sometimes. I don't know. Like, I get it. But also, it's not 1802 anymore, man. No one's gonna be on your brother's ass for *having a baby out of wedlock.* Randi's not gonna have to wear a scarlet A or something."

I can feel the defensiveness bleeding out of my throat. "I know that."

She raises her hands. "I'm not saying anything. I'm just saying I don't think it's all that bad. I think they're mostly cool. You know? They have their shit, your dad, especially. And Evian."

"I mean, I guess I would too if my name was *Evian.*"

She laughs, snorts a little. I do love that about her. "But they love you, right?"

"Yeah," I say.

Yeah.

"Sorry," she says. "We don't have to talk about anything. Let's just hang out? Have some tacos."

"You're always in the mood for tacos."

She cackles and her eyes sparkle.

The vampire ghost squid morphs into a lamprey.

I truly have no idea.

CHAPTER NINE

"I DON'T . . . I'm sorry; I don't understand."

I clear my throat and quite literally choke the words out. They're tainted with disingenuity and the desperate rattle of *Fuck you, Oliver West*.

"I simply don't have time—" I glance down at the floor. The ugly carpet they picked, because I guess no school on this entire, godforsaken planet is capable of picking non-ugly carpet. It's gray flecked with peach and pink and pukey, mustardy green. Good. It fits my mood. I shut my eyes and try to get a little less pukey-mustardy. Then I look Tanisha in the face. "I simply don't have time this year to dedicate to this contest the attention it requires."

I sound like a robot. Or a duchess. I sound like I've rehearsed this as many times as I have, indeed, rehearsed this, but I do feel sick to my stomach, so hey, that's something.

(It's not; it's not even new. I've felt like this every time I've practiced it, knowing I was about to give up my future for one tiny, little mistake. But I don't have a choice. The judge was clear. It's one and done, and I need my record erased. Both for my rep here at school and for my shot at college. This is just the way it is.)

Tanisha narrows her eyes and flips her hair back over her shoulder. She's got the shiniest weave, and it goes all the way down to her waist. To her waist! It's the envy of us all.

"Are you sure about this, Brynn? Absolutely, positively certain?" She looks around the empty civics classroom like she's about to commit espionage and then lowers her voice. "It's *forty thousand dollars*, Brynn. What the *hell* is student council going to do for you that competes with forty grand?"

I shut my eyes tight.

I take a deep breath.

Every molecule, every atom, every *electron*, every fucking quark inside every electron, rests quietly in the mantra: *I hate Oliver West. I hate Oliver West. I hate Oliver West.*

"I'm sure, Tanisha. My heart's not in it and I can't afford to take time away from so much of my other activities and academics"—*what other activities and academics could POSSIBLY—it doesn't matter. It doesn't matter it doesn't matter it doesn't matter; you're being blackmailed*—"when I don't even know that I'll win this."

She thins her lips and looks down at the sheet with all the finalists' names on it.

She opens her mouth like she's got something to say, and god, I am just *begging* her not to say it. I can barely stand myself right now.

It would just take admitting that I'm doing community service! Admitting that I'd made a mistake and was going to pay for it! That's all, and then I could switch volunteer jobs to one closer to home because who cares? Oliver would hate me, but he'd have nothing on me. And then I could really play ball on this scholarship I need—I *need*.

I think about it, just for a second. Just saying it, out loud. Just admitting to my failure.

But then I see them: the faces of my siblings. My cousins, whom I barely see, but whose name has tainted mine. The dread permeating every teacher's very soul the second they see my last name on their roster. And everyone, everyone, seeing me as one of them.

As another fuck-up.

My mom. My mom who works so hard every single day trying to make sure we don't have it as hard as she did, who's doing everything on her own because my loser dad can't seem to stop drinking long enough not to get behind the wheel of a vehicle *again*. Who's counting on me to be different. To be better.

Every human in my life watching my tiny, miniscule fall from grace and knowing in their bones that I have really fallen to meet all their expectations of me.

I can't.

I won't.

I suck everything back inside and let it lie trapped inside my lungs. And I stare back at her.

"Al—alright, Brynn. Okay. Fine. Well, I'm going to need you to re-run those applications and pick a replacement, or I guess I could do it. Jesus, this is such a colossal pain; I've got an AP exam in two hours and the first round of competition is in two days, so we absolutely *have* to have a replacement picked by—"

"I've got one. I have one. I ... I have him. My replacement."

Tanisha's shoulders drop from where they were by her ears, and she breathes an audible sigh of relief. I slide her Oliver's application. "Thank god. Oh thank—" She cuts herself off. "You serious?"

"As a heart attack."

She blinks down at the paper. "Oliver West? Oliver West. The same Oliver West who stole Principal Edwards's cigarettes to sell to the seniors when he was in the ninth grade? The same Oliver West who got the whole band together, snuck into school after hours, and covered the entire school, floor to ceiling, in bubble wrap? The same Oliver West who—" She glances around surreptitiously again, then leans in to hiss, "The same Oliver West who just got out of juvie at the beginning of the school year—god, Brynn, are you for *real*?"

I sigh. I hate that I'm having to defend him, that I'm having to defend my choice, that I'm having to do this at all, and not just do it quietly and with grace. But go *all in*. To convince her to take this from me and give it to him.

"Yeah, Tanisha. That Oliver West. Double-check behind me if you want. I'm telling you his application is stellar. And he might be ... a clown. Okay? I get it. But everyone loves him, even the staff, and you know that. He's not malicious, he just ... screws around. I'm telling you that this application is not something he's screwing around with."

Tanisha sighs.

She takes two minutes to look over his app.

And she says, "Alright. Okay, I'll call him."

"Cool."

"For the record, I think you're making a mistake."

Well, Tanisha, get in line.

I don't volunteer today. I can only go once a week, apparently, and even if I *could* just drop in whenever I felt like it, that day would not be today. Do I want to see puppies and cats? Yeah. Do I want that dose of fur-induced serotonin to come with a side of Oliver West, Supervisor? Absolutely not.

I'm so angry looking at my driveway and my living room and my siblings and . . . everyone. Everyone and everything to do with my life when the bus drops me off at home. I'm so angry that I probably shouldn't be working with anything that could cause me any physical harm, but the A/C's been out for two days and we are at least several more from the season shifting from blazing hot to freezing cold and no one wants to call anyone to take a look. That's a nightmare.

HVAC: Here's my Visa And Cash.

I've got a knack for this kind of thing, so I've been studying it for a while. I mean, mostly just screwing around on YouTube, but also manuals and written tutorials, that kind of thing. It might be weird, but this sort of work—the sort that requires you to work with your hands, to map out a plan, to solve a puzzle with your brain while your fingers physically put it together, well, it soothes me.

I've tried yoga and meditation and music, and nothing gets me in the zone like forcing my mind to do work.

No one expects it; I'm so *girly* and *cute* and *academic*. Like I can't be girly and cute and academic and love trying to figure out what's going wrong in machinery, and how to make it right so my family can have cool air in the summer and heat in the winter.

I ignore everyone gathered around in the living room and head back to tinker with the A/C unit for a while. I don't have to put on any kind of show for anyone. I just zone in on the wires and tubes and metal. I focus. I'm out here for maybe a half hour, until the loud buzzing roar dies down. I've made progress, I think, but I'm going to have to do a deeper internet dive before I can really figure it out. I look over the unit one last time before my stomach forces me out into the living room.

It's Kraft mac and cheese tonight. But my brother has dressed it up with tuna and cayenne, so, you know.

It's pretty good.

Randi says, "I don't know why on Earth this baby wants blue box and cayenne, but here we are."

Evian laughs. A cheesy dating show is on in the background, which is par for the course. "How far along are you again?"

"Oh, just a couple months."

"How you feeling?"

"Okay, actually."

Patrick pipes in, "She puked four times yesterday."

"Patrick!" she says. "Shut up; no one wants to hear about that."

I shrug. "It's fine." Everyone turns to me. I'm the quiet one around here, I think, because I love my family, but the older I've gotten, the more I've just kind of . . . resented everything, I guess? So sometimes I don't know how to act like a normal human. I say, "We can talk about morning sickness. It's supposed to suck."

The stillness, what feels like waiting for some kind of jab, something from me, makes me feel like crap, especially considering what Alisha told me the other day. But I let it hang. And the tension in the air releases.

Randi says, "You know what, little sis? It *does* suck."

And we relax.

We eat our mac and cheese.

Later, I shoot a text to Oliver West: *It's done. You're in.*

All he says back is: *cool*

Honestly, does anyone suck at texting more than boys?

CHAPTER TEN

SATURDAY MORNING, OLIVER PICKS me up. It's my first actual volunteer shift, and I'm weirdly nervous. I don't know why; it's not like I'm being monitored and evaluated by a boy who's actively blackmailing me and has every reason to force me to fail! Or who threatened to make my life a living hell! And it's not like I got into this whole situation in the first place with my illicit criminal activities!

The point is: It is not hot outside and I'm still sweating right through this very maroon Pibbles and Kits T-shirt that is decidedly not in my clear spring color palette. Ah well. I already feel like I'm dying, so my skin might as well embody the sentiment.

Oliver tips his chin at me when I slide into the truck and says, "Riley."

He, of course, looks fantastic in maroon.

Of course he does; Oliver looks fantastic in everything.

The freckles on his face stand out especially intensely in the storm gray morning light, dark irises blending nearly indistinguishably into his pupils. People go nuts for, what? Green eyes? But I don't know; I find dark brown to be almost unbearably mysterious. And Oliver's are that. Combine that with the wonders his close-shaven buzzcut does for his fine, sharp-boned jawline that's only hardened in the past year.

Jesus, what a walking nightmare.

I lean back against the headrest and buckle my seatbelt and Oliver pulls out of my neighborhood and onto the highway. "Hey," he says. "Thanks, by the way. I just, uh, wanted to tell you."

I feel my eyes narrow as they gaze through the windshield. "Thanks?" They slide over to look at him.

He shrugs a single shoulder. "Yeah," he says. "Just for . . . you know. For the scholarship."

"I didn't give you the scholarship."

"You know what I mean. For the chance."

I sputter out a laugh. "Yeah, you're welcome. I did it out of the kindness of my heart."

"Look, I'm just trying to say—"

"Don't." Fury bubbles up in my throat. "Don't say it. I don't want to hear it. You forced my hand here and you know it."

He purses his lips and his hands tighten around the wheel. He doesn't say much else for the rest of the trip. He just turns on some music—the Civil Wars, a choice I do grudgingly respect—and it is a very long, very quiet thirty-four minutes to the shelter.

I sign in at the front desk and Devika shoots me a toothy smile, bright as sunshine. The second I come into contact with someone who is not Oliver West, my chest lightens considerably. I can breathe. I can get through the day and maybe, just maybe, I can do it happily.

Devika's got this cute little pink nose stud in that winks in the light, and I say, "That's neat."

"What?"

"The stud."

"Oh!" she says, reaching up to touch it. "I don't even remember which one it is."

"Pink?" I say.

"Oh right, yeah." Her mouth slides into a grin. "Girlfriend got this for me." Her face lights up so brightly that I almost feel the need to squint. It's joyful and devilish all at once, just at the mention of the girl, and I feel a quick tightness in my chest, the smallest stab of longing, not for a person, really, just for being in a relationship? It's not a good reason to get into one; I know that. I feel like basically everyone has had to learn *that* one the hard way at one time or another. But I do miss it sometimes.

Eh.

Not like I really have the time *or* the inclination right now. Not with all of this plus the newly narrowed field of options in the *how the hell do I pay for college?* department.

I smile back at her. "Well, I'm into it."

"Thanks!" She sucks a tongue stud between her teeth, playing with the metal in a way that makes me shudder just a little—metal on teeth. I cannot stomach it; it feels like electricity shooting through every capillary.

Another employee shows up, then, a pretty, curvy Black girl with braids down her back and a smile, not on her mouth, but in her eyes. She's got the same kind Oliver does—that ~deep, mysterious~ dark brown that bleeds into her pupils. Devika stands and leans over the counter and says, "Girl. I have things to tell you," just as I say, "Hey, I'm Brynn. I'm volunteering," and stick my hand out awkwardly.

The new girl raises her eyebrow at me, probably because of the desperately awkward energy and weird boomerness of the gesture of a professional handshake upon meeting. She takes my hand and smiles, though, which is kind.

"Community service," says Devika, like that's not going to totally humiliate me. Like it's nothing and won't make me flash bright red from the crown of my head down to the tips of my toes. Just casual.

"Oh yeah, we got a lot of y'all! Honestly, no better place to do it. Play with puppies and kittens all day and call it paying off a debt to society or whatever." She laughs, and my full-body blush fades a little. "Jenn, by the way."

No one (but Oliver) knows my family here. No one has any expectations for me to fall to, so no one has any real reason to judge me, and the fact that my being here is court-ordered makes no . . . well, not a HUGE difference to anyone. I can relax. I can do this without wanting to crawl into the earth in shame.

I shake myself just a little and Devika says, "Well, or clean up shit and call it paying off a debt to society." She says it nicely, laughing, and I groan.

"Come on," says Devika. "I'll get you to the cleaning supplies."

From there, the day folds into lonely monotony. At least for a while.

The dogs are moved in and out of their cages, and it's my job to head into the empty pens and clean up any stray shit and/or pee and/or whatever unmentionable things. After that, I sanitize their kennels and beds and refill water and food, and then it's on to the next kennel, and the next. Someone else is taking the cats' rooms today, so it's me with the dogs.

Around lunchtime, I head to the break room and snack on a sandwich I brought, and Oliver says, "Riley," and cocks his head toward the dog room.

My heart flutters in my chest. I feel like I'm in trouble, suddenly?

I take a long swig out of my water bottle and swallow the last remaining pieces of my turkey sandwich and follow Oliver toward the kennels.

They allow me four volunteer hours per shift, so after lunch, I'm supposed to finish that out helping socialize the cats for an hour, which is really just translation for: play with the giant, fluffy fur beasts! And I've *really* been looking forward to that after a morning of being covered in cleaning chemicals and dog shit, so I swear to god, if he's going to do anything to take that from me, I'll . . . well. Do nothing, I guess.

There is no possible satisfying threat I can use to finish that sentence.

Oliver stands with his arms folded, staring into a kennel with an old, white pittie-boxer mix sleeping in it.

"That look clean to you?" he says, nodding at the kennel.

I peer into it. It's clean. I mean, mostly. There's a couple little streaks here and there, I guess, but I was in a hurry. It's a lot of work and—

"Brynn. Answer me."

I clench my teeth and my nostrils flare. "Pretty clean," I grit out.

He doesn't even say anything. He just stares at me and slowly, centimeter by centimeter, raises an eyebrow.

I try not to say anything. I try to hold my silence, to hang onto any power and dignity I have left. But his scrutiny is absolutely murderous, and he's so close, chest level with me, eye-to-eye, and I don't know how it's *worse* when he shifts that stare from my face to the kennel.

But the longer he looks, the more flaws he'll find, and I can't stand it; I can't *stand* it.

I say, "I tried my best, okay? I've never done this before."

He doesn't waver in his examination. He just says, without looking at me, "You've never cleaned up after a dog? Never done chores?"

It's incredible, how quickly he can take me from neutral to nervous to furious, but I'm a hotbed of frustrated, warping, swirling feelings. I say, "Of course I have, asshole."

"Watch it," he snaps. "You can be whatever kind of tight ass bitch you want at school, but here, I am your *superior.* You got that? This looks bad. You did a bad job. You want me to coddle you?"

I scoff and take a step backward. Great! Maybe I'll cry! Right here. I don't even know if the tears threatening me are sad or angry or embarrassed, but it doesn't matter. What matters is that I'm about to lose it right here at work in front of the person who, right now, I hate more than anyone on the planet.

His voice is a little softer when he says, "I'm not trying to be an asshole," but it still carries that hard edge of flint.

"These dogs are just really important to me, okay? They mean more to me than just about anything, and I don't think you're being malicious here, but I can't have you being lazy. When I say I need the kennels cleaned, I mean *cleaned*. I don't want something racing through here and all my babies getting sick, alright?"

There it is again: that hot shame. Not because Oliver disapproves of me—well, that might be a lie. No one likes disapproval. Especially not from someone like that, someone whose entire face and body and voice and *presence* are freaking designed to make you beg for their approval. But it's more because of the dogs. I let the animals down. Frankie's face flashes through my mind. His big muscles and his furious, big face, gone all gentle sprinting through the yard and frolicking with Oliver. I let these very good boys and girls down; I let Frankie down.

I chew on my lower lip.

I do need Oliver to leave. Now I really am going to cry.

I'm just . . . uh . . . not exactly used to failing at things.

Certainly not this many times in a row.

"Okay," I say. My voice is so small it's embarrassing. "I'm sorry."

Oliver sets his hand on my shoulder and says, "Listen, it's—"

"Don't touch me," I snap. He snatches his hand back before I even have the chance to instinctively shrug it off.

He says, "I'm sorry. It won't happen again." But his voice is so close. He's so close I can smell his deodorant. The spicy cool scent of Boy Anti-Perspirant That Smells Manly or whatever.

"I'll redo it," I say.

I look up at him and I just *know* my eyes are pink. He studies my face and suddenly I can't breathe.

Oliver opens his mouth like he's going to say something, then hesitates, and shuts it again. "No time," he says. "I really need someone to go socialize the cats this afternoon, and that's you, isn't it?"

"Y-yes."

"Well?" he says. "Go."

He turns on his heel, just like that, and leaves me standing there alone.

I blink into the room, nothing but dog sounds filling my head. And I leave.

When I cross the lobby to get to the cat room, Jenn says, "It ain't you."

"What?" I turn to face her.

"Oliver. He's *real* protective of these animals. He'll expect you to be perfect, and you can just come bitch about it to Danika and me. He's a good guy, though. He just . . . he cares a lot. About them, you know?"

"Oh." I say. "Oh sure, I'm totally fine. He didn't even bother me. I swear."

"Girl, don't lie."

I blink at the floor.

Then I look back up at her. "Okay. No, you're right, he was a complete asshole."

She grins, seeming both empathetic and ornery. "Like I said, he's a good guy. You can't let that protective shit get to you."

"Okay," I say. "Thanks."

It doesn't fix it, but it helps, I guess, to know I'm not the only one.

Then I head off to the cat room.

From the corner of my eye, I catch Oliver heading to the dog kennels with cleaning supplies.

My chest tightens.

I could take it as a sign of a lack of trust, I guess. But the way he looked at me in there, I think . . . I don't know. I think he was doing me a favor. Letting me decompress?

Maybe that's wishful thinking.

I don't know.

What I do know is that for the first time today, my heart isn't pounding out of my skin, and the gentle chorus of purrs and meows when I close the cat room door behind me lulls me into peace.

CHAPTER ELEVEN

MY SOLE JOY IN this life rests in the knowledge that Oliver West did not get enough time to prepare for round one of this competition.

No one did, frankly. That's part of the challenge. Once finalists are announced, you get ten days to prepare basically, like, a public service announcement explaining your project and why it's necessary, why it deserves forty grand in startup money.

That's one thing when you're presenting profit margins to *Shark Tank*, but it's another thing entirely when what you're asking for is a grant that needs to *keep* being granted. When what you need is money for something that is going to keep needing money and needs to help enough to justify the expense.

I scanned his application.

It's good.

It's worth the shot he's being given.

But there's no way Oliver West is going to pull this out of his butt.

Everyone goes all out for this thing—I'm talking, like,

professionally filmed productions. If you've got cash, that helps, but it's more about the connections than anything. Plus, local businesses like their names to be flashed around at the event. It's just one high school (the woman who funds it is a ~distinguished alumnus~) but it gets a lot of press. So what I'm saying is, businesses around here are all too happy to donate time and money to a bunch of students at the high school on the shitty side of town so they can get in the news for philanthropy and get advertising all over the place.

But a week before the presentation? There's no way Oliver has anything that's even close to slick enough.

The auditorium is filled with kids, some parents. A couple local news crews. We get an assembly day for this, because it's kind of a big deal here. A bunch of people choose to donate time to whatever causes and organizations the students in the grant competition draw their eyes to. The whole thing is kind of the school's claim to fame.

So all that to say: The auditorium is *packed*. Standing room only. It was supposed to be the gym, but a pipe burst and, well, here we are. About to listen to a number of heart-rending presentations, breaking fire code.

I'm lined up in the front with three other peer judges. Since I dropped out of the competition for what everyone *else* assumed were non-blackmail reasons and therefore I had the capability to be a totally non-biased judge, I was recruited. Alongside us are a couple teachers, the principal, three members of local government, and the woman who created the grant in the first place: Audra Robbins.

It's a rush just sitting this close to her, watching her

and hearing about her all over the place every year of my high school career.

The principal leaves his seat and takes his place at the microphone. "Welcome, welcome! Wow, can't believe we're to this place again." He launches into his speech, and it goes like it does every year. He always starts with that sentence, even. He explains why we are gathered here, as though we're eulogizing the grant, has everyone clap for Audra Robbins, then takes his place back among the judges.

The first contestant is Laura Kim, whose presentation is slick as hell. It's a good indicator of what's to come. Her organization is one that's built around the idea that food should be accessible and affordable, and it's essentially a large-scale community garden. It's really a *network* of community gardens she'd like to start, and she's already gotten permission from a number of growers in the area in exchange for press and a number of other incentives. It's really lovely, beautifully thought out, and like I said, *slick*. The TV ad is produced gorgeously; I think her older sister is a film student, so I'm willing to bet she got involved. There's moving music talking about hunger in the South, profiles of locals who can't afford food because food stamps suck ass and fresh ingredients eat way too much of the money for most people to afford them. She concisely establishes the problem, then lays out her solution: this network of community gardens, and another wave B plan that rolls out food trucks to fill in the gaps where the food stamps programs fail. They miss a lot of families and don't even allow you to buy, like, hot food. They've certainly never covered it for us. Heads nod around the room, moved, impressed, and I'm vitalized. I can feel the energy thrumming through my veins: being a part of something that might change things for people. It's exhilarating.

The judges mark down votes, numerical scores both on the idea and the presentation itself. I give her high marks. She's earned them.

The next student is polished, too, and stupidly handsome. He's on student council (of course), JROTC (unsurprising, given his straight gait, his broad shoulders, the air of authority he crosses campus with), any *number* of sports. His service organization is all about helping veterans with mental illness issues. Once again, top-notch effects, graphics, swelling music, and all the bald eagle American flag stuff that goes over real well in this part of the country. There's a kid with a cause dedicated to spaying and neutering cats in the area, one lobbying for better access to birth control and sex education and abortion (a tough sell in the South, but on the other hand, the people who jump in to work this contest are usually a little more open-minded than some others). Everyone, idea after idea, is just . . . killing it.

Audra is beaming several seats down. This is what she wanted. This is what she worked for and what she donates for and these students—my peers, my friends—are soaring.

Jealousy bubbles up in my chest when Oliver takes the stage. I can tell from here that he's sweating. His tie is listing to the side, and he's running his hands nervously down the sides of his slacks.

He's shaking when he sets his printed pages down on the podium.

It should be me. Talking to everyone about the lack of

access to plumbing and HVAC and electricity in the South, in the poorer areas—even the middle-income areas, the prohibitive cost, the absolute necessity of all of these things.

It should be *me* up there, so nervous I might throw up.

A voice in the back of my head says, *No it shouldn't. No it shouldn't, and you know it. You didn't give the guy a chance. You did this to yourself.*

I bite down on that thought—shred it and banish it from my mind.

Then I banish everything else—every bit of emotion I have attached to this, to this massive loss of opportunity, to Audra Robbins down the line, to Oliver West.

I clench my pen. Then I shut my eyes, take the deepest, slowest breath I can manage. And I open them again.

Every other entrant has had a presentation prepared. An advertisement, really. Music chosen and actors (actual actors or friends—that has varied) enlisted. Like . . . when I say people take this seriously? I mean they *take. It. Seriously.*

And Oliver West is up there in his sideways tie and his dark red slacks that I think might actually be skinny jeans and a button-down that makes him look, altogether, like an extra in freaking *Gossip Girl*, and his PERFECT smirk, and—Jesus, Riley, get it together. He's up there in his hipster-chic outfit, Converse and all, and the guy hasn't even made a PowerPoint presentation. He's got printed-out notes on a few sheets of paper.

Honestly, the schadenfreude was really getting to me before, but now I'm just feeling . . . embarrassed. And, god, I'm feeling guilty. He's not prepared for this. He's not prepared and it's my fault.

He's—

"Hey, so, I'm Oliver West," he starts. All he has to do is talk, take two steps out from behind that podium, and everyone falls silent. Everyone except a couple jock boys, who *whoop* from somewhere in the back. Oliver just laughs that dirty little laugh of his and tips his chin out to his cheering section in the dark ether of the auditorium. "Yeah," he says. "So." He glances down at his notes, shuffles them around for a minute, clears his throat. I expect him to draw attention to the fact the he got tossed into this competition at the last minute, to let everyone know that he's operating at a disadvantage. It's what I would do.

He doesn't.

I don't think *apologize* is really in Oliver's go-to list of plays.

He shoves his slender hands in his pockets and reads from the side of the podium, "I'm here on behalf of the organization I want to start. This organization is being founded with the mission . . ." He blinks, picks up his pages, glances back at all of us and narrows his eyes. Then he shakes his head and tosses the papers in the air.

A couple little gasps float up in the audience, which I think is a tad dramatic, but whatever.

"So let's be real about this—a lot of y'all know me."

Whoops from the jock boy section.

"A lot of y'all have known me for a long time."

More *whoops*.

"A lot of y'all knew me back when I was going by a different name."

A distinct lack of *whoops*.

Oliver's hands are back in those crimson skinny jeans of his. He saunters—truly saunters; what high school boy really has the confidence to *saunter*—to the front of the stage. "I want to be honest with you—being trans is not always a walk in the park, alright? Especially when you live here. Some of you know that because you're into social justice or whatever, and some of you know it because you've got friends or family who are trans or maybe because *you're* trans, and some of you—some of you know it because you've gone out of your way to make my life harder."

You could hear a pin drop.

Oliver rakes his hand over the back of his neck.

"So when I came out in the eighth grade, most of my friends were cool. Most of my peers were cool. It took my dad a full seventy-two hours to stop accidentally referring to me by my deadname, and it took him four minutes to acknowledge me as Oliver. I had it pretty easy." He takes a deep breath. "But not everyone does."

I vacillate between holding my breath and sucking in too much oxygen, feeling a little high. It's so . . . this is so personal. I feel like I'm watching someone rip his skin open on a stage.

"Did you know that 40 percent of the homeless population is queer? Forty percent. We're only like seven percent of the population. Did you know that queer youth are seven times more likely to be victims of violent crime than non-queer kids?"

It's so freaking quiet.

"My life expectancy? Well, it's—it's lower than yours. If you're cisgender. Mine is lower. And I'm white. Why don't you talk to a Black trans woman and do some quick math. Alright?" He scrapes his teeth over his lip. "I will. I have. I'm going to keep doing it. And that's what my project is about. I don't have a commercial for you. I don't have smooth visuals and audio effects. I don't even really have the security of knowing that I'm not gonna get my ass kicked—sorry. Butt. My butt kicked after this presentation or that a single one of y'all is going to care about this. What I have is my story. What I have is a desire to make sure that trans kids in the Carolinas get housed and get trained for jobs."

He takes a couple easy steps backward.

"My project is about bringing housing to kids whose dads didn't call them Oliver four minutes after they told him. And after that? It's about getting those kids into job training—I've formed partnerships with a couple big tradesmen around here to start youth in apprenticeship programs, and get them into careers that get them *paid*. Lifelong. That's it. That's what I'm going to do."

Those teeth on that lip again.

He stares down at the floor of the stage. Then he looks out over us all. "I'm going to do this. One way or another. With or without you, I'm going to do this. But, god, I hope you agree with me that it would be better if it was with you."

CHAPTER TWELVE

OLIVER IS SO COOL, so collected. He doesn't just exit the stage; he glides out of focus. Fades to stage left. And then he's gone. There is a smattering of applause, like there was for everyone else, but not *exactly* like there was for everyone else.

Because the other kids, well, let's just be real—a lot of the other kids, not all of them, but a lot of them, talked about issues they cared about, but issues that are easy to get behind. Issues that might be divisive when it comes down to policy, but that are easy to support one way or another. Animal rights, ending homelessness, stuff for women's shelters.

Not many kids up there hit issues that make people's hair stand on end, that draw a line and say, *This is right and this is wrong*, that ask you immediately where you stand, because even though it *seems* like it should be a united thing, there sure as hell are people on the other side of it.

But Oliver did.

As soon as someone says the word *queer*, people get their hackles up. Battle lines are drawn.

I'd like to blame that on living in the South, but come on. Let's be real; we didn't invent bigotry—that's around anywhere there's people. It's hard here, though, because it's in high places, too. It's in the government and the law books.

What Oliver is supporting, the organization he wants to start, that *should* be easy to get behind. Getting kids off the streets and into places where they feel loved and safe and can get the job training they desperately need. But not here. It's just . . . it won't be.

Oliver's was the last presentation, so the judges break. We're supposed to meet up in a half hour to discuss preliminary impressions, and yeah, I'm focused on that, my head is in the game, but I'm so distracted.

Not even because I'm jealous. Not because I'm upset!

Because I have this . . . this driving need to find Oliver.

I couldn't even tell you why. He didn't seem distressed. It's not like I feel like I need to comfort him or something. And it's not . . . I mean, it's not like I'm his girlfriend. It's not like I'm even his friend. So why would it be my job to go congratulate him on his speech? It's not. There's no reason for me to be doing this, to be searching the halls for him at all.

But the clock ticks down and I can't find him, and the longer it goes, the more I absolutely *need* to.

I find him in the band locker room, stuffed in the narrow space between the tuba lockers and the saxophones. He's got his knees up to his chest, hands clasped at his shins. Head down on them so all I can see is this prickle of dark hair close over his scalp.

He's quiet, and I don't think he's crying, but he's shuddering. His body right along with his breath.

I run my hand back through my hair and glance at him, then at the open door. I feel like . . . like I shouldn't be here. Coming was a mistake. I take a step back and he says into his knees, "Lyla?"

Suddenly my need to get to the door is overpowering, and what was going to be a stumble is becoming a scramble. I get one more step in before he glances up, eyes open and vulnerable, and then says, "Oh." He's instantly affronted, like I invaded him by being here, and he jumps to his feet and hisses, "Jesus."

I'm sorry for about a quarter of a second, and then I'm offended. "What, I can't be in here?"

He sighs and throws his arms up. "Yeah, Brynn, this is private property. Deeded to Oliver E. West. Get out of here or I'm calling the cops."

I roll my eyes.

"I'm fucking with you," he says. "I'd *never* call the cops."

My mouth twitches up.

There's quiet for a moment. Not easy exactly, but not . . . not scraping. Not stabbing. It's no longer a silence you feel like you're bleeding into.

I say, "I'm sorry. I just, I—" What am I even going to say? What explanation can I come up with that isn't creepy? "I just wanted—to see how you felt your speech went. Since, you know, it *is* my spot you're repping. I'm invested."

He purses his lips. "I feel fine. I feel good. So. Thanks."

It's a clear dismissal, and I intend to leave. I swear I intend to just immediately go. But then apparently my mouth opens and I say, "I just—it didn't look like you felt super great? Just now?"

"Brynn. Leave it. I was resting my eyes."

"Well, okay, but—"

"I'm a musician. So I like the band room. I'm hanging out in here. It's fine."

"It's just that—"

"Christ," he says. " I'm serious; can you get off my dick?"

"Oh," I say. "Oh, okay. I'm sorry? I'm sorry, I shouldn't have—I'll just leave. I'll go."

I take a couple steps backward, toward the door, and he runs his hand over the stubble at his jaw and says, "Sorry. You don't have to go. I'm just a little worked up right now."

It's taking every bit of strength I possess not to ask why. I'm trying not to be nosy. Not to pry.

I wait for him to speak.

He says, "Sometimes—okay, I know what I said out there is basically public knowledge. I've been out since the eighth grade, right? But it's always running through your head—who doesn't know? Who was this new for? Who does know and thinks you're lying to yourself or you're going to hell? I'm out, but it doesn't matter, because you're never *out* out. Never 100 percent. Being queer means coming out to a million different people a million different times, and I'm as out as I can be, but I've never talked about it to three hundred people and a news crew. And I've ever intentionally, actively just started shit with people about it. I saw some faces out there, man. This is starting shit. So I came here to just kind of be small."

"Oh," I say. I don't know what it's like to be anything

other than cisgender, but I know what it's like to need to be *small*. To tuck yourself into the tiniest place you can manage so that you will feel held by the walls, by blankets, by your own hands. Pressed into so that suddenly your chest opens and you can breathe. "Hey, have you ever thought you might have anxiety? Like, have you heard of—"

He spits out a laugh. "I'm queer; of course I know about *anxiety*. Why don't you ask if I've ever heard of depression next? Jesus!"

I would think he was offended, somehow, but he's doubled over laughing.

"Sorry, Riley," he says, "you're just—*Christ*, you're straight."

I sputter out a laugh. "Yeah, that's the rumor."

His eyes are sparkling when he looks at me, all mischief and play. He takes a step closer, and then they go a tinge sad again. Just the littlest bit. The smallest breath of depression, of the anxious thoughts I can read on him because I have them all the time. I say, "I wasn't trying to be nosy. Or a know-it-all or something. I just—I have anxiety. And depression. And I thought if you didn't recognize them, maybe I could help."

He nods at me once. "I can respect that."

There is a quiet between us, one borne of the specific camaraderie between those who have just exchanged *Oh, your brain is wrecked? Hey! Mine too!*

It stretches.

"What does the *E* stand for?" I say suddenly.

He blinks, dark freckles in his brown eyes popping. "What?"

"Oliver E. West, you said. What's the E?"

"Embry," he says, giving away his middle name, just like that. It's something people sometimes keep a tight hold on for one reason or another. But Oliver doesn't.

In fairness, if I had a middle name as good as Embry, I'd advertise it, too.

"Why do you want to know?"

"To steal your identity."

A smirk slits his face. "Think you're gonna wanna go for something a little more traditional. My social, my mom's maiden name."

"Oh," I say, waving him off like it's nothing. "I have all that already; what do you think this is, my first day?"

The laugh the comes out of him is almost a bark. It's hoarse, it's surprised, and it cuts through me like a knife. I feel it all the way in my stomach, in the deepest parts of my chest.

I feel it when he steps toward me in those crimson pants that now I *know* are actually skinny jeans, the button-down he's unbuttoned two down the chest, so his whole throat is exposed. The tie is hanging loose too, careless. Can't have something hugging your throat when you're in the middle of an anxiety attack. I'm sweating. Am I sweating?

I run my gaze up his chest, past the jut of his collarbone, his throat, the stubble at his jawline.

"Eyes are up here, Riley," he says, and when I meet his gaze, my cheeks are hot.

He's smirking, confident, but there's a tick of nervousness in his eyes, and I suddenly realize where my eyes snagged, and what that might imply.

"Oh shit. I wasn't like . . . I wasn't, I don't know how to phrase this."

"Staring at my chest?"

A wave of nerves rushes down my body. "Yeah. I mean no. It was just that I was—" I stop and bite down on my tongue. Unfortunately, telling him the truth means saying *I wasn't being an asshole. I was checking you out, and did you know there's a line of sweat collecting on your collarbone? Did you know your tie is askew and I don't know what on Earth has gotten into me but I want to tighten it and pull you into me by the throat?* I decide that I cannot let him think I'm staring at a part of him that he takes great care to bind, but that I also should not admit to wanting to pull him into me by the throat, so I grit my teeth and say, "I guess I was just checking you out, Oliver West."

His eyebrows fly up.

"You're—the tie. Your collarbone is nice and you look good in that stupid tie."

A laugh about chokes out of him. His hand absolutely *hurtles* to the back of his head and he puts a couple more inches of space between us and he—wow, I never thought I'd see the day, but he blushes.

"Well. I, uh—okay. Thanks. Ha." He glances up into the corner of the room and back at me, arrogance lighting up his eyes. And I'm so embarrassed because god, I can't believe I've made such a fool of myself so many times in the last five minutes, but I have.

I am desperate to get the upper hand.

I pull at anything I can.

I say, "Yeah. Anyway. I need to get going. I doubt that outfit did you any favors with the judges. Especially not when everyone knows I was supposed to be the one up there in the first place. So."

All the good humor slides right off his face and he says, "You're still on that shit? I was only out to begin with because *you—*"

"No, I'm not doing this with you again. I have judging to get back to."

He blinks hard and shakes his head, like he's clearing it of whiplash. "What the hell," he mutters.

I smile. "Hope the *outfit* doesn't kill your chances."

I know, and he knows, that it's a threat. That I'm reminding him of the power I have here. And he is not happy about it.

He is scowling when I turn on my heel and leave.

It's supposed to make me feel victorious. It should feel good, turning him on his butt like that. But if . . . if this was a victory, then why do I feel so shitty? Why do I suddenly feel a little sick?

I clench my fists and ignore it and move to make my way out of the band room.

And I hear Oliver's voice, echoing through the hall, "And I'll have you know! This outfit is fucking FANTASTIC."

CHAPTER THIRTEEN

I MAKE IT TO the student council room two minutes late. The time it took to stop in the bathroom and slow my pulse by activating the old trusty mammalian diving reflex screwed me, I guess. (The mammalian diving reflex: an anxiety trick for the ages. It's a way to trick your system into thinking it needs to slow, to preserve itself. It's worked every time I've tried it.)

Not to mention, it definitely left my face pink because it requires both holding one's breath and splashing one's face with cold water, so I'm sure I look completely ridiculous walking in there, the edges of my hair damp with water from the bathroom sink.

The point is: it calmed me down right when I was ready to spiral.

So at least, even if I might look absurd, I can walk into the classroom two minutes late with something resembling confidence written on my face. I take my seat next to the principal (the only one left) and face everyone else gathered around one of the lab stations.

It smells like formaldehyde in here, because the AP bio kids have been doing dissections, and this, the bio classroom, is where student council meets. We pretend, as a group, not to notice it. We are all consummate professionals.

Finally, Audra Robbins starts everything off with a mention of Shalise Friar, who gave a really polished, passionate presentation about her project, meant to get books to incarcerated youth as well as teens on probation.

There's a lot of approval across the board, both for her and her project, and I'm inclined to agree. We further agree that we're a little shaky on the food for the homeless project, just because there are a number of organizations around doing the same thing, approaching it the same way, and honestly, Eli just didn't exactly have a solid, well-researched game plan for how he was going to turn this into a self-sustaining organization.

A few names are thrown out as early frontrunners—Shalise, Laura Kim, Patrick Kite, who wants to partner with an Indigenous-run mutual aid project around here to kickstart a clean water initiative. All just . . . really good, really important, beautifully thought-out stuff.

But I hear the absence of his name. The specific space where it should be, because everyone is talking around it and no one wants to be, like, too controversial or something, I think. I don't know. I don't know, but it's sticking in my chest, the specific feeling of *cowardice*. Of cowardice in a room with a bunch of adults and other kids my age who shouldn't be afraid.

I say, "What about Oliver West?"

It's too quiet. Of course I'm too quiet; my throat's all dry and I don't know how to speak.

Audra Robbins is right across from me, and she raises an eyebrow. "Louder," she says.

I blow out a breath. I can't believe I'm sticking out my neck for him. After the blackmail and the . . . just the knowledge that he is absolutely capable of, and not just capable of, *likely to* wreck my reputation if his is connected with mine. Because he's such a slacker. He's such a freaking jester. Him showing up without a suit or quality production today wasn't his fault, but still. It fit. It fit everything everyone thinks of him, everything *I* think of him. And I'm pretty sure that's part of why some people aren't mentioning his name.

Like . . . Audra. She's not exactly afraid to make a statement.

A couple kids on the committee. Trey Gallegos is non-binary; they're probably just not speaking up because they freaking *know Oliver.*

But . . . shit. I have to. I have to mention him.

I see him, hear him saying, *I saw their faces. I'm starting shit.*

I have to.

I clear my throat.

"What about Oliver West?"

The discussion quiets.

Audra says, "I thought he had some very compelling things to say."

Principal Edwards purses his lips. "Mm. Well. He wasn't exactly professional, was he?"

Audra shrugs a single shoulder. "I'd rate that as less important than content, principal."

Ivy Pelligro rolls her icy blue eyes and chimes in, "Please. That boy has spent his entire high school career making sure he'd *never* get picked for something like this. There's no way he's going to do anything but squander this."

I can feel my fingers curling against the cool of the table. I should say something. I should. I will. Ugh. I should say—

It's Trey who does it.

Not me, and I should have spoken up.

Trey says, "That's not fair. To factor in right now, is it?"

It's quiet.

Trey is gentle and quiet and always wears shirts with puns on them. Shirts that say shit like *UNICORNELL* with a unicorn in a collegiate sweatshirt on it or, like, right now they're wearing an unbuttoned cardigan over a T-shirt with a whale on it that says:

What do you call a lying whale's butt?

A TALL TAIL

But there's steel there, behind their eyes. A firm resolution in their voice. "We're supposed to be deliberating on his presentation and his idea. And I don't know how everyone else in this room felt about it, but I think it's pretty *damn* important."

And this is important to know: if Trey Gallegos is saying "damn," that's like any other human saying . . . a word I don't care to even think about, it would have to be so filthy.

They shoot me a look and tip their chin, and I tip mine back.

Facts are facts, regardless of my feelings on him and

our up-and-down rollercoaster of a relationship: Oliver West killed that presentation today. Stupidly hot, slightly unprofessional outfit aside, his idea is important. He presented it with passion and backed it up with a written plan that's totally feasible and worth considering.

And he doesn't deserve to be overlooked.

He doesn't deserve to be *fought* because, in all likelihood, a number of people in this room and in that audience think who he is, and especially the idea of fighting for kids like him, is bullshit.

I don't know where everyone is going to direct their votes.

But I can leave the AP bio lab in peace, knowing that I've done what I need to do. He's going to be given a fair shake.

I can wash my hands of any further freaking responsibility.

My mom comes to pick me up in front of the school. She's got an hour between shifts at the hospital and her other job, which means she has just enough time to take me home, then drive across town to wait tables.

"Hey," I say, ducking in. The car is cool, and thank god; the A/C was on the fritz for two months before my brother ordered me the part I needed and we were able to tinker around and get it fixed for her.

"Hey, baby," she says. "How'd your presentation go?"

I blink. I told her already; I—oh. No I didn't. I barely told anyone, this whole thing is so fucked. I click my seatbelt into place and say, "Fine. It went . . . it was good."

I don't know why I do it, why I lie. But it slides out of my mouth a whole lot easier than the truth, and so I do.

Mom smiles, hands at the ten and two. She might play a lot in her life fast and loose, but she's always been an overly cautious driver. The crow's feet around her eyes crinkles, and I can make out new lines around her mouth. Her skin is a little dry and wrinkled from tanning when she was a kid, and from some hard living, I think, stuff she won't talk much to me about. But she's pretty. Pretty in kind of a . . . a tired way. The blonde in her hair is natural, like mine, but the lowlights aren't. They're nice, though.

Her makeup is nice.

And her uniform really does complement her skin.

It's hard with parents sometimes. Like, you get older and start to realize that they're not perfect and they never were and grown-ups don't really know anything either, do they? But they're still your parents. And your mom is still your mom and still gives the best hugs and is still the prettiest person you know.

She says, making the second of the two turns required to get from school to our place, "I'm proud of you, you know."

"Yeah?" I say.

"First in the family to go to college. Working on a scholarship. That's a big deal, honey. A college graduate."

My chest twists, and my heart jumps into my throat. It beats fast and hard and my palms sweat because the instant I even *think* about lying, my entire body goes into panic mode. I would have absolutely *failed* if I'd decided to go into the career I wanted in the fourth grade (spy). I just say, "Come on. I haven't even graduated high school yet."

She waves a hand in the air. "You will. Then college. Then gosh, who knows what? You're going to do big things, honey; I can feel it."

The pressure squeezes me until I'm afraid my throat will collapse and my eyeballs will pop out.

I say, "Yeah, Mom."

"Anyway," she says. "Don't let me go too Mom on you here; I gotta get to work."

"Thanks for the ride," I say, and I shut the door and head inside.

Patrick and Randi and Evian are all here, asleep in front of the TV, tangled up in blankets and an upended bowl of popcorn. *The Bachelor* is playing at too high a volume and I roll my eyes and shut it off. Sometimes, I kind of wish they spent a little more time at their own place instead of, like, parenting me.

I glance down at the blanket, where Patrick and Randi's torsos disappear beneath the fluff. I feel . . . I don't know. Disappointed, I guess. That things are going to be hard for them, because they may not be ready for this. But more than anything, I feel pressure. And just knowing that the negativity in my brain isn't *really* about them, isn't really about the baby or anything—it's about me and my selfishness—makes me consider what Alisha said. That I'm too hard on them. That it's me, that I'm the problem.

And I can't—I can't do it; I can't think about it.

Everything feels so freaking heavy sometimes.

I mercifully avoid talking to anyone on my way back through the tiny hallway to my room.

I don't have anything to say to any of them, to anyone

outside my own brain, which is being loud enough for three of me right now.

First college graduate.

I swear I'm going to suffocate.

I don't know how I'm going to pay for college without the big service project I was planning, or at least a sponsorship like most finalists wind up getting one way or the other, and my academics are strong but not strong enough to compete with, like, prep-school kids and the cutthroat valedictorians out there who have filled their entire high school careers with studying and forty-seven extracurriculars. I haven't. So much was riding on this stupid competition.

Why did I do that? Why did I plan my entire academic life this way? Why have I made half the decisions I've made in the past year. The past month. The past *week*.

Everything was perfect, and now I don't . . . I don't even know if I'm going to college at all.

CHAPTER FOURTEEN

VOLUNTEERING IS A COMPLETE nightmare.

We had an adoption fall through, and now we've got a huge, anxious dog freaking out because he's been moved from place to place, and now he's back in the kennels after spending four days on someone's couch. Plus one of the Maine coons is sick, and she's been yowling for hours, and we have a vet coming, but god, I'm tired.

It's a full moon, and Mom told me there really is something to a full moon; it makes the patients go completely batty. I think it's the same thing with animals. Even the totally chill, peaceful ones—the ones that are so sweet and docile that sometimes you have to throw in a treat and give extra pets to them just to make sure they're breathing? Even a couple of *them* have gone after each other! I'm worn out. Just ready to melt down and into my bed, seep all the way into the mattress and stay there and never get up again. I will make it to my bed and I will live there.

But it's not even the animals, really. They're not the living creatures making me lose my mind. My muscles are burning and my brain is turning to mush from trying to keep them all happy and safe today, but it's Oliver who is making my life hell.

He picked me up five minutes early, then got on my ass because I wasn't quite ready. Barely even spoke to me the entire ride to the shelter, and the whole day, he's been barking orders at me and assigning me all the shittiest jobs—literally and otherwise. I had to clean up after the cats, which, okay, sure. But then the dogs, too. And when one of them threw up? Me. I've had to go back in after myself and a couple other volunteers to re-clean kennels and to handle the hardest dogs on walks. To do the crappiest transfers from the cat room to their little kennels, and I've got scratches all up and down my arms from cats. And it's all been at Oliver's behest.

I leave the cat room, grumbling under my breath and stretching out my arms and hands. They're burning because cat scratches *suck* and what sucks even more is having to disinfect them a million times until your skin is on fire. I'm staring at my arm and the ground, about to finally duck into the break room to eat my freaking lunch, when I hear Oliver's voice. It's sharp and smooth and echoes across the tile. "Brynn."

I hesitate. No. No, I'm starving. I'm not stopping. It'll be like I didn't hear him. He'll buy that. He definitely will. I just keep on walking.

"Brynn," he repeats.

Nope. Nope nope nope I hear nothing. He's not even there. Not until I get my lunch. I speed up. He sidles right up next to me and blocks off the break room with his arm. *"Riley."*

"What?" I snap.

He straightens and raises an eyebrow. "You heard me."

"I don't know what you're talking about."

He breathes out a little disbelieving laugh. Fine. He doesn't have to believe me; it doesn't matter. What matters is that I am challenging him, jaw jutting and staring straight into his stupid, smug face. We're at eye level, and even though I always feel like I'm looking up at him, this puts us on more even ground, in the most literal sense. And that's something.

His voice lowers, so I have to lean in to hear him. "You're not done," he says.

"I'm sorry?"

"With The Enchanter Tim."

The Enchanter Tim is the biggest cat we have here. He's the size of my torso, just the most *enormous* chonky boi. He's also utterly well-mannered. Super affectionate and perfect and precious. It's just that he's also arthritic, so can't groom himself normally, and what that results in is . . . a persistent chronic butthole issue. It's a gland expression thing, but it just means that while petting him is lovely, taking care of him is a stinky experience. "I wasn't aware that I was supposed to—"

"You were. I told you. Two hours ago."

I lock my jaw. My teeth are grinding against each other in a way that would make my dentist's hair stand on end. "I don't remember that."

He laughs again, in that specific, assholey way. "Well. He needs groomed, and you need to do it."

"I'm starving."

"Okay?"

"I'm not . . ." I glance at his nametag, the one that says *manager*. He could screw me over, he really could. And I need to tread carefully. But also, screw this. I'm not going to be treated like crap. I say, "I'm not doing anything more until I get my lunch."

He looks at me, pointed and contemplative. Then he lets his arm fall and slides back, leaving the doorway open. He says, "Have at it."

I eat my stupid lunch.

After work, cat buttholes and all, when I push myself up into Oliver's truck, he doesn't even wait for me to shut the door. He yanks the car into reverse, reaches across my chest, and slams the thing. I blink and stare straight ahead. The windshield is cracked in two places, and I can't stop looking at them, thinking about what exactly would happen if we got into a fender bender. Would it shatter from the smallest impact, because its integrity is already compromised? Maybe it would. It probably will. Great.

I blink hard and shake my head. That's anxiety. It's anxiety, and it's not real, and the meds I'm on usually help me with that but not always. Every once in a while, something peeks through and climbs out of my ribs and I have to recognize it and bite down on it so it doesn't spiral out of my control. This is nearly impossible to do right now, because if I'm not focusing on the windshield, I'm focusing on Oliver, and the tension in the truck that is so thick I'm choking trying to breathe.

I dig my nails into my hands and tap my heels, jiggle my knee until I'm sure I'm shaking the whole car. Then I finally just blast out with it: "This is unprofessional!"

A frown flits across Oliver's face, then he turns to glance at me. "I'm sorry?"

"It's unethical. It's unethical that you're my supervisor and that—that—it's . . . it's unethical."

He says, voice low and raspy, "Yeah, like you and I have ever been overly concerned with *ethical*."

I wrinkle my nose. "What do you mean?"

"I mean it sure as shit wasn't ethical for you to toss my app in the trash without even reading it because the applications you got weren't anonymous. But that didn't stop you, did it?"

"Oh my god," I say. "We've gotten past that. You're in! I'm out! I had this whole plan worked out; I was going to get a low-income utilities thing going and partner with local trades companies and it's all gone up in smoke, and . . . it doesn't matter. You *won*, Oliver. You won. What the *hell* are *you* even *bitching about*?"

He makes a noise and shakes his head, turning back to face the road.

It's dark outside, industry and trees flying by the windshield in dark, quick blurs.

The quickest, most horrifying thought enters my head when I notice the speed because my anxiety is all over the place. And I wonder, suddenly, what it might be like if I reached over and jerked on the wheel. Not that I want to, just wondering. Thinking about what little force it would take to cause a catastrophe. Wondering how much it could *really* hurt to slam into a tree.

I shut my eyes tight and breathe. They're called intrusive thoughts, and they're one of the worst things about anxiety and depression. These random, terrible, violent things that I have zero interest whatsoever in doing. They just jump in with questions like that and leave me to wonder. The meds usually take care of them, too, but I'm having . . . a hard time lately.

I breathe.

I push it away.

I focus on Oliver.

"You made it into the next round!" I say.

He says, "No thanks to you."

"No thanks to—" I laugh. I am noticing that he and I spend a lot of our time together laughing, in the very worst possible way to laugh.

"What?" he says. It's not a question. It's an accusation.

"I stood up for you," I say.

This time, when he says, "What?" it comes out different. Low and . . . something a little more open than suspicious.

"I—I stood up for you. No one was talking shit or anything, but no one was talking about you at all, and I stepped in to push you and your project."

"I don't need your charity," he bites out.

"It's not charity. You fucking asshole. It's a good project and it needed to be paid attention to. Christ."

The ride falls completely silent.

It's nothing but the road noise and the breeze outside that comes with the speed on the highway.

The tiniest shove on that wheel.

Jesus, that semi is close.

I wonder—

After several minutes in the dark, he says, "You brought up my project?"

I'm leaning against the window, and I blink away the quietly destructive thoughts in my brain. I say to the trees outside, "Yes."

"Were you . . . were you like . . . the only one? To take up for me? It, I mean?"

"No." I shake my head against the glass. "Trey Gallegos."

I glance over at him and see a small smile curling his mouth. "Yeah? Of course, Trey."

"Of course Trey? Trey's like the quietest, sweetest thing."

Oliver laughs, and this time it's not bitter or mean. It's loudly, shockingly amused. "*Trey?* Is quiet and sweet? Haha, Jesus, okay. I wish I wasn't driving. He needs to hear that shit. No, like ten of my friends need to hear that shit."

I don't know what to say to that, so I just shrug.

And then Oliver says, "Thanks. For doing that. You didn't have to."

I don't even accept the thanks. I'm too furious, still. Too worn out and sad. I just say quietly, "Stop treating me like shit at work."

He runs a hand over his jaw. That's a thing he does a lot, I notice. Not that I should be noticing things like his little physical habits. But here I am, noticing them. Noticing him.

"Yeah, I—I deserve that. For what it's worth, it's not just you. My dad—it doesn't matter. I've got some personal stuff going on and I've been kind of on the razor's edge lately. And then after the whole thing with the presentation in the band room and everything leading up to it, I guess I've been . . . I've been taking everything out on you."

I'm silent. Truth be told, I'm not used to boys accepting when they screw up and actually apologizing. Honestly, how often does that happen?

"I'm sorry, okay?"

He meets my eyes in the dark and I say, "O-okay."

Maybe this is a truce. Maybe we can survive each other for the rest of this.

Maybe . . . no, I don't think *friends* is what we will wind up being, but maybe we can make a mutual decision not to be mortal enemies for the next month.

I open my mouth to sort out a verbal contract to that effect, and then I can feel tears stinging the back of my eyes.

He, of course, picks that *exact* moment to look over at me, and I am livid that it's not dark enough to camouflage me. How dare my face betray me like this?

"Shit," he says. "Are you okay?"

"I'm fine."

But my voice is hoarse.

Talking about it made this whole situation real, and I've been panicking about losing my chance at that service project for weeks, but saying things to him, and then being forced to confront, like, vulnerability? Brought it bubbling to the surface.

He doesn't push. Just drives.

I sniffle and say, "It's nothing. It's just . . . I don't want you to feel bad. I screwed you over and I deserve this and I accept it, but . . . you taking my place in this competition has wrecked so much for me. I needed this on my applications to school to even begin to be considered for a scholarship, and like . . . you've seen where I live. I don't—I'm afraid I'm not gonna be able to afford school at all. I don't exactly come from money. Like some people."

He does a double-take. "Hold on. Are you—are you implying that those people are me?"

I shrug. "Well, if the Louboutin fits."

Then he throws his head back and laughs so long and loud that I wind up yelling at him to get his eyes back on the road.

He wipes his eyes. "Shit, Riley, and I thought the stuff about Trey was funny."

"I didn't—"

His phone buzzes in the middle console, and he glances over at the preview. Then he breathes out a curse. "Change of plans."

He wrenches his truck off on the nearest exit and I say, "What the hell?"

"You're about to see why what you said was so damn hilarious."

His voice . . . does not sound amused.

CHAPTER FIFTEEN

WE PULL INTO A trailer park that's, like, two miles up the road from mine.

"Wait, I'm sorry, what are we—"

He doesn't even wait for me to finish my sentence. He yanks his car into park, and gravel goes flying. He jumps out and slams his truck door and I just sit there, blinking. Staring straight ahead.

Am I . . . am I supposed to follow him? I don't know, that seems a little intrusive. A little personal for someone with whom most of my relationship has consisted of mutual irritation or downright hatred. Certainly majority betrayal.

I just wait in the quiet, in this row of trailers.

A dog barks.

A car backfires.

It's . . . god, it's cold for October.

No, screw this; I'm going in.

I slide out of the truck and crunch across the gravel and stop at his door.

There's a lot of . . . voice-raising going on inside, and I fear that if I knock, it's going to be swallowed.

I grit my teeth and prepare to open the door to a battle.

But that's . . . not what happens.

The ones yelling are Oliver and a very muscular man in a trucker's hat, who I assume is his dad, based on the entire face and body movements. They gesture wildly in the exact same way. His dad has a good six inches on him, both vertically and horizontally, but *wow* are they related.

"Dad, seriously, what were you thinking?"

His dad throws his arms in the air. "I was *thinking* that I'm a grown-ass man who should be able to do repair work on the damn car without my son ripping through the drive coming to check on me—"

"Oh my *god*," Oliver says. He's about to rip his hair out.

I hover awkwardly in the doorway.

"You think I can't take care of myself?" his dad says.

"I know you can take care of yourself. I don't know why you *don't*. It's freezing out there! You thought it would be a good idea to get under the car with your arthritic hands—"

"Oh, hell," his dad says, gesturing like Oliver's being ridiculous. When he gestures, the wrap on his hands becomes visible. It's red, nearly soaked through.

I decide, even though it might be an overstep, that my talents will currently be best used in gathering a fresh wrap and antiseptic. I'm no medical professional, but I can definitely obtain supplies. I slip into the tiny corner kitchen and start rifling through cabinets. Their first aid stuff has got to either be here or in the bathroom.

"Who the hell is this?" I hear from the little dining nook behind me, and I about jump out of my skin.

Thankfully, no one hears him. I don't know why that feels like a blessing except that I just don't want my presence here to be any more evident, any glaringly weirder, than it already is. I don't want to draw Oliver's attention. It's like the scene with the T-Rex in *Jurassic Park*. Move slow enough, and he won't see me.

It's another guy in his fifties, just as big and brawny as Oliver's dad, but with a big red beard and a plaid shirt. He looks like a lumberjack. Underneath that mass of facial hair, he's got the same mouth as all three of them. And he and Oliver have the same piercing eyes.

I say, "I—I'm Oliver's . . ." I stop. What do I say? Friend? Volunteer? Mortal Enemy? I settle on the most comfortable lie: "I'm Oliver's friend. We work together at the rescue."

The man's face softens. "Oh, you're up at Pibbles? Then you know what a royal pain in the ass my brother is."

I laugh, like I know what he's talking about. Like I'm not clenching my teeth until they hurt because I don't know how to exist with anxiety, this boy I barely even like, and two large men I don't know, one of whom is bleeding and yelling, all in one little single-wide.

"I'm, uh," I say. "I'm new. So."

"Oh," he says. "Well, sweetheart, welcome to the family." When he laughs, his eyes crinkle.

And he doesn't say *sweetheart* the way some men do: like they're trying to make you smaller, lesser. He says it like he means it. Like he's apologizing for the uncomfortable circumstance, like he's trying to be gentle. My teeth unclench the smallest bit.

"I'm just—I'm—I'm looking for a change for the wrap."

"No, you let me take care of that. Why don't you sit down? You're lookin' a little green around the gills."

I'm embarrassed, but I take the seat. Blood doesn't bother me. Well, not *that* much. Not like the whole situation is bothering me.

It's just that I know I shouldn't be here. I should be home.

Maybe I'll walk home?

I know I wouldn't want Oliver inside my house watching this all go down.

I wouldn't want anyone in my house at all. Except maybe Alisha.

I pull my feet together and my knees up and try to make myself small.

Oliver says, "Dad, you have rheumatoid. You just have to accept it. And you're on blood thinners, and we can't afford to make these kinds of mistakes; you know that—"

"It's not a big deal."

"It's a big deal."

"Son—"

"Dad." Oliver rakes his hand through his hair. "If Uncle Beau hadn't—"

"If Uncle Beau hadn't called you, I would've been fine."

The man I assume is Uncle Beau says, "Now hold up. When I texted him, it was when we thought that gash went down your arm, and you were being a stubborn ass about going to the hospital."

"Well, shit," says his dad.

The pressure in the room has lessened by a few pounds; it doesn't feel like the roof and walls are about to burst outward.

I unfold just a little, just enough that I don't feel every muscle fiber in my body coiling, about to pop.

That's when Oliver's dad turns his head just a little and says, "Well, who's this?"

He's not embarrassed about all the booming earlier, the blood on his hand. His voice doesn't change a tick, and neither does his posture.

I think it's because . . . well, because the fight I just stumbled into wasn't a fight. Not like the kind I get into with my family. It was three people saying they loved each other in unmoderated tones. Three people caring, and doing it loudly and aggressively. So it hits different.

I meet Oliver's eyes. He only holds my gaze for a second before he looks away. There's something in him that won't let him look me square on, stare me down like he usually does. I furrow my brow, but I decide to be brave, to get past the stranger danger burrowed in my DNA.

"Mr. West, I'm Brynn Riley. I'm Oliver's friend from school and the new volunteer at Pibbles and Kits."

Mr. West's face has been neutral, if just a little guarded, and when I mention his rescue, he immediately opens up; his whole countenance relaxes. He says, in that huge, gruff voice, "So you're an animal lover."

The corners of his eyes wrinkle when he smiles, too, just like his brother. The anxiety doesn't go away altogether, but it starts to melt. I don't feel like I want to peel off my skin.

"Yeah," I say. "Especially big ones. There's this one dog there—"

"Frankie," all three of them say at once, and I'm struck

by the astounding adorableness of three dudes just hanging out here fawning over animals. It's too much.

"Yeah," I say. "How'd you know?"

"Frankie's my favorite," says Oliver.

"He's all of our favorite," says Mr. West, but I catch Oliver's eyes, and they say, *He's mine.*

"Anyway," I say.

"You gonna be alright, Dad?" Oliver says.

"Shit," he says, "if I have to tell y'all to stop babying me one more time . . ."

"Just don't know how he's gonna get to work tomorrow," Beau mumbles.

Mr. West rolls his eyes. "I'm tellin' you, it's not your problem. I'll figure out. I'm gonna get back out there tonight and—"

"No, you will not," says Oliver.

"I swear to Jesus, boy—"

"Are we seriously going to get back into this? In front of . . ." He lowers his voice, but I can hear him; it's not like this place is big. "In front of her? Come on." He runs his hand over the back of his neck and glances at me.

I get it, but honestly, there's . . . nothing to be embarrassed about. This house is warm and comfortable. And it's so evident that everyone in it cares about each other.

You can see it in the lines indented into the old couch in the living room, the family pictures on the wall. You can smell it in the cinnamon and cloves on the stove. You can *feel* it in here. This is not a fight; it's a warm battle of wills.

Now that I've settle into it for more than three awkward minutes, I don't even think I mind bearing witness to it.

I glance out the window at the old truck out back and say, quietly, "I can take a look."

I am entirely ignored, due to being, I'm pretty certain, unheard.

Mr. West just glances at me and says, "You gonna try and stop me from doin' what I gotta do to get to work tomorrow? A dog rescue doesn't exactly make a full-time living, boy; you know that. Ain't like I can just not show up to that big commercial job on Monday just because my hand got a papercut."

"A papercut, *Jesus*—"

"Well," he says. "You call John. You tell him I'm not gonna be there to supervise the job I promised him months ago and see how his building goes up, and then—"

"This is the whole reason you started the rescue, Dad—"

"Tell that to the heating company. I don't wanna worry you. This ain't your fight. Just be the kid and you let me be the dad and fix my damn—"

"I CAN TAKE A LOOK," I say.

And the room falls silent.

Suddenly everyone's eyes are on me. Beau's and Mr. West's are open and questioning. Oliver's are . . . Oliver's are full of a hundred things—questions and curiosity and a little embarrassment and . . . something I can't put my finger on.

That familiar anxiety bubbles up in my stomach and chest. But I don't mind it so much this time. Because I know what I'm doing. I say it in a voice that is very intently clear and confident. I stand straight. I project. I've rehearsed it twice in my head while they were arguing: "I'm not formally trained, but I know HVAC and I know cars. I bet you my very tiny college savings that I can fix whatever you've got going on."

Mr. West's eyes brighten and start to twinkle. "I—well, I don't want to put you out."

"You don't have to do that, Brynn," says Oliver, but it comes with a question mark attached. Because how else is his dad going to get to his job without risking life and limb?

"No, I know. I have nowhere else to be. Let me at it. Where's your toolbox?"

"It's out by the truck."

"Okay," I say.

Oliver clears his throat and approaches me. "You sure? It's late and it's cold, and I can just . . . I don't mind taking you home. We can figure it out. I can just—I can pay for an Uber for him tomorrow. Seriously, it's fine."

"Nah," I say. "Let a girl get her hands dirty."

CHAPTER SIXTEEN

I POP THE HOOD of his dad's truck and roll up my sleeves. It's kind of grungy in here, but not too bad. It's obvious that no one in the family has the money to keep everything top-of-the-line; no one's dumping thousands of dollars into maintenance or something. But Oliver's dad takes care of his stuff, and I can appreciate that.

I leave the hood up and slide the key in the ignition. Nothing. There's no telltale clicking or anything, and it's not even giving me a growl. I flip on the headlights to see if they'll even come on. I hope they won't. If they don't, that means it's gotta be a battery issue.

They come on immediately, no problem at all.

I narrow my eyes.

Damn. A battery replacement would have been so simple.

I slide out of the truck, leaving the headlights on. I'm gonna have to spend some time investigating under the hood, and it's going to be a huge pain in the ass to try to do that with a cellphone light. The headlights are bright, but they work, and that's what matters.

I have no idea *what* Mr. West was doing *under* the vehicle.

Sounds like a man, honestly. Think you know about a thing because it's a thing men ought to know about, then wind up with your hand shredded, not even close to the field you were supposed to be playing in the first place.

I'm guessing hard that the issue is coming from in here.

I lean over the hood, touching the serpentine belt to check it for wear, though that really shouldn't be the issue here, not if it won't start at all. The battery looks good from this end too.

Already, my nails are getting that familiar line of black under my DIY manicure. I don't know why I love it so much; it's kind of gross. But I do.

I'm happiest when my fingers are stained.

I yank a scrunchie from my wrist and throw my hair up (now grease is going to be in my hair, and that I could do without, but ah well. Who am I trying to impress?), then duck back under.

There's a crunch behind me and a shadow falls over the vehicle, and I jump so hard my head about hits the hood.

"Shit!" I yell. I get so in my head doing this kind of thing. My gosh.

"Sorry!" It's Oliver, of course it is. I shoot a look at him, and he's raising his hands up in a gesture of surrender. A jacket is hanging from his left. "I just thought—I thought you might be cold."

"Oh," I say. I take another look at the jacket; it's his—leather and worn and familiar. I've seen him in it at school a hundred times. "Oh, well I—"

I don't exactly know what to say. Him offering me his jacket seems like too much. Taking it seems like . . . it feels like a lot. Feels like letting him under my skin. Letting him warm my blood in a way that usually only happens in secret.

"Take it; it's cold. You—you have goose bumps."

His gaze lingers on my biceps, then travels up to my throat, and I say, "Okay."

It comes out too fast, almost panicked, because that's how my mouth reacts when he looks at me like that.

I blink and study the gray-green siding of Oliver's trailer when he moves to slide his jacket over me. It's soft and warm and fits me like a glove. I slip my arms inside, and he runs his hands from the back of my neck over my shoulder, so close I can smell the cinnamon on his breath from the gum he's chewing. I have to clench my teeth to keep from shuddering. I pull away and back to the truck, sighing out a breath when I'm far enough away from him that I physically *can*.

The jacket smells like him, too. Like old, worn leather, and the clean spice of his deodorant, and that specific combination I can't put a name on. The smell of Oliver. I've come to learn it the past couple weeks, spending all this time in his circles, in his world at work and school, in the closeness of his truck. I could sink into it right here, right now.

Shit, this is dangerous.

"Thanks," I manage.

He says, "I don't know what you're thanking me for; you're the one making sure my dad gets to work tomorrow."

I shrug, eyes on the engine. "It's nothing. I like doing this kind of stuff."

"Not when it's forty degrees out."

"Your jacket helps," I say and glance at him out of the corner of my eye. A tiny smile curls his lip, and I look away again. Focus.

He leans against the passenger's side door. "How long have you been working on cars?"

"Since I was a kid. My dad taught me. It's cars and HVAC stuff, but it was mostly YouTube that taught me that."

Oliver says, "Goddamn," and does this low, surprised laugh.

"What?" I say, ready to bristle. Ready to fight at the assumption that I can't do this because I'm a girl. I can feel my hackles rising, and I don't mind verbally eviscerating a boy while fixing his dad's ride.

"It's just kinda hot."

I choke.

"Not trying to get into your pants," he says, raising his hands. "I know there's lines."

"Why would that be a line?"

I don't even think about stopping myself until it's already out of my mouth, because the idea of there being a line that says we can't is so immediately . . . alarming. Alarming? Is that the right word? It feels like it. What matters is that apparently, I hate it.

It's Oliver's turn to look a little taken aback. "I just mean—come on, you're like Princess Manicure of House Student Council and I'm . . . well." He gestures to himself like it's self-explanatory. "Me."

"Princess *Manicure* of House *Student Council*?"

He laughs and leans back against the truck, hands shoved in his pockets. "Yeah," he says.

"I don't even know what that's supposed to mean."

"It means," he says, staring up at the sky, smile in his voice, "that the second you walk into class, every teacher wets themself with happiness. *This semester is gonna be a smooth ride.* You prance down the hall—"

"I do not prance."

"—in your pretty little heels and your pretty little hair with all your perfect, pretty little makeup, going from good-girl extracurricular to good-girl extracurricular. You're like . . . you're just, like, untouchable."

I nearly choke a second time. Untouchable? Please. No one has ever called me that in their life.

Because I'm nosy, I check the oil while I'm in here, and grumble when it all comes out black. The shit gets all on my hands and streaks up my arm.

I glance over at Oliver. "And what, you think you're, like, a bad boy? Is that it?"

"Sounds stupid when you say it like that," he says. "Just—come on, as if you and I have ever been playing in the same league."

I huff, and I'd like to be offended. I'd like to be more genuinely taken aback that he'd even think about us like that, but what was I doing just a couple weeks ago? How was I thinking of him?

As the class clown. The kid who'd been arrested more than once, never took anything seriously. I'd thought of us as operating in two separate worlds, and now, what? I'm allowed to be offended because he's thought of us that way, too?

"That's silly," I say. "To think of people as running in leagues."

I'm a hypocrite. So fine, send me to hell, I guess.

Oliver shrugs, and my gaze slides to him. I can't help it, he's like a freaking magnet. A lean, sinewy magnet with eyes so bright they shine in the dark. With a blade of a jaw I can never seem to rip my attention away from. Shadows splashing on his collarbone, where his Henley unbuttons.

Oh my *god*, when did he change into a Henley?

When did that happen and who allowed it?

I turn back to the engine, face filling with heat.

"That not how you see people, Riley? In leagues?"

The silence hangs between us, and I know exactly what he's implying. It's about that stupid night in the stupid classroom with the stupid applications, and I get it. I get that it was shitty. I get that I judged him, misjudged him really, and I shouldn't have, but god.

"I'm sorry," I say. "I'm *sorry* for what I did, okay? I shouldn't have put us in two different realms like that and it was wrong of me, but I just don't know how many more times you want me to apologize—"

"No," he says. "I'm not . . . I'm not trying to start shit. I'm not looking for another apology from you; I'm just telling you that of course you see people like that. You sure did that night. You're a human; everyone does it. And if there's leagues, you and I don't play in the same one."

"I just think it's bullshit."

"Yeah?" he says. He springs up off the side of the truck and comes to stand by me. His shadow makes it harder to see what I'm doing, but who are we kidding? Not like I was super focused on that anyway. "You a rebel?"

I purse my lips. "Sure," I say, staring down at the engine.

"How many times have you cut class?" he asks, voice low because he's close enough to afford to whisper.

"Cut class?" I say. "Listen, some of us care about our grades—"

"Smoked?"

"Smoking gives you cancer."

"Weed."

"There's nothing prim about not wanting to engage in the consumption of mind-altering substances."

He leans a little closer, shadow brushing my skin. "How many times have you been arrested?"

It comes out as a whisper: "Once."

"See? You're good. You're precious."

His hand is dangerously close to my hip, on the truck. Fingers over the lip of metal, tip of his thumb a breath from my jeans. I take a breath. And I turn around to face him.

"And you're so *edgy*? You work at a rescue for dogs and cats. You're in the running for the most prestigious grant in the city." I look him up and down, tight, black pants to the fitted blue Henley. "You're smart and funny and a killer ball player."

His face twitches. There's a scar on his eyebrow I never noticed before, this vulnerable glint in his eyes that I have, this edge of a smirk always curling on his mouth. I can barely breathe. He shifts, so his hand *is* brushing my hip now, and the other braces him on the popped hood.

"I bet you haven't even been to juvie. I bet the rumors about you are bullshit."

He's staring at me so intently, I've forgotten about the truck. I've forgotten how cold it is. I've forgotten that I'm supposed to hate him, that he's supposed to hate me, that because he's my supervisor, getting involved in anything beyond casual acquaintanceship would be unethical. I've forgotten everything except the racing of my pulse, my throat and mouth going dry, everything but Oliver West looking at me like that. Caging me.

I swallow. I say, hoarse and trying like hell to cover it, "I bet those stints where you were gone had you caring for a sick relative or something."

"Which one?"

"Grandma."

"No dice," he says, shaking his head, muscles flexing by my ear when he shifts his weight. "One grandma died when I was a kid. The other one still runs marathons."

"Aunt, then."

"Alright. Aunt. So I'm caring for my sick aunt."

"Yeah," I say, struggling to swallow. What am I doing? What are we doing? What is happening here? "So you're caring for your sick aunt and probably volunteering at the local homeless shelter, and like, knitting on the side."

He barks out a laugh, and I can taste the cinnamon of his gum in my mouth when I open mine to breathe.

"Then you come back," I say, "and you want to seem cool. So you let everyone think you just got out of juvie. But every time, it's Aunt and Knitting City."

Oliver glances down at the ground, grinning. He runs his tongue over his lip and says, "Wasn't bullshit, Riley."

"No?" My voice is shaking. I'm shaking.

"No. Wanna know how many times I've gone?"

I blink. Again and again; too many times. It's an anxiety

thing, and I'm riding so high on adrenaline I don't think my body knows the difference. "Okay," I say.

He says, "Four," and leans into me.

"Why?"

He shrugs.

There's more to it, but I don't care right now. I'm sure I will later. I'm sure I'll spend hours mulling it over in my head, mulling over all of this—every interaction, every twitch of his muscles, every little catch of the breath and slip of his feet on gravel. But right now, I can't think past the immediacy of Oliver West leaning over me like this. Looking at me like he wants to eat me alive.

I say, "Why would you admit that?"

He smiles, all soft and cocky—languid. "I think you like it."

"Not as much as you like my manicured nails and the fact that I've never skipped class."

He slips his hand from where it's grazing my hip over to my arm. Runs his fingers down my forearm to my wrist, and loops his fingers around it. He turns it over, so my palm faces him. Fingers lightly curling. His thumb is on my pulse, and there's no way he doesn't notice that it's going wild.

His fingers on the soft skin there light up my nerves, and I have to remind myself to breathe. To balance. To focus—on what?

Oliver looks back up at my face, pressing his thumb into my veins, and opens his mouth like he's going to say something.

Then, the floodlight comes on, and Beau says, "How's it goin' out there?"

For the second time tonight, I leap up, and whack my head on the hood. "GOOD GREAT GOOD GOOD GREAT."

That's what I say.

That's what happens.

Oliver has flown several steps back from me, gravel has gone flying, he's pacing with his hands linked behind his head, like, *What the fuck?*

And in his defense: What the fuck?

What's happening here? What was about to happen? Did I want it? Did he? What do I want now—what am I even asking, exactly?

Jesus, I have no idea. All I know is that my pulse is absolutely ripping through my throat, and the buzzing on my skin is just this side of physically jarring.

I say, to Oliver, "It's the timing belt."

He blinks. "I'm sorry; what?"

"The—" I clear my throat. Shut my eyes to clear my head. Take a few seconds to reorient myself to something that is not Oliver's face and Oliver's presence and *kiss me kiss me kiss me oh god, kiss me right here against your dad's truck or I'll collapse*. And when I can at least lie to myself well enough to claim that I have it together, I say, "The part. It's the timing belt. That's what you need."

"Oh," he says. At least he looks as disoriented as I feel. "Oh yeah, of course. Cool. Timing belt."

"He also needs his oil changed; that stuff is toxic sludge."

Oliver's hand is back on his buzz cut, stroking the edge at the base of his skull. That's his comfort position, I'm learning.

Not that I should be learning about him. Not that I want to. Not that it matters, that he matters, at all.

"Yeah," he says. "Cool. Cool cool. Well, I'll just—I'm sure we can manage."

"No," I say. "Just pop over to the auto parts store and get a belt, and get me some oil, and I'll do it."

"You don't have t—"

"Seriously. Oliver? I don't offer to do things I don't want to do. Pick it up, and I'll get it done. And then you can take me home."

"Okay," he says. He sucks in a breath that suggests he's been running for two miles. Then he heads into the trailer to report on the findings.

I decide to accompany him to the auto parts store, but apart from a brief debate over the music selection, neither of us says anything. What are we going to say? We're both a little busy, I think, figuring out what the hell happened back there?

And, for my part, I am trying to figure out if I want it to happen again. And if so: why?

Oliver gets what he needs, and we drive the few minutes back to his place, and I leap out of the truck like it's about to catch fire. I can get to work and not worry.

Except I can't. Not in these clothes.

No, I have to borrow some of Oliver's old, ratty pajama pants, and one of his older, rattier shirts and hoodies, because I'm not about to wreck real clothes. So here I am, doing my favorite thing in the world, covered in Oliver West.

When I finally get out from under the hood, the vehicle is running again.

His dad and uncle thank me profusely, and I'm back in the truck.

I'm only a few minutes up the road.

It's quiet again, which is how I need it; I just don't know what to do with all of this and there's no way I can process it until I'm by myself in my room.

We pull into my place.

I move to just . . . to just leave.

Then Oliver catches me by the oil-slicked wrist. He says, "Brynn?"

"Yeah?" I say. It comes out too loud in the quiet dark.

"Thank you. For what you did."

I meet his eyes.

Silence hangs.

I say, "You're welcome."

I slide out of the truck and cross the gravel to my front door.

I should shower, but it's late.

I should change, but I'm tired.

I compromise and wash my hands and face.

Then I slip into bed wearing Oliver's clothes.

CHAPTER SEVENTEEN

TONIGHT IS SADIE HAWKINS. It's one of my favorite dances, mostly because people aren't restricted to the most formal of formalwear, so it's like . . . I don't know. People show up acting normal. Like it's a party, rather than a school-sanctioned event. I still look good; I mean, come on. I'm in jeans (that I got from Goodwill and artfully ripped myself—and did an absolutely banger job, thank you very much) and they show off my butt, which is the purpose of jeans. Heels that I'll slip off the second I really start dancing but that make my legs look a mile long. I've painted my toenails this super pretty, subtle shimmery shade of ballet pink just two ticks off from my actual nail color, and the red, off-the-shoulder shirt I picked up for four bucks is classy but also a little ~scandalous~, and that's exactly what we're going for here. I feel *good*.

Plus, I got tossed into the whole arrest and volunteering mess just as the planning for this thing was starting to wind down, and I'm extremely proud of myself for making it work.

It's good.

Tonight? Is good.

Evian jumped at the chance to give me a ride here, and I took it. Usually I don't. I love her. I love all of them. But, I don't . . . I know, I tend to keep my distance. Just a little. Just enough to keep them from rubbing off on me. Tonight, though, everything is stellar, and I took the ride. It's not personal, not really. She supports me. And I do love her. And it was nice. And so is this.

Alisha and her girlfriend are here, matching—it's part of the Sadie Hawkins theme but only like half the paired up folks do it here. Paige insisted. Alisha is . . . tired. There are little dots of matching colors here and there, one trio passing me to the snack bar in matching outfits, which is mildly scandalous but in a "Hell, good for you guys" way. The music is smooth, the snacks are smooth, the minimal décor has worked out, and I'm just . . . proud. I'm proud of the work we've done. Laura Kim is here with her boyfriend and she pops up behind me.

"We did it."

I turn out, beaming. "Hell yeah, we did."

She bounces on her toes and stares out over the crowd. "Miss you lately, though. I haven't seen you at the last couple meetings."

I shrug. "I know," I say. "I've been so swamped."

"Yeah?" She's not accusatory; Laura really is just extremely kind. But still, my pulse jumps dancing this close to my big fat secret.

"Yeah," I say. I feel a shadow pass behind me, one I'm more aware of than I am of random couples and throuples and students I don't know. Just as I say, "I've just been working on college stuff on the weekends, and that's been kind of eating into my weekdays; you know how it is," that shadow chokes and laughs.

The pulse spike morphs into sharp heat, traveling down from the crown of my head to the tips of my toes. Laura doesn't notice, thank god. At least she doesn't act like it.

Her date whisks her away, and I whirl around. "You alright?" I say to Oliver.

He's standing there, having the audacity to wear another Henley that hugs his biceps, done in a lazy open button at the top, Vans, goldenrod pants that should look stupid, but only manage to look stupidly good. I hate it, and I hate him.

Or . . . or something.

He smirks. "I'm fine. Thanks for asking."

"Just sounded like you had something caught in your throat there."

He cocks his head, eyes sparkling. "Did it?"

"I'd hate for you to choke and die."

He laughs, big and genuine, and says, "Yeah, you would, wouldn't you?" Then Oliver's hand is on mine, and he's linking his fingers around my wrist and pulling me from the sidelines to the center of the dance floor and, my god, I'm going to let him.

What am I doing?

I'm being pulled against Oliver West's chest, so close I can smell his deodorant, so close I can feel him breathing. I'm pushing closer to him, hipbones rolling against his, fingers pressing into his shoulder blades. I'm losing my breath because, for a split-second, while his right hand is playing at my waist, his left slips up my back and neck and his fingers tangle in the hair at the base of my scalp before he drops it.

That's what I'm doing.

Fuck.

I manage to inhale. I say, "You smell like weed."

He runs his tongue over his bottom lip and grins. "Well, I was smoking weed earlier."

"Jesus."

"You smell like Bath and Body Works."

"Get your nose out of my neck."

"It's not in your neck."

He's right. It isn't.

But metaphorically. Or something.

The beat is low and solid and pulsing and Oliver's hips brush into me. I could be offended, I could call him presumptuous, but I don't want to. I'm quite suddenly drunk and pushing closer to him than he is to me, so maybe I'm the one presuming. I'm dying, and he looks utterly unaffected, completely confident. Unflappable.

But I can see the pulse pounding in his throat.

His hands are shaking at my back.

I want him to kiss me, even if it tastes like weed, even if that Henley is close-woven with smoke.

I've always thought it was so cheesy when you watch, like, a school dance scene in a movie and suddenly the music swells and the lights dim and they're the only two in the whole room. But god, I can't remember anyone else here.

I can't think past his fingers, the cut of his jaw, the bass pounding through both of our chests. His gaze slips past my eyes, down to my mouth.

He says, voice low and throaty, "You're not my type, Riley."

My fingers curl against his skin. "Good. You're a delinquent."

Even he has to be able to admit how shaky his breath is when he inhales.

He laughs. It's a little smoky, raspy. I'm so keyed up, *god*. He glances over my shoulder for a second, brushes his fingers up just under my shirt to my skin. I shiver, and I'm hoping it comes off as some kind of gyration for the music.

"What's that on your arms?" I say. "Smoke stuff?"

He busts out a laugh. "Smoke stuff? This is black paint. I was dipping my drumsticks today; I wanted them two-toned. Before all the *delinquency*."

Cool. He's a drummer.

That doesn't matter. I don't even care. I don't suddenly want to watch him play so badly I can taste it.

I don't.

I'm not his type.

He's definitely not mine.

What are we doing?

The song ends, and I stumble back.

His eyes are dark and wide and almost confused. Desperate. That's it. They're desperate.

"I've, uh—I need to—"

I do not finish that statement.

I leave.

I meet Alisha at the little indie coffee house on Main, and when I finally make it from the bus stop to JAV (it's JAVA, technically, but the A got torn down by some kids six months ago and no one's bothered to fix it), Alisha's already there.

I say, "I don't know what to do," at the same time she says, "I don't know what to do."

"You first," I say.

She runs her hand through her long, dark hair and peers up at the menu, even though we both know exactly what she's gonna get.

"Let me get a large Van Gogh, heavy on the raspberry."

I mouth the order right along with her.

I smile brightly at the barista, who has eight piercings in her face alone. I admire her. That many needles, I could not do.

"Can I do a Gaudi? Extra whip?"

"Sure thing, babes," she says to both of us.

I hand her some cash, and so does Alisha, and we find a table to wait it out.

This place is the best in the area. It's all wooden beams and warm light, and there's twinkle lights in the windows. The walls are decorated with works of art everywhere, some of which have been painted right *on* the walls. Even the ceiling is artwork: dark with pinprick stars, so it feels like you're having coffee in a painting.

"Why didn't they call this place INK?" says Alisha, dreamily looking up at the ceiling.

"Hmm?"

"INK," she says. "It's black, like coffee, you know? And with all the art."

"I like JAV."

"You don't know genius when you see it."

I laugh and head to the counter to pick up our orders, and when I come back, I say, "So. Shoot."

She sighs and takes a sip of her coffee. "Paige? Said she loved me."

"Oh, shit," I say. "Last night? At the dance? Well. That's good, right?"

Alisha wrinkles her nose. "No, it's not good! Paige is, like, adorable, and a great kisser, and fun, but I'm not there. And if we're being real, I don't think we're ever getting there. I'm having a nice time and all, but . . . I don't know. Paige is so . . ."

"Paige?" I say.

"Paige," she confirms.

I get it. They've been dating for a few months, and Paige can be . . . exhausting. She goes to school with us, and she's chipper in a way that makes you want to dress in all black and start smoking those cigarettes with the long handles and get super into black-and-white photography just to kind of balance her out. She's super sweet, but she can be kind of a lot.

Alisha sighs. "Seriously, she doesn't suck. She's smart and cute and funny and the ray-of-sunshine thing can be nice when it isn't making me crazy. I like her. I *like* her. But I . . . she's more into me than I am into her. That's it. I said it."

I nod and swirl my drink. "This have anything to do

with the person I saw flirting with you at the party? As *always*?"

Alisha blushes and tries to turn it back around. "The party we do not speak of? Your rebellious debut?"

"No, no, no," I say. "You're not getting out of this that easy."

She rolls her eyes. "I don't even know who you're talking about."

"You absolutely do, you dirty, rotten liar. About a foot taller than you? Hair down to their chin? Deep, soulful eyes that make you want to get lost in them and never find your way out? Ring a bell?"

"I *suppose*," she says, "that you're referring to Jistu, but I'm not saying that because I agree with the assessment." She primly sips her drink again.

"Mmmhmmm. You're not blushing all the way up to your hairline at all."

"Ugh," she says. "What do you want from me? They're gorgeous."

"Listen, *I* know."

"How am I supposed to resist that pull? Have you seen them jingle dance?"

"No, never. Not like they invite us up to Cherokee every year for the pow-wow explicitly so they can show off for you."

"Ugh, please," she says, but her smile is so big and bright and sly that I can see it around the lip of the coffee cup.

Jistu is just stupidly pretty—legs and biceps for days, and a smile that absolutely swears you will get in a world of trouble if you spend more than five minutes in their orbit, and you won't regret it when they ruin your life.

"It's just . . ." she says. "Jesus, do you know how *hard* jingle dancing is? The hours and *hours* it takes to sew those costumes alone. Imagine dancing like that, in the summer Carolina heat, in all that weight and fabric. And . . . god, doing it like Jistu does."

She's right. When they dance, they dance with their whole *soul*. And they had to want it. Jingle is traditionally a women's dance, and Jistu was, well, expected to get into something male. Something like fancy dancing, or maybe hoop. But Jistu's heart was in jingle, and they're asegi, which is Tsalagi (Cherokee) for *strange*, essentially: queer. Like, Two Spirit, but tribe-specific. And they're incredible. They place in the competition every year.

The power is astounding, and the passion that radiates off them when they dance. They're swept away and laser-focused all at once. Watching all the dancers is a revelation, but Jistu—Jistu is special.

Frankly, I don't know *how* Alisha hasn't caved already.

"Listen, I'm not saying you should absolutely go for it, but you should absolutely go for it."

She shrugs, but I can see the wheels turning from here. "I gotta break up with Paige first."

"You gotta break up with Paige first," I confirm.

"Shit," she says, head falling into her hand. "I really do."

I reach across the table to pet her head.

She says, to the fake wood, "Tell me about your troubles; I need distraction from mine."

"Oh," I say, "nothing really. I just might be extremely into the dude who's supervising my court-ordered community service and who stole my spot in the grant competition

I've been prepping for since last year after I absolutely screwed him over and he blackmailed me into it."

There's a very long pause.

I say, "And also, I'm thinking about doing my own highlights."

Alisha raises her head and says, "Rewind a minute?"

"Which part?"

"So, the court-ordered community service. This part, I obviously knew. The grant competition . . . you—wait, you didn't just drop that? You were blackmailed out of it?"

"Well," I say, drumming my hands on the table, "I wasn't *not* blackmailed out of it."

"By your supervisor. At . . . at the cat and dog place. Okay, well, I'm just putting this out there: the way you were dirty dancing last night with *Oliver West* sure made me think—"

"Yes."

"Yes to the Oliver thing or the supervisor thing?"

"To both."

She furrows her brow and drops her forehead into her hand again, starts massaging it. She says, "Jesus, Brynn. Oliver is a weird choice for you, but he's better than your *supervisor*. Please, please don't tell me he's like thirty. Do not tell me you have the hots for an old man who is supervising you, god, don't do this to me."

"No!" I say. "Oliver. Oliver is the supervisor. I didn't want to tell anyone; it's such a mess. And I didn't even . . . I didn't think there was anything to tell about me and him because I didn't *like* him, I didn't. Except. I think I do. I don't . . . god, I don't know what to do here."

She just blinks at me, jaw open.

"What?" I say, throwing my hands in the air, even though I guess there are like, a million reasons she might have to be shocked that this is the guy I'm announcing I might be kind of, sort of, somewhat, the tiniest bit interested in. "What's so weird about that? He's hot!"

"Exactly!" she says.

"Excuse me!"

"You're just—I'm just proud. That you're admitting it out loud. Brynn, listen, I don't want you to take this the wrong way, but you're into the worst guys."

"Oh, thank you," I say flatly.

"Complete douchebag player boys who aren't even cute; they're just like, guys with jawlines."

"Well."

"Just absolute dick weasels."

"Alisha! Jesus!"

"Sorry," she says. "Sorry sorry." She's laughing now.

"Ethan wasn't bad," I say.

"Alright, fine, I'll give you Ethan. Ethan was cute."

"See?"

Alisha says, "Oliver West is stupid hot, and he's hilarious, but not in the ridiculous way you like to pretend guys are funny—in like, an actual cuttingly funny, havoc-y way. He's like . . . sly. He's so—he's so *fucking hot*, Brynn, *I* want to bang him, and I am just honestly shocked because this has never happened before."

I drain the last of my coffee. "Well," I say, glancing at my nails, "there's a first time for everything."

Alisha leans back in her chair and says, "I'm proud of you."

"Thank you."

She leans forward again, length of her hair brushing the tabletop. She gets this conspiratorial grin on her face and says, "So? Tell. What happened that's got you all hot and bothered?"

"Nothing," I say.

It's not a lie.

And it is.

"I—seriously, nothing. Nothing."

And now that I go to explain, it does sound so stupid. So very *nothing*. What am I going to say? We had some super intense eye contact last week? We danced together? A lot of people dance together.

I don't even know if I like him.

I don't know if I hate him.

I have no idea whatsoever how I feel about him and how he feels about me and how either of us is supposed to feel and I just . . . want to go to bed. I want to crawl in bed because it's too intense trying to puzzle it out.

I say, "Nothing happened. I just fixed his dad's car—"

"A power move."

"—and we got to talking while I was out there, and he gave me his jacket or whatever—"

"Oooh, he gave you his jacket? That's a move."

"—and there was, just, like . . . chemistry. There was chemistry, I guess."

She just sits and waits, eyebrow raised.

"That's honestly it," I say, shrugging. "It'll pass. I'm not into the bad boy thing."

It's a lie. I never would have thought it was one before,

but even as I say it, I can feel the heat off Oliver's chest when he leaned over me, small of my back digging into the hood of the car. I can see him grinning, asking how many times I've smoked, if I've ever been arrested, saying, *It's not bullshit, Riley*, and my pulse rises so hard and so fast, I'm afraid I'll rupture a vein. Just bleed right out on this table.

"I'm not trying to beat a dead horse," she says. "But. The dance. Listen, I was pretty sure you guys were going to get right down to it on the dance floor. Right there at school. In the dirty, sweaty gym."

I plunk my head down on the table.

She says, "Well, hell. Enjoy it while it lasts."

"Oh, I won't," I say. "The guy makes my life a waking nightmare"

Alisha shrugs. "That's half the fun of it."

I roll my eyes, and Alisha and I move on to other things. This girl in one of her classes who's being a bitch, my brother and his girlfriend and their pregnancy, her mom's business and some new federal shit they're implementing at the rez, everything. And after my second cup of artist-themed coffee, I get her to take me home in her mom's car.

When I get in, I check my phone.

For a blissful hour and a half, I haven't thought for a second about Oliver West.

And I'm sure he hasn't thought about me.

My phone informs me otherwise.

I have two texts, both from him.

The first one: *Thanks again for what you did for Dad. Car's running great.*

And the second: *Hey, are you free tomorrow night?*

Oh god. No. No, I'm definitely not; I'm booked. Nope.
Nope nope nope not in a million—
Yeah, I write back. *As a matter of fact, I am. What's up?*
Shit.
Well.
The game beginneth.

CHAPTER EIGHTEEN

TOMORROW NIGHT, AS IT turns out, is a basketball game.

And I guess I'm going.

I guess I'm going to a game of sportsball on purpose. Because Oliver is gonna play, and he wants me to be there, and apparently that means I actually care and want to be there? I've been killing myself today, filling out college applications and doing some work for student council to make up for the time I've spent volunteering, and filling out paperwork for a new healthy food cafeteria campaign that I should have gotten done two days ago and should have taken me at least a week, but I've done it in three hours. I'm exhausted before the game even begins. But I'm determined to be there.

Alisha was already going because it's a social event, so she's absolutely thrilled that I've chosen to come out of my Boring Introverted Academic Hole and join her in the land of the living.

I hitch a ride with her, though I'm pretty sure Oliver is the one taking me home.

Not because this is a date.

It's not.

It's because he wants to repay me for fixing his dad's truck with, like, you know . . . coffee or something. With a ride. With a hangout. It's friendly. Super normal and platonically friendly, and I absolutely did *not* spend a good half hour on my nails and makeup and hair and changing outfits eighteen times because I wanted to be sure I looked good enough to catch a cute boy's attention tonight.

Why . . . why would I do that?

I run my hand through my hair for the fortieth time this evening, which I'm sure is doing wonders for the oil content, and take my seat next to Alisha and the slowly wilting hot dog between us. I've sucked down a whole large Cherry Coke already so I'm kind of jittery (yup! Because of the Coke! 180% because of that ONLY).

Alisha is here with a few other theatre kids, kids I don't know, really, but who have always been nice enough to me. Paige (fellow theatre kid) is notably absent, and when I raised an eyebrow about it, Alisha slit her finger across her throat, either because she murdered her or broke up with her.

I'm assuming the latter, but I guess I'll find out later.

I fix my eyes on the court.

Oliver is absolutely destroying tonight. Just sinking layup after layup. Watching him move down the court is like watching a professional. He's a good half-foot shorter than basically everyone else out there, and that should make a difference, *does* make a difference, I'm sure. But that's not what the scoreboard indicates.

I'm mesmerized watching the power of the ball when

he chest passes, the intense focus on his face when he picks up a catch down near the hoop and the ball sails in. The trail of sweat traveling down his neck, his throat, pooling at his collarbone. Jesus.

Suddenly it's so hot.

It's the crush of bodies in here, the adrenaline, the thrill of the crowd.

It's not . . . it's not Oliver, dribbling low to the ground, eyeing his opponent like he's about to go in for a kill. Not the flex of his forearms as the ball transfers from one set of fingertips to another. The expertise with which he wields . . . every single freaking part of his body.

I don't even really care about basketball, but my gaze is absolutely glued to the court. The scoreboard. Not that it matters; this isn't a sports movie. It doesn't come down to the last few minutes, down to one final jump shot.

Heading into the final quarter, we're up thirty points, and everyone in this room knows it's largely because of Oliver West.

Pride swells in my chest, as if I have any claim to him. Any stake in his victory. As if a single shred of it is mine.

I shake my head, clear it, and the clock ticks down.

A minute left in the game.

Thirty seconds.

Fifteen.

It's Oliver's ball, and I swear—I swear he looks up in the stands and sees me. And when he does, his grin widens, sharpens; his eyes get this cocky glint and he takes off like a gunshot down the court.

He doesn't need to; McKinley is up by thirty-four now.

He should take it easy.

But I . . . if I didn't know better, I'd say he was doing it for me.

My pulse jumps, heart catching in my throat, heat in my cheeks.

Oliver fakes left, then spins right, body between the ball and the monster of a boy guarding him. He takes four leaping steps, and a half a second before time runs down, fluidly jumps for a layup. The ball leaves his hand as the buzzer goes off, and the ball circles the rim.

He comes down.

The right post is there, just an inch closer than he should be to Oliver.

So when Oliver's feet hit surface, ninety percent of his sole finds the rubber. It's the other ten that's the problem.

His foot catches on the other boy's ankle.

The other guy is lucky. He snatches his leg back, swears loudly, but apart from that, he's fine.

Oliver hits the ground yelling.

He's clutching his ankle, knee to his chest, and he's fallen into silence with the crowd.

The ball falls through the net.

The whole gym is quiet when the scores finally change.

Shit.

I'm clutching at my own throat; I hate this. I hate this I hate this.

Is it . . . god, it can't be broken. Not his senior year—the scholarships he could get . . . fuck. I'm leaning forward, like being a few inches closer to him can change the course of his fate.

Everyone is hanging on it—our team, theirs. . . . I don't spend a whole lot of time in the sports world, but the time I have: someone gets injured, everyone comes together.

A medic comes to check him out, and then two teammates let him take their shoulders and help him hobble off the court.

It's a win for McKinley High, not that that was why I came in the first place.

The mood is measurably damper than it typically is after a win.

Everyone's wondering if Oliver's okay or if theatrics killed the school's shot at a state championship this year.

I wait outside in the hall with Alisha and her theatre friends, but I can't hear a word they're saying.

Good lord, when did I get so invested?

Why does this even matter to me this much?

When on Earth did this happen?

Finally, finally, the team comes out of the locker room.

Oliver's still in his uniform—purple and gold, both of which manage to look good on him. The collar of his tank shows that collarbone that continues to subtly murder me, tips of his sports binder peeking out of the armpits of his shirt. He's sweaty and disheveled and favoring his left leg, but he looks alright.

I try not to read too far into it when he makes a beeline for me.

"You came," he says, wincing and correcting his stance, then pulling the pained stretch of his mouth into a grin.

"I did." I smile, and it comes out all shy and small. Like this is acknowledging something.

"West!" someone yells. It's Absalom, drummer and theatre extraordinaire. The guy stands out because he's in the tenth grade, and, I shit you not, has a full-on mountain man beard. ABSALOM with a MOUNTAIN MAN BEARD. It's incredible. He's joined by DeAndre, head of the drumline and lead in at least half the shows here, Trey Gallegos, and Ilsy, the tiniest, most elfin platinum blonde with an undercut. She does tech, I think. Then, as a group, the rest of Alisha's typical flock descends on him, Alisha following behind and shooting me waggle eyebrows.

I throw my hands up in a shrug and say, "I didn't—I didn't even know you did theatre."

"I don't," he says, as DeAndre throws his arms around him in a congratulatory hug.

Absalom glances over at me, like he's just now realizing I'm there. "Queers of a feather, baby," he says. He tugs DeAndre to him by the arm and DeAndre catches Absalom's jaw in his teeth.

"Oh!" I say, "sorry, I didn't even realize you were—"

Absalom winks at me.

Oliver slips through them and pulls in toward me. "I don't hang out with many cishets."

"Gross," says Ilsy. "Absolutely not."

I chuckle, and my hand scrapes the base of my skull. I'm just not sure what to say to that. I'm not, like, offended, I just don't know how to respond.

Oliver wrinkles his nose and says, "Don't worry. Sometimes I make an exception."

So is that—is that what I am, then? Someone he hangs around with?

I make it a point not to think about what that does in my chest. How unsettling it is that this is pleasing to me, not maddening.

"I'll catch up with you guys tomorrow?" he says.

DeAndre gives him this look I can't interpret, eyes twinkling, slides a glance at me out of the corner of his eye.

Oliver scrapes his teeth over his lip and gives him a single shake of his head, and DeAndre just says, "Mmmhmm," and that's the signal, I guess, for the drama kids to make their exit.

Oliver looks at me, duffel bag thrown over his shoulder, and says, "You wanna get out of here?"

"Yeah," I say. "Yeah, I do."

Oliver says he needs to change, and he does it in the bathroom—locker room shit can be kind of uncomfortable, especially in the Carolinas, I gather. And then we hop into his car. We run through Cookout, the south's cheapest, Christian camp-themed (???) restaurant, where you can get the best milkshakes on the planet for like two dollars, and roll down the road. Oliver glances over at me in the quiet and says, "You need to get back home?"

I shake my head. Bubble fizz in my chest.

"Don't mind hanging out with me in this sweaty, post-basketball state?"

"I'm disgusted," I say, "but boys are disgusting, so I've learned to tolerate it."

He throws his head back and laughs.

"Let me show you something cool," he says.

I don't ask where we're going; I guess it doesn't really matter. What matters is that we're here, hanging out, like friends, or—or, god I don't know. Something I'm too afraid to name. And I like it.

And shit.

So does he.

Neither of us says much. I think we can both feel it, or at least *I* do; I haven't stopped feeling it since the dance. No. Before that. Since the night with his dad's truck. So we just . . . drive.

The cool thing about South Carolina is that you can be in the city one second, make the correct turn, and within a mile, you're in the middle of nowhere. Or at least, it feels that way.

That's what Oliver does. He hangs a right, and suddenly, we're surrounded by trees and kudzu on one side, farmland on the other.

He makes a sharp left, and we're traveling down this old cow path, way back through some undeveloped land, and when we're far enough that we can't see the road anymore, he stops.

"You trust me?" he says. His eyes are glittering.

"Maybe."

"It's illegal," he says.

"Well then, yeah, definitely."

Oliver laughs, and the sound fills the cab.

"Are you serious?" I say.

He shrugs. "Technically, it's trespassing."

"What is it in non-technical terms?"

"Taking a girl out somewhere cool and doing something edgy."

I lean my head back on the seat, taking in the smell of Oliver's truck, the humid cool of the night, the mingling sweat and deodorant. It's pitch dark out, apart from the wide, smiling moon and the stars.

I shouldn't, probably.

I should tell him no thanks and ask him to take me home. He'd do it.

And because he's left the engine running, hasn't even unbuckled, because there is not a doubt in my mind that if I asked him to take me home right this second, he'd do it without complaint, I say, "Okay."

And I jump out of the truck before I can change my mind.

Oliver kills the engine but leaves the headlights on, slides out, and shuts the door behind him.

"Come on," he says, tilting his head to the dark.

I don't know why I agree. But I do.

He locks his fingers and thumb around my wrist again—which is such a murderous move and I don't know why—and leads me over the smooth grass, steadying me so I don't trip, and just when the headlights fade from helpfulness, he says, "Hell yeah, here we are."

I look up. We're at this ramshackle building, full of holes and wood rot. It looks about a million years old, looks like it'll cave in if too strong a wind comes along.

"Wh—is this a murder shed? I swear, Oliver, if you brought me here to murder me, well . . . in all honesty, I think I'm stronger than you."

"One," he says, holding up a finger, "try me in the morning after I've recovered, we'll see about that. Two, I'd never murder someone here. This is sacred ground."

"Oh yeah?" I say.

"Yeah."

He takes a second with the door, shoving just so—careful and strong all at once. The door gives and he flips on his cellphone light, illuminating what's inside.

"*Oh,*" I say.

"Right?"

It's . . . it's an old cabin. Half falling down, full of dust, but it's like a piece of history. Which . . . I'm a total nerd for this kind of stuff, for falling into the past, but I—I didn't think he knew. Didn't think he'd even noticed. That would require his paying more attention to me than is necessary for blackmail and passing each other in the hallway. I can't even fall very far down that train of thought, because I'm too pulled in by all of the stuff in here. There's a bunch of old bottles lined up on the floor, labels yellowed and peeling, a few bottles cracked but some totally intact.

"Holy shit," I say, completely ignoring the safety hazards present in, like, whatever dirt substance is covering the ground and coming from the rafters and the tetanus probably sticking out of the wood in ninety-four places. "Are these bottles from when they put *coke* in Coke?"

Oliver spits out a laugh.

"Look, 1902!" I shout, thrusting a bottle into the air, like the guy at the end of *The Breakfast Club*. "Hell yes, 1902!"

Oliver shrugs and just says, "I—?"

"They didn't take the cocaine out of this stuff until 1903."

"Are you trying to get me to do hundred-year-old coke, Riley?"

I roll my eyes. "These bottles are empty, you miscreant. And I'm not that kind of girl."

"Eh," he says. "Community service and all that? Could have fooled me."

"I thought I was a goodie two-shoes."

The corner of his mouth pulls up and he shoves his hands into his pockets, meandering around the little building. Then he winks at me.

It's freaking *wrong* that a wink can have me doing this. Have my palms going sweaty and my pulse slamming through my throat, my blood running suddenly hot and my face warming with it. I swallow.

A wink.

A wink!

"These newspapers are from like, a million years ago, too," he says.

"Read me a headline."

"Can't."

"Read?"

"Ha ha," he says, giving me the finger. "The print is too faded. Paper's pretty rotted, honestly."

I mourn this fact quietly and move to join him. "Well, hold on," I say. There's a dry stack in the corner that looks pretty well-preserved. Looks like it just *might* be possible to touch without it falling apart in my hands. Maybe I'll be able to actually read it—which seems like hoping too much. But: "Oh my god."

"What?" Oliver says. He's standing just behind me,

leaning over my shoulder. I can feel the stubble of cheek just beginning to kiss mine. The shadow of his jaw slipping over my collarbone.

I force myself to swallow. "This—well . . ." I slowly reach out to touch the paper and pick it up more gently than I'd pick up a newborn. It, happily, does not disintegrate. "This is . . . this is a copy of the Katzenjammer Kids."

"Oh," he says. "Yes, the Katzenjammer Kids. Sure. Of course."

I glance back over my shoulder to roll my eyes at him and the shift of my face, the push closer to him, makes him jump back. He sucks in a breath and stumbles, that hand catching on the back of his neck.

"The, uh, the strip. It was drawn by Rudolph Dirks. He was such a force in comics, like, he was the first guy to use speech bubbles! That's cool, right? It's cool. He's just . . . this is like holding something revolutionary, Oliver."

I hope that this set of geeky factoids gives some sort of explanation to my shaking. I can't just feel it; I can see it. I can hear it. I'm rattling the paper.

"You're kind of a dork. Did you know that?"

I shrug, still staring at the page. "My dad was really into this shit." *Was* doesn't feel completely right; he's still alive. But he's . . . for all intents and purposes, he's practically gone, so present tense doesn't feel right either. I try not to dwell.

Oliver doesn't ask me about it, doesn't ask about the quick catch in my voice or the use of the past tense, just kind of grunts and lets me have this moment of quiet.

I'm grateful for that, too grateful, and I am getting dangerously close to *liking* Oliver West. Not just liking.

Shaking because he's so close to me, breathing, existing in this tiny space.

Because we are breathing the same air.

Because I want to know what my face will look like after it's been reddened by the stubble on his.

Jesus.

I set the paper gingerly back where it came from.

"This is really freaking cool," I say.

"Yeah." Oliver's voice is low when I turn to look at him. The headlights are still coming through the doorways, the lines where the wood has shrunken or rotted or gotten holes. So I can see him, but it's not like it's bright. He's all dark and shadowed like everything else in here.

"How did you even know I'd be into it?" I say.

He shrugs. "Like I said. You're a dork."

"Nah," I say. "That's not all it is."

He grins and takes a step closer. "Fine. You wanna hear that I've been paying attention? To pick this up? You got me, Sherlock. You're always wearing these nerd-ass t-shirts when I come pick you up to volunteer. The library check-out card one that just has ALEXANDRIA at the top? The menu at Donner Bar and Grille with all the clever cannibalism puns?"

"I bought that for Halloween!" I say. "I just wear it as a pajama shirt now! Well, or when everything else is in the wash, and the washer was on the fritz because it's always on the fritz and—"

"You're a sick fuck," he says, but he's laughing. "Or wait, shit: *In Soviet Russia, you do not gaze into abyss. Abyss gaze into you.*"

He laughs harder at that one—tears actually leaking out of his eyes.

"In fairness to the Soviets," I say, "they didn't even really like Nietzche."

He shakes his head and kind of rolls his eyes. "You're always hand-up, jumping out of your chair in class."

"Okay, now that's just not fair."

"Yeah, alright," he says in that specific mocking voice. "Your eyes always light up the second any teacher brings up anything even vaguely historical. Like they're telling you you just won a free double-scoop of ice cream."

Now it's my turn to roll my eyes. I do this kind of offended snort thing, but I'm not offended, not really. I feel . . . warm. The tiniest bit closed in, but not like the walls are caging me. Like when you're being wrapped in a blanket. Fuzzy and secure and—safe. Safe. That's how I feel.

Safe and deeply, profoundly off-kilter, because Oliver is standing there saying these things to me like I'm a full human, and more importantly, like he *sees* me as a full human. Not just any human. One worth knowing.

I glance at the dusty floorboards and let my hands slip into my hoodie pocket. I look up through my eyelashes at him. Very, extremely aware I'm doing it. The coquettish thing. But, like, I can't get myself to stop.

I say, "Are you saying you've been paying attention to me, Oliver?"

He kind of laughs and looks at the ground. Kicks it. There's this little smile tugging at his mouth, one he's not really acknowledging. He's just standing there all bashful for the first time since I've met him, and I find myself moving closer to him, and what. What is happening?

I can see his jaw shift when he swallows, the little balance shift in his chest and feet. He exhales slowly, and when he looks up, I realize we're a little closer than I intended. And those eyes—those confident, unflappable, cool eyes, spark and light. It's panic. I register it when he blinks and stumbles back and stutters, "I—I should, uh. Yeah, we should head out. It's getting late, right?" He mumbles under his breath, "It's getting fucking late," and whirls around to the cabin door, yanking it open with enough force that I'm a little nervous the whole thing will come down around us.

"Oliver," I say, and I start after him.

"Sorry," he says, wincing, because I figure the speed of his exit reminded him of his injury.

He limps down the path, and I catch up to him by the bed of his truck and press my fingers into his arm. He spins and says, "Jesus, Riley. Jesus, don't touch me unless . . ."

I step back. Have I—yeah, cool, I've misread everything. Oh my god, this is humiliating; I could have *sworn*, but . . . no. Nope, I'm not his type and I don't know why I ever thought I could be and when it started to matter, but it does, I guess. It *does* and I hate it.

"Unless?" I repeat, wincing against it. I don't even want to hear this answer! Why am I asking! Why am I doing this to myself instead of having him take me home immediately so I can nurse my platonic, he's-just-not-that-into-you wounds?

He does that thing, hand on the back of his head, and leans against the truck. He stares up at the sky. It's black now, which almost makes it easier. Not being able to see each other outside the haze of low light.

"Unless—here's the thing, Riley. I just, uh, I know you're straight, and like, I know what that means, what it *should* mean. But I guess I don't know what *you* think it means and if—and like, even if you are, even if you're not—shit. I never know how to figure this thing out and how I'm supposed to . . . ha. Christ."

He runs his hand down his face.

This is the least smooth I've ever seen him.

His hands are shaking and it's almost like he's mad, but he's not *mad,* that's not it.

It clicks for me, all at once, what I think he's trying to say. And it kind of makes my chest hurt. It hurts and blooms with anxiety because, what if I'm wrong? What if this is absolutely not stress because he's interested and I'm about to make a fool of myself?

Cool.

I hate this.

I look at the ground for five full seconds, count them out, before I look him right in the eye. Like I'm bold. Like I'm the kind of person who looks guys right in the eye and tells them she's into them.

I say, "I'm, yeah, I'm straight. I'm into guys. I'm—I can't believe you're going to make me say this out loud."

His nostrils flare and his breath shows up on the air. It's only now that I realize how cold it is.

"I fucking like you," I say. Turns out I'm not that kind of person because I look at the sky when I say it. Like I'm Romeo. *I FUCKING LIKE YOU, STARS.*

There's a beat of silence.

The longest silence that has ever beat.

Finally, Oliver says, voice all low in the dark, "You cold, Riley?"

I laugh. White in the black. "I guess."

"You want my jacket?"

I look up. "Okay."

"Why don't you come get it?"

I bite my lip, heart going eight thousand beats a minute. I'm freezing and too hot all at once. I think—yeah, I guess I'm doing this.

I take a step toward him, two, three. His eyes are locked on mine, deep hickory brown and glistening and focused in the dark. He shrugs out of his leather jacket and stands up straight from where he was leaning against that truck bed.

I hold out my arms, which, frankly, feels a little dorky. But I don't have time to get too anxious over that, not with the intensity of Oliver's stare and the wry tilt of his mouth.

I wonder if—I hope—he'll touch me with it.

The worn leather slips over my arms and my back. It fits me like a glove.

Oliver's smell wraps around me. It's a smell that, apparently, makes my breathing come too fast and shallow.

"Thanks," I say.

"Yeah."

He searches my face, gaze dipping from my eyes to my mouth.

There's this beat of quiet, his gaze lingering there.

I run my tongue over my bottom lip.

Then, his hand is sudden and strong around the back of my neck, and he pulls me toward him. My mouth crashes into his and I don't even know how he does it, but he has me flipped around. One second my back is free, nothing at it but leather and air. The next, Oliver is leaning over me, hips pressing into mine, and the truck is digging into my back.

It's quick, desperate, a little dirty. And I'm so . . . I'm so freaking into it I can't breathe.

My hand is fisted in the hem of his shirt, the other tugging on a belt loop. He still has his fingers locked around the back of my neck, pressing one and then the other, strong and fluid, to make the smallest, most pointed suggestions to my muscles that move my jaw, my face, my mouth, exactly where he wants them. I'm a little embarrassed when I actually *sigh* into his mouth, but then he sucks in a breath and it shakes.

I can feel it hitching when he kisses me, air juddering in my mouth, on my lips, my tongue, and *god*. It's intoxicating.

I feel halfway to drunk. On the way he tastes, what his fingers are doing in my hair, on the way he kisses me. It's not exactly like kissing a cishet guy. At least, none of them that I've kissed. I don't know why, exactly—if it's because they've all been cis and straight or if it's because they've all just been . . . inferior to him. If it's a trait or if it's an indictment on them all individually, as humans. Oliver kisses me like it's not a step he has to get through to get to the other stuff. He kisses me like . . . like it's not a means to an end. Like the kiss in and of itself is something that matters. All on its own.

He kisses me like's he *needs* to, like he's caught up, like his blood is running just as hot as mine is. But not fast. He doesn't *rush*; he just slowly leans a little more of his weight against me until I'm melted into the frame of the truck. Until all I can feel, all I can think about, is his tongue between my teeth, his hand pulling at the hair of my scalp, the other slowly, lazily traveling up and down the stretch of skin between my underwire and the low waistband of my jeans. Skating over my hipbones.

Somehow, we've migrated.

Where we started out just behind the cab door, just where the bed began, now we've turned the corner so I'm pushed up again the very back of the bed. He takes a step back and pulls me into him, pulling his lips away from mine and scraping his teeth down my throat, tongue ghosting over that spot where neck meets shoulder, and he pops the bed so it opens. Then he takes me by the thighs and lifts me up so I'm sitting there, legs hanging off it. It makes me just a little taller than him.

I say, "Christ, you're strong."

He says, "Thanks, I work out."

I throw my head back and laugh. I can feel the pink from his stubble running up my throat, raising around my mouth.

He takes a second to breathe, hands resting casually on my thighs, and looks at me, then at the truck bed. Then he raises an eyebrow and cocks his head toward it. Smirking and confident and flushed.

I say, "Okay."

He hoists himself up into the truck bed with me, careful

to avoid that ankle, and then his mouth is on mine again so fast it's like he was just dying for it the last twenty seconds.

His hands are fucking fantastic. They're nowhere they shouldn't be, nowhere I'm not yet comfortable with, but it *feels* like they are. It feels like they're all over me, like we must be doing something more than kissing. But we're not.

We're just . . . we're just making out in the back of a truck, and my whole body is on fire.

He's on top of me, ridges of the bed in my spine, kissing me like we'll never get the chance again. Like he's been imagining this for ages.

And I'm going to say something I may never have said about a high school guy: he uses the proper amount of tongue.

It's a revelation.

He pulls back at one point, braces over me, biceps flexing, and says, "How you doing?"

I blink. I don't think I've ever been, like, checked in with while fooling around before. It makes me smile like an idiot when I say, "Good. I'm . . . I'm great." I laugh, the sound riding on the waves of my pulse. "You?"

He laughs with me, and brushes a tendril of hair out of my face.

I've always wanted a guy to do that.

I grin and I know it's goofy, but I hope he doesn't notice. If he's psychic and hears the desperately romantic thoughts rushing through my head, I'll die.

"Yeah," he says, "I'm good."

He lets his gaze brush my eyes, my mouth, my throat, my chest. Then, slow, right back up again.

"Jesus," he says, "look at you."

My face gets hots. "Oh god, stop."

"I should get you home." He's still all silly, smiling, and so am I.

It's nauseatingly adorable.

I don't even care.

"Probably," I say.

"Come on," he says, descending, then he holds his hand out to help me down from the truck.

We make our way back to the cab, and he starts it up. We're not too far from my house, which is good, because who ever knows what to say after they've kissed someone for the first time? It's the most awkward thing. Even if you're happy about it.

I am.

He's got this total shit-eating grin on his face that he can't seem to get rid of no matter how many times he actively tries to wipe it off, and at one point, over the music he's put on, I say, "What?"

He says, "Nothing!"

I say, "It's something."

He glances over at me and says, "*Nothing.*"

I narrow my eyes.

"I just . . ." He looks out the window and back over at me. "I'm just having a nice time."

He shrugs, and that warm glow that's been melting through me for hours lights up even brighter. What is happening to me?

I realize, then, that we've rolled to a stop. We're sitting in the gravel lot just outside my place.

"Me too," I say. My voice comes out all quiet. "I—yeah, I should probably get inside."

"Yeah," he says. "Sure."

"So, I'll just—I'll see you at school? Or this weekend? Or. Whatever."

"Yup."

He grips the wheel, twists his hands over it.

I unbuckle.

"Hey," he says, "one quick thing?"

My stomach dips and swoops. Oh god. *This was a one-time thing. Let's not make something of this? Don't tell.* Any number of quick things tumble suddenly through my anxiety brain. I say, forcibly light and breezy, "Hmm?"

He unbuckles his seatbelt and says, "Let me just—" and he locks his fingers around my jaw. He kisses me again and I can feel it everywhere—in my head and my chest and my stomach and my toes.

Holy god, I just . . . I guess I did not quite understand what kissing was intended to be.

That it can absolutely knock your feet out from under you.

That it *should.*

All other kisses should be ashamed of themselves.

I kiss him back, losing my breath, losing my cool, utterly high.

Then he pulls back and says, "So, yeah. Uh. Goodnight," and laughs his way through it.

I'm stupidly giggly, just entirely *drunk*, when I make it through my front door and close it behind me.

CHAPTER NINETEEN

I PRACTICALLY DANCE INTO my house on a hormone cloud. Evian is still up, doing some knitting or something and watching a true crime documentary on the couch. She lives with Patrick and Randi, but she stays over sometimes, especially when Mom's working nights (which is often). I don't think she likes leaving me alone all night, even if the others leave.

That thought briefly warms my chest, so I hesitate in the living room long enough for her to say, "Baby sister."

I tip my chin up at her and pause behind the couch. I want to say hi, but I also want to just go to bed and rehash everything a hundred times before I fall asleep.

"Oh," she says, fake scandal in her voice. "Someone's looking kissed."

"What?" I say.

"Your mouth." She laughs. "And, uh . . ." She gestures at her own collarbone. "This whole situation."

I frown and turn on my selfie camera. Oh god, there's definitely a hickey there now. GREAT.

I blink, then straighten and smirk. "Well. I've had . . . a nice evening."

"Yeah, looks like it." She grins. She smells a little like weed, because she always does. I'm reminded of the huge chasm between us in that smell. And the catch of my eyes on the note Mom left on my door that says, CALL DAD.

"It's good for you," Evian says. "To have fun sometimes."

I don't even mean for it to come out bitchy when I say, "Yeah, that's advice I'm gonna take," but it does, because it *was* kind of bitchy, and her face immediately shutters.

She says, "Consider the source, right? Forget I said anything. Have a good night, Brynn."

And she goes back to her knitting.

That's what I wanted: privacy. The ability to go back to my room and mull it over in peace. Read or something.

But now she's given it to me, and I wish I hadn't gotten it.

I feel like a complete jerk.

I run my hand over the back of my head. "Hey, sorry, I—"

"No, Brynn, seriously. Forget I tried to offer you any kind of advice or support. I'm just a thirty-year-old screw-up and honestly, things are going well for you, right? You don't need shit from me."

"I didn't say that."

She says, "Okay," and focuses on her project.

I should leave her alone.

She's being too sensitive.

But I feel bad.

So . . . great, guess I can't.

I say, "What are you working on?"

"Knitting."

"Duh," I say. "What, though?"

She glances up, eyes me. "Socks."

"Oh," I say. "They're . . . they're small."

She sets the needles down. "Well, Brynn, they're for a baby. Your brother's baby? You remember? Or did that get lost in all your academics and whatever?"

I flinch. I remember. Of course I do. "No, yeah, that . . . that makes sense. Sorry. They're cute."

She stares at me, hard, for ten seconds. Which doesn't seem like a long time, but let me reassure you: it's a *long* time when you count it out.

I count it out.

"Go to bed," she says. "You have school in the morning."

"Y-yeah," I say. I want to tell her she can't tell me what to do. But I think that'll make me sound and feel more like a baby than I already do. So I don't.

I just head quietly into my room.

Considerably more deflated than I was five minutes ago.

I don't know whether my sister has done this to me or I've done it to myself.

What I do know is that I don't want to think about it.

That's . . . usually where I land when it comes to my family: I don't want to think about it.

I don't even know why! It's just that I'm . . . I'm tired all the time. And embarrassed. I'm embarrassed to talk about where I live, and I'm embarrassed that my dad is in jail, and I don't even want to pick up the phone when he calls because I'm *embarrassed* to tell everyone I'm a Riley at school because of all the shit they pulled. And then I'm embarrassed for thinking that way. That I'm so much better than them or some terrible shit. That's horrible of me and I know it. It's just . . . I don't know. Complicated. They support me. My family isn't bad; I don't have some kind of Matilda walking to the library at four years old begging her teacher to adopt her backstory. It's just that I don't know how to sort out the way they treat me (good) from the way they paved this rocky road for me (bad), and the way I feel like I have to distance myself from this name at school, and all the million complicated feelings in between, and it always comes out of my mouth completely, terribly bitchy.

I breathe. I push back quick tears that I have to admit are borne of shame. And I resolve not to think about it.

I walk into the bathroom, pulse heightened and face hot, and splash my face with cold water. My pulse begins to slow. I cool down. I wash, I brush my teeth, I do everything I need to do to slip from Daytime Brynn into Sleepy Nighttime Brynn Who Doesn't Worry About Family Conflict, But Worries Instead About the Guy She Just Made Out With and How Her Dreams Tonight Will Go In the Aftermath.

I focus, as I slip out of my clothes and into bed, on what it felt like. When he kissed me and touched me. How the intensity of the anger I've felt about him for weeks didn't exactly go away; it just transformed. So now, Oliver, who's been keying me up forever every time I think about him, getting me so livid I can't think straight, is keying me up again. Muddying my thoughts and wrecking my heart rate.

Somehow, I think that texting Alisha: *WELP I KISSED OLIVER. APPARENTLY* will help calm me down. It only gets me jacked up even higher seeing it written out like that.

It's at least an hour before I can calm my thundering heart into allowing me to sleep.

I get up at the butt crack of dawn, as per usual, because the time listed on my bus route at the beginning of year was "lower back tattoo of dawn," which means that, typically, "butt crack" leaves me a safe amount of time to get ready for school.

In the bleary, early morning dark, I open my eyes to see there's a text on my phone.

I both desperately want it to be from Oliver and absolutely *need* it to be from someone else.

Just in case.

Just in case he's rethought everything.

In case it's a joke.

In case I absolutely nailed the first kiss, but when the second came around, I totally faceplanted and ruined it all and he just had the grace not to tell me in the moment, to my face.

My heart is strangling me when I open my messages, and it does not say: *Hey thanks for the tongue but NO THANKS you SLOBBERY FREAK get your whole mouth together*, as I feared.

It just says: *hey im about to pass out, but let me give you a ride to school tomorrow?*

I am beginning to think it's time to request an adjustment to my anxiety medication.

I blow out a frankly far too relieved breath and slam my head back on the pillow, blinking up at the ceiling.

If I catch a ride with Oliver, that gives me a good extra hour to lie here. And, you know, not sleep.

There's no way I can now; I'm too keyed up just from seeing his name on my screen.

Gracious, when did this even *happen*?

I blink up at the popcorn on my ceiling, the little glowy stars that have been there since I was a kid, and I shove my hands under my pillow in an attempt to get them to stop shaking. When I'm at least satisfied with my potential ability to get through sending a text message, I write back: *sounds great!*

Then I wonder if that was too peppy.

Did the exclamation point make me sound, like, clingy? Or weird?

Oh god.

My brain pipes in with a very helpful: *What if you sent him a nude right now? Doing something* REAL *fuckin graphic. Enough to make him blush. What if you—*

I grit my teeth.

I hate these.

I swear, I hate these more than the anxiety that's something so bad I can quite literally feel it scraping over my skin, picking out the little hairs one by one.

Nothing makes you feel more like an absolute weirdo than your brain sending you deviant signals in the middle of nowhere, for absolutely no reason, and you having to remind yourself that that doesn't mean you're going to act on it, doesn't even mean you *want* to act on it.

Not that nudity is just such NIGHTMARISH, HORRIBLE behavior. But ha. Right now? Absolutely freaking not.

I shake my head and shut my eyes. The one nice thing about the intrusive thoughts is their tendency to disappear in a flash.

This one, mercifully, follows the trend.

I wait, wondering if somehow he knows about my bizarre, inappropriate thoughts.

He writes back: *sweet. 7:15 work for you?*

Yes. About that dosage switch . . .

I send back several thumbs up emojis and yank the covers over my head.

Sleep isn't going to happen, but I can at least just lie here in the dark for a while and be quiet. Breathe.

That is what I do. I'm not hit with anything else unsettling, any unhinged questions or anxious thoughts, just the happy anticipation of seeing a guy who likes me, who is cool enough to offer me a ride to school so I don't have to suffer the bus, even though I'm not even really his girlfriend. Even though we just made out in the back of his truck.

The scenarios I wonder about are nice, soft, safe. Scenarios where we kiss again, in his truck, in the school hallway, in my bedroom.

Scenarios where he just coolly says, "So, you wanna do this thing, or?" and laces his fingers in mine as we pass row after row of lockers and he pulls my head toward his and kisses my temple through my hair.

Just . . . sappy stuff, honestly.

I don't care.

It makes me feel warm and comfortable, and that is what I want.

I finally peel myself out of bed and get dressed and when I hear his truck idling in the drive and jump up into his passenger's seat, that's how it makes me feel, too.

When his face brightens and he says, "Hey," with this big, sunny smile and then he says, "Hey, can I—uh, yeah, I'm just gonna say it. Can I kiss you?"

And I say, on a relieved exhale, "Yes."

And he laughs out a similarly reassured, "Cool," and leans in, lips on my mouth, taste of cinnamon gum on my tongue.

My pulse is dancing in my veins, nerves lighting up over my skin, and I *love* it.

He pulls back and yanks the truck into gear, and we pull out, rumble of gravel vibrating below the tires. And we're both just . . . stupidly happy.

I lean my head against the seat and blink up at the roof of the cab.

He says, "Whatcha thinkin' about, Riley?"

I shrug. "Just, I don't know. I feel good."

A smile curls his lip and he says, "Yeah? Why?"

I roll my eyes. "I swear to god, if you get *any* cockier . . ."

He laughs.

We roll down the road.

Alisha about tackles me when I get to school and we spend breaks going over every last detail. Oliver and I don't hang out after school, because he's got a service project to do, apparently, and that's fine. It's one of the biggest facets of the competition: actually serving. You have to get twenty full hours over the length of the competition, and I honestly don't know how the heck Oliver is going to manage it with school, basketball, and his job at the shelter. Frankly, kids with jobs usually are not this competition's target demographic.

But like . . . when *are* we?

I'm not working this year because 1) community service made that pretty much impossible, and 2) my siblings have been able to band together with Mom and make sure I don't have to during my senior year. It's so freaking impossible to manage that and extracurriculars and . . . well. Everything leading up to college. They all want me to be able to make it, go to school. First Riley to really make it happen. So I'm lucky. But if you think I haven't busted my ass making coffee and burgers every year but this one since I turned fifteen, well, you would be wrong.

So, yeah, I just have no clue how Oliver manages it.

But he does.

And I have student council stuff to work on anyway. Laura Kim is *very* excited to see me and makes a point of hugging me around the neck, which makes me feel a little bad, but I have been shirking my duties. She's right. She's not actually trying to guilt me; she's just flipping excited enough to see me that it suddenly hits me how absent I've been while trying to manage all of this and . . . god, I need to pull it together.

I focus as hard as I possibly can for the three hours I'm there. I write a revision for the healthy lunch options pitch we've been working on and go over an impassioned proposal a big group of seniors has made for more parking options, though I have no idea how we can swing that. The parking lot has finite space. I don't know; maybe eat into the teacher's lot or . . . expand bike parking? I noodle on that for a while, call Laura and Matt White over to help. Tanisha has some ideas that involve working something out with the middle school next door to negotiate for space in exchange for auditorium usage since they have to use the cafeteria for their productions and it's not like middle schoolers have cars. I think that's got some traction, so we all bust our butts creating a proposal for this. And then it's on to planning the next dance, because Alisha was right when she called it dance season. We've got homecoming, Sadie Hawkins, and then Snoball is basically right around the corner. We're brainstorming candy décor since this year's theme is Candy Land.

By the time seven o'clock hits, I'm wiped. Patrick picks me up to take me home and I kiss him on the cheek, because bless him. Then I get very unattractive and very braless in my own room immediately.

I pretty much figured I wouldn't be seeing Oliver until tomorrow when he picks me up for my shift with Pibbles and Kits, but then it's 8 p.m. and he texts me and invites me over for dessert.

I don't care that I'm wiped out.

Suddenly, I have all the energy in the world.

I don't bother asking permission. Mom's at work, so who am I supposed to ask?

I just immediately agree and change out of my PJs, which I'd slipped so happily into, prepared to settle in for a long and wild night of researching reasons that women had been locked in mental institutions during the Victorian era.

I would like to tell you that this was for a project.

It was not.

When Oliver pulls up and asks what I've been up to, under no circumstances do I tell him. I just immediately change the subject, ask what we're doing for dessert and whether this is, like, a regular thing because, if so, he can expect me over eight nights a week.

Then I briefly panic that perhaps I have said something too stalkery, too overly committed, even though it was a joke, I swear it was a joke, but we get to Oliver's before I can follow that rabbit trail beyond the point of no return, and Oliver doesn't act weirded out.

He just shrugs and says, "It's every Friday. But, like, obviously come over."

Then we hop out of the truck and he slips his hand in mine as we crunch across the gravel to his front door.

I'm giddy with it, just blown away by the touch of his hand and the still-heady whiplash of hating this guy to taking solace in his hand while we go into his home for family dessert night.

We head into his trailer, and I'm blown away by the warmth here. It reaches out and grabs me when I walk inside, the smells of apples and butter wrapping me in the sweetest, softest hug.

I can't believe a house can feel this way.

Oliver's dad flashes me a smile when he sees me, even though his smiles are more like hints. Suggestions that he might smile if the opportunity presents itself, but he's not inclined to give away the game. His uncle is there again, and I wonder if they live together or if he's got his own place.

Not that it matters.

"Well, well, the girlfriend."

"*Dad*," Oliver hisses, and his palm immediately goes clammy. "We're not—well, maybe we're—Jesus. Dad, can you just?"

His dad comes out with a round, barrel laugh, and I guess that swift denial should send me into a panic like everything else does. But it doesn't. Because it wasn't a denial—it's not, like, a shame thing. Oliver is pink with embarrassment at his dad assuming.

He looks at me apologetically and leans down to whisper in my ear, "Sorry, uh, I guess we should . . . sorry."

Yes, the fragmented anxiety speech, with which I am intimately, terribly familiar.

His voice caresses my ear and sends goose bumps down my back and arms. I just shake my head, hoping the smile cuts through the silence, and say, "Well, what's for dessert?"

"The chef," Oliver's uncle says, "has prepared for us this evening: apple crisp a la mode. Plating, of course, in a homey nod to the humble surroundings, generously apportioned and accented with a delicate caramel drizzle in an homage to—"

"Aw, hell," says his dad. "Sit down, shut up, and have some pie, goddammit."

His brother loses it and Oliver says, "Dad went through a cooking phase."

Oliver's uncle pipes in, "A fourteen-year cooking phase."

I'm giggling along with everyone until his dad says, "And Beau's going through a forty-seven-year-long asshole phase. Drop it."

He's not mean about it, but there's the tiniest edge of pain behind his voice that I kind of wish I hadn't detected; it feels too private. It sobers things considerably.

Until Mr. West takes a huge bite of the apple crisp he made and says, "Well, Beau was right. I shoulda gone professional."

The tension snaps, just like that, and we can eat.

He's right. It *is* incredible. It's the perfect combination of sweet and tart, butter melting on my tongue and cinnamon marrying the salt. The caramel, which has got to be homemade, is something they should write songs about.

No one even speaks while we eat, and if that's not a testament to perfect cooking, nothing is.

Oliver's fingers graze my knee under the table and I smirk into my bowl and lean my leg just a little closer to him. His mouth tilts up and his nostrils flare.

That's the only indication.

"Son," Mr. West says, "tell me about volunteering."

"Not a lot to tell. It was good."

I furrow my brow. "That's it?"

Oliver snaps his head to look at me, affronted. "It was good!" he says. "What!"

I shrug. "You're not going to get the grant with *It was good*, that's all I'm saying." I shove a spoonful of vanilla bean into my mouth and say, "I'm trying to help you."

Oliver's eyes glint, amused and challenging, and I smile around my spoon.

"Oh," says Beau. "I like her."

"Fine," says Oliver, that little cheeky grin still on his mouth. "It was exhilarating. Inspiring. It was like being in a living, breathing spread of *Humanitarian Weekly*. I can still feel the *Good Place* points running through my veins like magic."

"Jesus," I say, rolling my eyes.

"Seriously, what do you guys want!" He laughs, and I'm beginning to understand that this is just how his family communicates. Ribbing and yelling and sarcasm and warmth. Gosh, I . . . I think I love it.

"We want to know what you were doing all day!" says Beau.

I point my spoon at Beau in agreement and we all look expectantly at Oliver.

"Good god, can a guy have his privacy?"

"He cannot," says Beau.

Mr. West chuckles.

"It was kids. Just, like, this theatre program for lower income kids? The one you and Mom—yeah, the one you and Mom sent me to when I was little. Kind of cool, I guess, to be helping out at a place I used to go. Neat being on this side of it."

I love this, too.

I love all of this and I can't believe I ever found myself doing everything I could to avoid Oliver West.

"You were in theatre?" I say.

"Yeah. Shifted, though. I'm mostly into music now. Drums, yeah? Queer kid requirement: you must do some sort of performing art. It's in the bylaws."

My gosh, between him and Alisha, there's apparently a very specific type of person I like to hang out with, and that type is: drummers. I laugh and his dad and uncle chuckle and we eat this incredible dessert.

"That how you feel about it, Blondie? Nice to help out?" says Beau. "Volunteering at the shelter."

I laugh. "Sure? I mean, I like it. A little different when you're doing it because a judge wrote your ticket, but yeah, it's cool."

A silence falls over the table and Oliver and his dad exchange a look, and I almost choke on my pie.

Did I . . . did I say something?

Oh god.

Now it's my hands' turn to sweat.

Shit, did I ruin everything somehow?

Beau says, "Well, I'm getting seconds. Anyone else? All of you. Good," but when he takes all our bowls to the kitchen, I can feel it. The solid moment of concern. Of his doing that to soften something, to smooth it over.

It almost works.

We eat seconds, and everyone is friendly and comfortable but everyone is also . . . wary. Careful.

Was it the judge thing? I wouldn't think . . .

Oliver's hand is at my knee under the table again, and I try to be reassured by it.

When dessert is cleared, I quietly say, "I should go."

Oliver says, "I hear you. But. Counterpoint: you should stay."

"It's . . . it's late, and I—"

He leans in really close. No one is at the table anymore but us. "If you wanna go, that's completely cool, but if this is about . . . about the weirdness while we ate, it's not you. My dad's in a bizarre mood tonight and I promise you it's not your fault. And he's fine. They're fine now, I swear. You can go, I'm not going to pressure you." He smiles, teeth and dimples dazzling in the yellow kitchen light. "But it wouldn't suck if you stayed."

"Ugh," I say, but my mouth is smiling. My eyes are smiling. My face has clearly decided for me: I'm staying.

CHAPTER TWENTY

THE THING ABOUT TRAILER walls: they're really freaking thin.

So when I go to hang out in Oliver's room and he leaves to run to the bathroom, I hear it when his dad says, "Oliver. Listen—"

"Dad, I know what you're thinking. But—"

"No. I cannot have you doing this again."

"I'm not—Dad, I can't—I can't do this right now."

A silence.

I am frozen on Oliver's carpet.

This is about me; they're talking about me.

Oh god.

This is my anxiety brain's worst nightmare: finding out that all the unreasonable shit I'm worried about is true.

I curl up in the throw at his bedside, and his dad says, voice low, "We just got back on track."

"She's not like that." A beat. "I *swear*."

Silence.

"Dad. You have to trust me."

Something mumbled that I can't hear, and then Oliver comes back into his room.

He leaves it just barely cracked. "Rules," he says, hand where he likes it to go when he's nervous—the base of his skull.

"I don't want to cause problems," I say.

He furrows his brow. "What?"

"I just . . ." I pull that throw even tighter around myself and tilt my head toward the wall. My eyes find everything but him to focus on. The sports ball stuff on the wall. The navy comforter haphazardly tossed across the bed. The beat-up trap set and sticks in the corner. I glance back at Oliver.

That furrow runs deeper, and then understanding falls over his face. "Oh. Oh, shit, you—okay, no. Listen, that really has nothing to do with you."

I raise an eyebrow, shaking everywhere.

"I—" He crosses the room and sinks down beside me on the floor, hand searching for me across the carpet. He slips his fingers over to my leg, tips brushing it through the blanket. "My dad's . . . nervous. I had a pretty rough go of shit for a while, and he's—he heard the community service thing, and figures I'm gonna be drawn back into stuff. And he just doesn't want me going back. To juvie."

I'm quiet.

He's quiet.

"I'm going to talk to him."

I look over at him. "You don't have to. It's not like . . . it's not like we're dating."

"It could be," he says. Then his eyes widen. "Cool, I'm glad I just said *that* out loud." Then he stops, considers. "Well. It's out there. Date me."

My eyes are as round and baffled as his are. "Are you—really?"

"Yeah. Date me. You should. Have you seen us making out? We're so good at it. It would be a shame to waste that."

My instincts say to be nervous about his dad, to dwell in the shame of this mistake making me the kind of girl who concerns parents, who gets accused of being a bad influence on their sons. But a much stronger drive is punching through that specific anxiety. It's that drive that has me saying, "Well, I can't argue with that logic."

He says, "Yeah?"

I tilt my head back against his bed. "Yeah."

"Okay," he says. I can hear the smile in his voice, and when I tip my head over to look at him, I see it. The blanket falls from my shoulders, because in this second, I don't need it as a shield.

Oliver scoots over next to me so we're shoulder-to-shoulder, his pinkie the lightest touch against my thigh.

There's this nervous thread between us, that one that asks the question: What do we do now? What happens?

I take more time to look around at his room, for lack of answer. Beyond the basketball stuff, it's plastered in posters of punk bands. From a million years ago—Rage Against The Machine, Dead Kennedys, that kind of thing—and from today. Salient Narcolepsy. Drowning Effigy. Bands I've never heard of. What isn't covered in punk is covered in . . . succulents.

As in, like, the little desert plants. Pictures of them on his walls and real living ones on his windowsill.

"Don't judge me for the plants," he says, following my gaze. "Succulents are queer culture."

I laugh. "Noted."

I'm struck, in the moment, by how intimate this is. Being in someone's room, I don't know. It's just . . . a different level.

He says, "It's not just that he's afraid you're gonna, like, influence me."

Immediately, the cords of my muscles tense up and my jaw tightens. It makes me nervous to even talk about it. Because I'm going to have to face Mr. West when I leave this room, and that fills me with—you guessed it—anxiety.

"He can't have me going to lock-up again. Frankly, *I* can't. The fallout just—it fucking sucks, and my dad's exhausted and I guess I'm exhausted. Like . . ." He sucks in a breath, breathes out slow and shaky. His throat moves and his jaw clenches. Then he says, "It's not like they're sending me to a guys' lockup, you know?"

"Oh," I say. "Are you—seriously?"

He glances over at me and raises an eyebrow. "Come on, man. In *South Carolina*?"

"Yeah. Okay, good point."

"Honestly, I can't believe they let me on the guys' basketball team. Consideration in juvie would be asking too much."

I kind of laugh, because it seems like it calls for that, and he's laughing a little, too. It's sort of haunted, but sometimes that's just the only way to deal with shit.

"So yeah," he says. "My dad really is cool, I promise. He's just . . . yeah. You get it."

I nod. "I get it." Then I say, "Four times, man, what the hell have you gotten up to?"

The laugh this time is deep and loud, like a bell. It's authentic. It unwinds my muscles.

He says, "Some shit. Vandalism, mostly. Petty theft. Got into a huge fight, and that didn't go great."

"Damn," I say, and I shove his shoulder, "Oliver, get your *shit* together."

He snorts. "Listen, man, I was off the rails for a while. After my mom died. What do you want from me?" He drops it like it's nothing, casual, just a part of who he is, and something in my chest twists at that, because it's the same voice I use to talk about my dad.

I say, "I get it. I had a rough time after my dad got locked up."

"Shit," he says. "Sorry."

"For what?"

"I, uh, I don't know. Just seems like that's . . . what you're supposed to say."

"Fair enough."

After a moment, he says, "What kind of trouble could you have possibly gotten into? Did you cheat on a test? Forge your mom's signature on a permission slip? Wait. Did you . . . oh god. Brynn, did you . . . ditch school?"

"Fuck you," I say, without any heat. Just laughter and a middle finger in the air so that he catches my wrist and pulls me a little closer. "Some of us don't do grief with busted knuckles and a can of spray paint, you ass."

He says, "Your loss," and I say, "Ugh."

"Ha," he says, "god, this is not how I planned for this evening to go."

"How did you plan it to go?"

"Well," he says, turning toward me, thumb still running up the vein in my wrist. "I'd planned on plying you with food and drink, welcoming you into my sumptuous abode, and using the punk band posters to seduce you."

I choke. "Well, you're halfway there."

"To a seduction? Doubtful."

I laugh.

I've laughed so much this evening, even with all the stress and the . . . dark topics of conversation. And that pull, that pull that for weeks felt like a push, it's as strong as it always was, and it's so intense here, in the dark.

So when he looks over at me, shadows and light playing on his bones, that almost elfin smile on his face, a question written on his mouth, I kiss him.

He sucks in a breath and frames my face with his hand, fingers soft on my jaw and cheekbone, and then urgent.

He shifts toward me and pulls me onto his lap, and I wrap my hands around his neck, edges of his buzzcut tickling my wrists and palms. His fingers are trailing up my spine, under my shirt, and my breaths are coming so hot and fast.

I can't possibly consider anything besides Oliver touching me.

Wanting me.

Kissing him is a revelation.

I'm so freaking glad I came over tonight.

I don't even mind facing his dad when I finally leave.

I'm floating.

CHAPTER TWENTY-ONE

IT'S ONE THING TO trudge toward community service, death knell playing in the background. It's another to look forward to it.

Oliver's dad is here today, and he's clearly keeping a weather eye on me, but I'm not nearly as bothered by it as I thought I would be. I think . . . I don't know, it's gotta be because it has nothing to do with my siblings. He doesn't know them, he doesn't care about them. He's a little suspicious because of me, because of the thing *I* did. And I'll take that.

I'm working with the cats for the first half of the day, and The Enchanter Tim and his problematic butt in particular, but even that doesn't bug me today.

At least The Enchanter Tim is pleasant to be around. He's so *huge*, just absolutely monstrous. But he, like, doesn't know, so he likes to hop (leap, majestically soar) from one surface to another in the cat room and gently crest upon your shoulder.

I've only had the chance to witness this from a distance before, but today, The Enchanter Tim has seen fit to let me in on the ritual.

I stumble when he lands and let out a stream of swears.

Oliver happens to be walking by at this specific moment, and I see him suppress a cackle. Jenn is cleaning cat kennels with me and glances at me, grinning. "Girl, that cat will absolutely break your back."

"It's too late for me," I say. "Leave me behind. I'm broken."

"Tragic, but sometimes a person's gotta make sacrifices."

I laugh and start feeding the cats one by one.

Princess Mimi is my favorite in here, because she attacks shadows. Just jumps headfirst into the floor and squishes her big old face, trying to murder them. Then she looks at you like *Why? Why did you personally do this to me? What did I do to deserve this?*

I respect it.

After the cats, I move to the dogs and start the work of exercising them.

Oliver's dad meets me in the room when I'm between dogs.

My pulse instantly spikes, just anticipating some kind of judgment, interrogation. Something to the effect of *Stay away from my boy, you miscreant.*

But he doesn't say that.

He folds his huge arms and stares down at me and says, "You think you're ready?"

"W-what?"

He nods toward Frankie's cage.

Frankie is staring at me, his big eyes narrowed and suspicious. His lip curls. He does not want me around.

I say, "For—Frankie?"

"No, for an ice cream sundae. Yeah, for Frankie."

"I don't know," I say.

He looks at me, then back to the dog. "Then you ain't ready. Move on to the next one. I'll take him."

I deflate, like this was a test and I failed it.

Should I have said I was ready?

Should I have lied?

Should I have . . . been ready?

Maybe this does say something about my character; maybe I'm a coward.

. . . Or maybe I am, once again, overthinking everything and all Mr. West wanted to know was whether I wanted to take a tough three-legged dog on a walk, and what he has learned from this interaction is "not yet," and there's nothing more to it.

Jesus, I gotta get it together.

I take another dog—Chewie (short for Chewbarka) out of her kennel instead. She's a big girl, lots of loose skin from having a gazillion puppies, and she's about the gentlest giant I've ever come across in my life.

She looks at me with the warmest brown eyes and straight up *smiles* when I hook her onto her leash and let her out back. Chewie is kind of old, but when she smells the trees, when she sees the sky, she turns into a puppy. She doesn't just go for a walk. Chewie takes you for a bound. Just hops and hops and tries to eat little butterflies that fly too close to the sun, and it's the purest joy on the planet.

I could get used to this.

I . . . I see why they love this—the Wests. Why Oliver's dad decided to get into this for a living, even though it's not like he's making bank on it. Even though he's got to hold two jobs to keep the place running. Chewie and I make a loop around the grounds, then I take her for an extra, just because I can. Because she's the very best girl. And because I like watching her ears flap and her skin jiggle when she leaps and runs.

I tuck her back into her kennel, smiling, and find Oliver staring down at me, arms crossed over his chest. His eyebrow is raised, whisper of a challenge on his face. He says, "I hear you're being a chicken shit."

I sputter. "Excuse me?"

He inclines his head toward Frankie.

I throw my hands in the air. "Frankie hates me! He's huge!"

"Frankie's got three legs!"

"UGH."

He steps closer to me. "Seriously. After your shift, come out back with me."

I say, "Well god, Oliver, that's forward, but I'll think about it."

"Jesus." He laughs and rolls his eyes. "I'm gonna get you and Frankie acquainted."

"Okay," I say, trying to keep the shaking out of my voice. "Cool."

A small laugh escapes his lips, which I can only assume means that I suck at sounding tough, but, well. You win some, you lose some.

I finish the day out and get my four hours approved, then Oliver says, "Alright. Time to tame the Black Stallion."

"His name was just *The Black*, you know."

"Neeeeerd."

"PROUD OF IT."

He lets out that loud and clear laugh. It rings out of the yard, vibrates in my chest. I want to grab him and run my hands over his hips, feel that laugh in his throat, feel it in my mouth. But I resist that urge and follow him to Frankie's kennel.

He gets right in there with him and links a leash into his collar, then brings him out with me. I walk straight ahead, eyes on the prize. I'm walking way too rigidly, like a robot on a mission to find and kill Sarah Connor. But I'm nervous.

I don't need to be; Frankie isn't *vicious*. He's just . . . slow to trust. And he's on a leash. And he does, in fact, have just the three legs. Plus, Oliver is right there, and while a week ago, I would have said he very well might loose an entire pack on me out of vengeance, I know him better now.

He wouldn't let anything happen to me.

I follow him out into the yard.

"Stand where you are," he says. Oliver shoots me a look, then takes Frankie around the grassy, fenced area in the back, winding him up and getting him happy.

"Good boy!" he says, when Frankie sits still, then dives dramatically to the ground in the most victorious "lay down" I have ever witnessed. He feeds him a treat, then says, "Stay."

Oliver says, "You got any treats in your pocket?"

I shake my head.

"That's fine; come over here and grab some of mine."

I'm so nervous about my impending meeting with this gargantuan dog that I don't even bother to make a slick joke about grabbing his treats; I just follow instructions.

"Don't be nervous," Oliver says when I come close. "Frankie will sense that on you and it'll make him suspicious."

"Oh good, yeah, that helps. Now I feel super comfortable."

Oliver looks me up and down. "If you don't want to do this, I'm not gonna pressure you. You don't have to. But I think you want to."

I curl my fingers into a fist, then unclench them one by one. Again and again.

What if you just ran right up to that dog and absolutely sucker punched him?

I blink. Christ. There is not a single iota in my body, in my brain, in my soul, that has any interest whatsoever in punching a dog. But intrusive thoughts are the most distilled agents of chaotic thought.

What if I did? Well, I'd go to jail for animal cruelty, and Frankie would bite my hand off, and Oliver would definitely defend the dog, which he should, because I'd be the person who, unprovoked, punched an adorable three-legged dog.

I shake my head hard and blink even harder, trying to get the possibility out of my brain. Not because I'm concerned I'll do it. Because I just don't even want the image in my head.

"No, I'm—I'm fine. I can do this."

Oliver says, "That's my girl," and smiles, and I light up from the inside.

I take a few steps toward him and Frankie stands. He starts to growl, low and targeted.

I stop.

"No," Oliver says, sharp and low. "Back down."

Frankie's nose twitches and he glares at me.

"Back. Down," says Oliver.

Frankie side-eyes him and grumbles, then he lies down on his stomach. This time, he is considerably less enthusiastic about it.

Oliver takes a few treats from his pocket and hands them to me.

"Hand out," he says. "Palm down."

I breathe and do as he says.

"Not the hand with the treats; Frankie's shit at depth perception. You really *will* lose a hand."

I snatch it back and present Frankie with my left hand, knuckles facing him. My breath is cold in my throat and warm on the air, coming out in visible puffs against the chill of the night. I crouch, and Frankie stares at me.

Oliver says, "We gonna behave?"

Frankie flashes him a penitent look.

"Alright, then," says Oliver. He looks at me. "I'm not going to let anything happen to you, yeah?"

I nod.

"Frankie," Oliver says, shooting him a nod, and Frankie stands. He takes a couple small steps toward me, if you can call anything this dog does small.

I'm nervous, and now I have it in my head that he can sense that and that's making me more nervous, but it's okay. Oliver won't let anything happen to me.

The dog stretches out his neck. He approaches me, so slow and nervous, and I can feel it then. He's not mad; he's terrified. He's shaking. He's huge and he's got a massive, powerful cave of a mouth. He's *made* of muscle. But he's afraid of me.

My heart twists.

He stretches just a little further, then his nose is at my skin, sniffing.

I smile up at Oliver, all teeth.

He smiles back down at me, just the littlest curve of his mouth.

He's had this moment.

It's nothing; I know it doesn't mean the dog magically trusts me now. But still. I don't know; it doesn't exactly feel like nothing to me.

It feels . . . like the brightest spark in an exhausting couple months.

I relish the feel of that wet, sniffing dog nose.

"Try a treat."

I move my right hand to hold a treat out to him and he leaps backward and starts growling again.

I jump up and Oliver says, "Back down."

He's so authoritative *I* want to back down. But I'm busy panicking. Shaking.

"Toss a treat on the ground," he says.

I do it.

Frankie approaches it warily. He looks up at me before he snatches it, then he does, and he retreats to a safe distance.

"He'd be dead if it weren't for my dad," says Oliver.

I look at him.

"Dad took him in when someone called about a dog being rescued from a fighting ring."

I grimace. I *hate* dog fighting, god, what kinds of pieces of shit—

"He's so jumpy," says Oliver. "Fucking terrified of people. And no wonder, you know? His whole life's been being beaten and yelled at and fighting and living on a chain. I'd be jumpy."

"Yeah," I say quietly.

"He's not even mad at you; he doesn't want to hurt you. He's just—"

"Scared," I finish for him.

Oliver says, "Yeah." Then, "He's risky. Most pitties are friendly as hell, like, honestly the nicest dogs on the planet. But this guy . . . he's sweet, too. I can get him playing like a puppy out here. But he's way too high-risk. And it's been so much work even getting him to where he is. But he's not even *close* to being adoptable yet. He'll get there. Because my dad took one look at him and refused to let him down. I'm not talking shit about kill shelters; eventually little guys like us run out of room and it's like . . . I don't know. It sucks. But I don't know a good solution to that problem. What I'm saying, though, is that if my dad hadn't stepped in and said, *I wanna do the work on you*, this guy would be dead."

Oliver crouches and Frankie immediately lays his big, square head on Oliver's lap. "And what a shame that would be," says Oliver, "huh, boy?" He scratches Frankie's ears, and I see it: the puppy he used to be. He's shaking his ears around, smiling that big old goofy pit smile, working as hard as he can to leap up and lick Oliver's face.

"You lick your own butt, man, no!" says Oliver,

collapsing backward and laughing so hard it echoes when Frankie tackles him.

I stand back.

Not perfect. I didn't conquer this fear on my own or earn his trust in minutes or something. But it wasn't nothing.

Frankie took my treat and let me touch him.

It was a good day.

CHAPTER TWENTY-TWO

THE NEXT FEW WEEKS are a whirlwind.

For me, for Oliver, for the school, for everyone, pretty much. It was Thanksgiving, and I've been busy with Snoball, and Oliver's been killing himself trying to get in all the volunteer hours he needs to qualify for the third round of the grant competition. I'm not even upset about it anymore; I don't have the time. And Oliver wants it so much worse than I ever did.

I've basically been doing nothing but eating, sleeping, breathing, volunteering weekends (and, unofficially, a little more often than that because it's the only way to hang out with Oliver right now), and trying to help Randi with the morning sickness and everything involved in the first trimester of pregnancy when she's at the house. The beauty of the miracle of life.

So when Alisha asks if she can come hang out, I absolutely *leap* on it. I shouldn't. I should throw myself into more Snoball planning (legit, who would ever think coordinating a freaking school dance would take *this much effort*?). I should fill out any one of eighty thousand college apps I have opened, at least the common app, god. I should get a head start on my FAFSA. I've barely even *thought* about college in, like . . . weeks. I'm so behind. I see my mom, this perfect balance between pressure and support, beaming about me being the first in the family to go to school, and my siblings busting their butts to make sure I *can*, that I have time to do things like, you know, fill out a FAFSA!

But, nope.

No, I push that out of my head and ignore the anxiety. I'm taking nineteen seconds to hang out with my best friend.

Randi is puking in the bathroom, and she comes up wiping her mouth. "My gosh," she says. "Two more weeks of this."

"Fingers crossed," I say. "You need anything?"

"My boyfriend to not be working sixty hours a week? A magic solution to capitalism?"

I shrug. "Anything *I* can get you?"

"Ugh. A ginger ale."

"Okay." I get up off the couch and get her a cold RC ginger ale. I don't really know what else to say.

Alisha shows up in her mom's car, and I about fall out the door, ready to leave.

"Babe!" Alisha says. She doesn't even wait for me to get in her car; she leaps out and practically tackle hugs me. "I feel like we haven't gotten to hang out in ten years."

"That's only because we haven't gotten to hang out in ten years."

I squeeze her around the neck and she smiles into my hair. "I miss you during school dance season."

"Tell me about it."

She runs around her car and jumps in, and we set off.

We're going hiking, even though, frankly, Alisha isn't really into hiking. She says she's not into eating bugs or potentially diminishing her thick thighs with too much harassment.

But neither of us has a dollar to our name, so hiking it is.

I myself am a fan of the trees.

We find a little trail behind a school and walk off into the woods.

"Why," says Alisha, "did I let you talk me into this?"

"Oh please. You're as broke as I am."

"Well then we should have done something free and fun. You know. Like sitting in an empty parking lot watching grass grow."

I shove her shoulder. She wrinkles her nose and we walk on.

"How's your sister-in-law?"

I say, "Fine, I guess. Puking her guts out." She's not technically my sister-in-law, but like, close enough.

"Sounds right. Patrick doing alright?"

"He is, actually. Working all the time, but he's all in. Did I tell you I caught him the other day tearing up looking at tiny little baby socks?"

"Oh my god," says Alisha. "That's the cutest thing I've ever heard in my life."

"Seems like Paige is doing okay," I say.

She nods. "Yeah. Breakups suck but like . . . she said hi to me after gym the other day. So it might not be a total disaster."

"Yeah?"

"Well, nodded at me. It's close enough."

"Fair enough."

"On the plus side, I, uh, I got accepted."

I stop walking. "You got accepted?"

She bites her lip and her eyes brighten. "Yes. To engineering school. Early acceptance. On scholarship. SCHOLARSHIP, BRYNN. I'm gonna be an environmental engineer. I'm going to do the thing."

"Oh my god," I say. "Oh. My god. Alisha!" I tackle hug her for the second time in an hour, and Alisha isn't one to cry in front of people, but my shirt comes away wet. We don't talk about it too much, but I know she wants this so bad. "I'm so proud of you, dude."

She smiles, huge and sunny, then shifts her face so it goes all cheesy and goofy.

I roll my eyes and laugh. "Still can't believe you want to be an environmental engineer when you think *hiking* is torture."

"Listen," she says, back to walking ahead. "Wanting to save bugs is different than wanting them caught in your hair."

Point: Alisha.

We walk in the quiet for a while, just kind of enjoying the woods. At least, I am. I think Alisha enjoys it more than she lets on; she's just gotta fake hating it to save face or something. Either way, she's not complaining right now.

The silence is comfortable, but it gives too much time for worry and questions to fester in my brain. One in particular that's been blooming there since Oliver and I got together.

It's fast, too soon to even worry about this, but honestly, I've always moved kind of fast. Waiting when it came to physical stuff is a lot of people's style and that works for them, but it's never really been for me. I used to be embarrassed about it.

I'm not anymore.

And in that arena, I've always been at least *halfway* confident.

But . . . not right now.

"Lish," I say. I'm looking straight ahead because this is a little embarrassing.

"Mmhmm."

"You've had, like . . . you've been with people."

"I've . . ." She peers at me. "Yes. I've . . . been with . . . people."

My hand presses my forehead. I meet her eyes. "I had sex before you did; I just can't believe I'm coming to you for advice."

"Oh shit," she says. "The juicy stuff. Tell me what's up. I never thought I'd get to be on this side of it."

Alisha's always been kind of wild, but when it comes to sex, she's pretty reserved. That's been *my* area of expertise. Some people, people with what Alisha calls "a heteronormative view of sex", wouldn't even really call what Alisha has done sex but she says they're wrong, and so do I. The point is, I've only slept with two people, but I've fooled around with a few more, and I am so not used to playing any role in this conversation that is not The Wise One.

The grin on her face can be described as nothing other than "shit-eating."

I groan. "I've just . . . we haven't had sex. We haven't even talked about it, really. I don't know if he's ready or if it's gonna be a week or six months or a year or, I don't know. But I've just been thinking about this and it's freaking me out because, well, I've never had queer sex before."

Alisha's smile softens. "I'm so proud. My baby is growing up."

"Oh, get fucked," I say, laughing the smallest bit.

"Sounds like that's your department."

I flip her off.

We pass through a section of trees that's more the world's largest thicket than anything else. Trees that tower above us, vines and kudzu winding everywhere. Brambles and briar sticking in the undergrowth. I take comfort in the shadow.

"It's nothing, babe," she says.

"No," I say. "It's not nothing. A penis is simple. It's pretty, like, standard form. A vulva is such a different thing. I've done like, fourteen hours of research and I don't know how I'm supposed to . . . how I'm supposed to touch one or how to make it work or—god, I'm panicking, Alisha. Things have been going so well. And what if it's perfect and great and the conversation is great and the volunteering is great and the kissing is great but I suck at fucking him?"

Alisha laughs out loud. She grabs me by the shoulders. "Brynn. Oh my god. You're overthinking this. You didn't know what to do with a penis the first time you touched one either, and, frankly, you have a whole lot more experience figuring out what to do with Oliver's equipment because you've got the same equipment. And don't try to tell me you don't masturbate."

"Please, Lish," I say, hand over my heart. "I would never lie to you."

"So just . . . do that. And if it doesn't work, okay. Talk to him, man. All sex should involve talking. Straight sex should involve talking even though, shit, I *swear* it doesn't, like, half the time because everyone's dumbasses. Talk to him. See what he wants. He'll tell you, or don't sleep with him."

It's so nerve-wracking. I'm not even sure it's relevant. I might not need this information soon or, like, ever.

But even if I do, like, gosh, it seems simple.

It's . . . it's so simple. And it shouldn't be hard.

It shouldn't be.

In my bed that night, I'm still thinking about what Alisha said, about the talking, which I can't really practice, and about the fact that my equipment matches his, which, well, I can.

I've been texting with Oliver, and it hasn't even been dirty, but well, I feel like practicing.

I've masturbated like a zillion times because, frankly, orgasms are things I'm pretty interested in obtaining, as a rule, and el oh el as though teenage boys know how to do *that* without step-by-step instructions. But I've never masturbated with a goal in mind. Not a goal that didn't involve my own orgasm.

I blow out a breath because suddenly, now, my own sexual exploration is coming (ha) with the slightest hint of pressure attached. I need to catalog all of this. I need to remember, to figure out how to work this; it's just never occurred to me until now, and now is the time.

Figure it out, Riley.

I slip my hand down under the comforter, under the slick bamboo sheets, into my underwear. And I slide them out on the other side, running them up my thighs. Such a big mistake people make, thinking the only place they should touch you is where it *counts*. It just . . . it counts in so many places.

I touch my legs, and I run up between them when I'm dying for it, thinking, as best as I *can* think right now about what it feels like on every single piece of me. What pressure I want, where I should move in circles, how fast, and what it feels like when I *like* it. What it feels like on my fingers when I'm almost there.

I'm listening to my own breathing, wondering what I look like when I'm getting close, feeling feeling feeling.

Until I can't think anymore. Can't observe because my thoughts are running into each other, galloping over each other, and they're a blur. And I'm lost, back arching and ears legitimately ringing.

I only do this once, because I'm so exhausted from all the study involved that I don't know that I want to go for the usual two or three.

But it's enough.

I curl over on my side and sleep so deeply I don't even wake up to my alarm.

CHAPTER TWENTY-THREE

I'M FINALLY THROUGH WITH all my service hours, but frankly, I like volunteering so much that I stay on. It's not like I really have time for this. It just doesn't matter; I can't stop. I love the travel time with Oliver and hanging out with the girls at the front desk, and I'm getting *so close* to getting Frankie to like me.

Well, to tolerate me, at least.

I can't let that go.

This is more fulfilling to me, as it turns out, than, like, any of the extracurriculars I've done for school—to try to prove my worth to colleges. So I'm going to keep doing it.

Today, Oliver and I head in together for the morning shift, and Mr. West meets us at the door.

"Jesus Christ," he mumbles. "A week. A week! This is an emergency; what the hell am I going to do waiting a *week*? What, Oliver?"

Mr. West looks at us, eyes all wide and pissed, as though either of us is supposed to be able to answer that question.

I say, "Uh."

Oliver says, "Well."

Mr. West takes his hat off and rakes his hand through his matted hair.

"Listen," I say, "we both wanna know what you're talking about, but it's, like, extremely cold out here and—"

"Oh," he says, half-laughing. The laugh borders on hysterical. "Yeah, go on in. It's not gonna save you."

Oliver glances at me and then we walk inside.

"Christ!" he yells.

"YUP," his dad shouts.

It's glacial in here. The inside of this building feels like the outside, which is: cold. Unseasonably cold. Charlotte is usually pretty mild, even this close to Christmas, but this week-long cold snap we're having is *wicked*. I immediately bring my hands to my mouth and nose, breathing into them to warm up my insta-freezing nose.

"Did you—" Oliver lowers his voice and steps in toward his dad. He doesn't lower it quite enough. "Did you get the heating bill paid, Dad?"

Mr. West scoffs, even though I'm sure this question was borne of experience. "Course I did, son. Heat's just out."

"Well," says Oliver. "Shit."

He looks around, like the answer to the problem is painted on the walls. Then he says, "Shit, what about the animals? They're gonna freeze."

"I'm tryin' to handle it," says Mr. West, panic in his eyes. "Shortest I got so far is a week, which is useless. Weather'll be gone by then. There's one company that . . . I can't pay it, the emergency charge. It's—shit, I don't know what we're gonna do."

"Let me fix it," I say.

"Brynn—" Mr. West starts.

"Let me do it," I say. I straighten and cross my arms over my chest. "I'm not just some kid, Mr. West. I've taken classes at the technical college! I've spent hours researching it. And I do, like, all the maintenance on our trailer. I know what I'm doing. Let me do this."

Mr. West cuts a look at Oliver, and Oliver looks right back at him, then shrugs. "Sounds like she knows what she's doing, Dad. She sure knew how to handle your truck."

Mr. West lets out a sigh. He's not great at accepting help, I've learned.

I don't wait for more confirmation than that. It's all I'm getting, and if I wait any longer, he might change his mind (or his pride might).

I just signal for Oliver to come with me, because *Oliver* won't change his mind, and have him direct me to the furnace. Then I roll up my metaphorical sleeves and get to work. The filters are clean. The switches are clean, everything is clean, which is a bummer because that's such a common reason heat fails and it's the easiest fix ever.

Curse you, Mr. West, for being efficient on equipment upkeep.

I'm absolutely in the zone.

The work here, with my hands, settles me. I don't even care that my fingers are cold, that they're moving a little slow, that I'm, honestly, pretty uncomfortable. I don't care because this is something I'm so good at, and it's something that . . . god, I don't know. It's weird.

No one says, "Hell yeah! I just love to work on HVAC! I do this for *passion*."

And I guess it's not HVAC specifically, but it is mechanics. I love the way things work. I love to manipulate them with my hands. I love to follow the roadmap that wires and metal create and get to the root of the problem and see it come together.

I love that, and so I love this.

I love the thrill in my chest when, after an hour of cold work, I come back out with, "Welp. It's your capacitor."

"It is?" says Mr. West, but the blank look on his face tells me he knows not of what he speaks.

"Yup," I say. "I'm glad I found this, actually. Getting this one from a regular HVAC guy would cost you around five hundred bucks."

"Okay. Okay, if . . . shit. If I need to pay that, I'll do it. We'll make it happen, I just gotta find some room *some-where* in the budget and I can. I can."

He's starting to panic, so I cut him off. "Mr. West. The part costs like, twenty bucks. I'll write it down. You pick it up at Home Depot. I'll get it done."

"I can't let you do it for free."

I hold out my hand and say, "I'm doing it for Frankie."

Within an hour, the heat is back on and the day is saved, and I'm absolutely beaming. The rest of the day goes smooth, like clockwork. (And I can use that expression authentically because I have smoothly taken apart and put back together at least nine clocks.) Even The Enchanter Tim keeps his butt in check.

At day's end, Oliver looks at me and says, "You ready for this? I think tonight's the night."

"Yeah?"

"Yeah."

I take a deep breath.

Okay.

This is it.

The moment of truth.

Oliver leads me out into the yard, then disappears.

He returns with Frankie.

Frankie takes a moment to size me up, scars protruding in his face when he starts that low growl. They match the scars that stand out on Oliver's arms when he flexes, holding Frankie back.

I steady myself.

He approaches me and I give him treats like I usually do, let him sniff my hand, make myself as non-threatening as possible.

And I just . . . I try to let him *feel* that I like him. That I'm gentle, that I love him, even. I try my hardest to radiate it.

And suddenly, all at once, something changes.

He sniffs the air, looks right at me. And the biggest, dopiest, pittiest smile spreads over his blocky face. He licks me. Right over the eye.

I laugh out loud.

Maybe he knows. Maybe he knows I'm why he's been warm all day and he's decided I'm not out to get him.

Oliver doesn't say anything; he just steps quietly back and smiles while magic happens.

They told me: this is how it is with Frankie. He hasn't taken to anyone but the Wests, but for them, it was overnight. One minute, he was suspicious and angry and wary, and the next, they were best pals, inseparable by mere inconveniences like time and space.

He crouches, in that little tail-wagging, butt-in-the-air stance that puppies do, and hops. Then he noses his ball toward me.

He's playing with me.

Oh my god, he's *playing* with me.

I refuse to let Oliver see me tearing up just a little, and I throw the ball across the yard.

I throw and throw and accept tackles and messy kisses until Frankie and I are *both* so exhausted that neither of us can move another inch.

Oliver lets me lead the big boi inside the kennel, and I drop him off there with one last treat. He gobbles it down, gives me the warmest look, then drops onto his bed. He's curled up like a chonky cinnamon roll and asleep inside a minute.

When we leave the rescue, I'm twirling like a Disney princess.

Like woodland creatures should be lighting on my fingertip and singing me a happy tune while we sew dresses the old-fashioned way.

I'm tiptoeing on a cloud, a huge, tripod-formulated cloud.

"Did you see that, Oliver? Did you see?"

He's smiling, and it's all indulgent and sweet and half-sleepy. "I saw," he says.

"He played with me! I have dog slobber all in my hair! Oh my god. I think I'll cry. Just kidding, I won't. Probably. Wow. Wow wow."

He throws his head back and laughs, and then I slide up into his truck and he gets in the driver's side and we head out.

"You were great today, by the way."

"I know," I say, tossing my hair. "Just ask Frankie."

"Well, I mean, yeah, with him. But also with the heat. You just . . . you have no idea the level of pressure you took off my dad."

I shrug and my face heats. "Oh, it's nothing. It was easy. Seriously, don't worry about it."

"I'm not worried about it," he says, putting on his blinker. We make a slow turn left. He hesitates. "I do wonder, though . . ."

"What?" I say.

"Just, like . . . I don't know. What are you planning on going to school for?"

I frown. "Why? Why does that matter?" I don't know why I'm so immediately defensive. But, I don't know. I am. It's unreasonable.

Oliver says, "It doesn't. Just—I guess I'm just wondering because whenever I hear you talk about school, it's about just . . . going to college, like that's something you have to do. But I see you working on things, anything—the truck, the heat, the shit we build in tech ed at school, and you just—you light up. And I just wondered if—"

"If I shouldn't go to school?" My stomach drops and twists. I choke out a laugh. "No one in my whole family has gone to school. And now—now you're saying I shouldn't go?"

"No," he says. "That's totally not what I'm saying. I'm just—"

"You're just suggesting that maybe school *isn't for me.*"

"No. Brynn, I'm not trying to say that. I was just asking if you'd ever thought about a trade, like—"

I turn very deliberately away from him, facing the window. My forehead rests against it and it cools on contact. That helps the rising tide of anger and anxiety in my chest. I say quietly, "Business. I'm majoring in business." I don't say that I have no idea what I'm going to do with it. That I only picked business because it seems like a safe major, like a major I can do pretty much anything with, and it's nowhere near as thrilling as putting mechanical systems together and taking them apart. That maybe I'm freaking out and furious so immediately because part of me thinks he's right. That, frankly, I've been considering this for a while, because I still haven't managed to do that FAFSA and deadlines on all my college apps are coming up and I haven't found the time to turn them in. That my mom's supportive, *You're gonna do great things, baby!* has, somewhere along the line, turned into pressure on my bones. I don't say anything else at all.

"Shit," Oliver whispers, focused on the road.

I have to fight tears.

Even though . . . I know. I know he didn't meant anything by it, and ultimately, he's right about some of it. I do love mechanical stuff. It's just an instinct—to be hurt, to react like this. I don't know how to reprogram my own brain.

We ride in silence for a while.

Then Oliver says, "Hey, Brynn?"

I say, "Mmmhmm."

"I think you can be whatever the hell you want."

We've been driving for longer than I thought. We're turning into my trailer park.

"I know," I say.

"Do you?" he says.

At that point, he puts the car in park, and I turn to look at him.

He says, "I can be stupid sometimes. I'd never—I'd never want you to feel like I didn't believe in you or something. Like if school is something you want, you couldn't get it. Trades are really hard, too; you have to know so much stuff to be an HVAC tech or an electrician or a plumber."

"I know," I say quietly.

"And you have to be so good with your hands. And jobs are easy to come by and you make killer money. So I was just—"

"Oliver," I say. "I know."

"I'm sorry," he says. It rolls off his tongue so easily. That's a new one for me. From, like, anyone.

I say honestly, "You don't have a reason to be."

Oliver says, "You know I'm crazy about you?"

I grin and he curls his hand around the back of my neck and pulls me in for a kiss. "Yes," I whisper.

Then he looks up and pulls his car forward a foot. My mom's leaving for work.

She rolls down the window and says, "Well, we finally meet," and flashes Oliver a bright red lipstick smile.

He smiles back and says, "Hi, Ms. Riley. Oliver."

"Well, Oliver, I'd love to chat but I'm afraid I'm late for work." She looks at me. "See you tomorrow, baby girl."

I groan and she laughs and heads to work.

"Well," Oliver says, "I guess I ought to let you get inside?"

He says it like a question.

I move to exit the car, then I see that all the lights in the house are off.

Is it . . . is it actually empty?

I swallow hard.

Take a deep breath.

I say, "What if you stayed?"

CHAPTER TWENTY-FOUR

OLIVER HESITATES. "LIKE . . . stayed?"

I shrug. Suddenly I'm shaking just a little. Blood is rushing to my face, and I feel like I've said something wrong. Well, not wrong exactly, just . . . a lot. Vulnerable. That's it; that's the word I hate.

Who *doesn't*?

I'm struggling so hard to be nonchalant that I'm positive it does not come out nonchalant at all when I say, "Yeah, I mean, sure. Like, if you wanted. I don't mean—well, I kind of mean—but not necessarily." What possessed me to follow up that disaster of a proposition with, "Does that make sense?" I do not know.

And yet.

Something does.

And I do.

Oliver laughs, that ever-present hand on the back of his neck. "Yeah. I mean, yeah, okay."

"Okay," I say.

I slide out of the truck without looking at him. I don't know how I managed to ask him if he wanted to come hang out in my empty house and heavily imply that maybe we could potentially hook up without passing out if I can't quite look at him now.

But he's not really looking at me either; he's just looking at the door of the house, making his way toward it, breathing. Smiling, kind of—that little turn of the mouth that tells me he's pleased without spreading into something silly. I don't think he's scared. I'm not scared either.

It's just a lot. To say to a person, to invite them in, to say it all looking right at them. It's like being naked before you even have the chance to strip.

I slip in front of him and push the door open, and I'm immediately kind of embarrassed. I shouldn't be; it's not like Oliver has a huge mansion at the edge of town with a picket fence and a swimming pool. And honestly, his place is great. But, like, I don't know. It's how I feel.

And my mom left dishes in the sink and the TV blaring (bad habit of hers)—some trashy reality show that I suppose highlights the living room as the background, and like, well. I don't know.

I don't know, and it's probably shitty to be embarrassed, probably some kind of internalized something or other. But I am.

I say, "Well, uh. Here it is."

Oliver shuts the door behind him.

It's so quiet, except for the *14-Second Bride* or who knows what is on the television.

"Sorry," I say, reaching for the remote. "Sorry, sorry."

"About what?" says Oliver.

"I don't know."

Oliver's fingers brush my lower back. Tingles travel up my spine. "You alright?"

"Yeah." I shake my head. "Yeah, of course I am."

"Are you—" He presses my back and I turn to face him. He's scraping his teeth over his lower lip. "Are you, like, having second thoughts? About asking me to come inside? Because I know what it sounded like and what you maybe wanted it to sound like or maybe didn't but it doesn't mean anything. We can hang out and play video games! Seriously, I don't, uh . . ." He peers at me and I think maybe I'm waiting for him to continue but he's waiting for *me* to say something, and when I don't, he draws the wrong conclusion, which is: "Or I can head home. I can totally—that's fine, too."

"Oh!" I say. I reach for his arm. "Oh gosh, no, it's not you." His shoulders visibly drop. "It's just—I don't really invite people here, I guess? Except Alisha."

"Mmm," he says. He glances around. "Yeah, I get it."

Suddenly, I flush, because what's that supposed to mean? I mean, I can pretty well figure, but like, Jesus.

"That's a pretty embarrassing picture to have hanging on the wall." He tips his chin at this old family pic hanging in the hall. We're all much littler, and everyone is at least *some* degree of embarrassing, but I'm the easiest one to pick out of the crowd, because my face practically looks the same, just tiny. The difference in this picture being the literal gingham dress with a square of lace at the neck, the bangs that are so short I don't even know if they can reasonably be called "bangs." Plus, I'm smiling so hard that my eyes have disappeared entirely and it looks like I'm a lion baring my teeth (my only half-existent teeth; they'd like *all* fallen out at once).

"Oh my god!" I say, immediately laughing and hitting him in the arm, tension breaking in me like a dam.

He laughs with me and I say, "Shut up, I was precious."

"You were!" He holds up his hands in a display of innocence and says, "I love the lace square thing you got going; why don't you wear that more often?"

I get my hands about an inch from his throat and mock choke him. He laughs again, harder, then takes me by the wrists. "Really, why, though?"

"Oh," I say. "I dunno. Just—" I don't know how to finish that sentence. What am I supposed to say to him? Especially him? *Oh it's simply that I am but a pauper, and mine possessions are meager?* He is but a pauper as well and he truly does not seem to give a fuck.

Oliver walks slowly through the living room, fingers brushing over the furniture. He waits for me to speak.

"I don't, uh, I don't even know how to show people where I live?"

He glances at me, then back at the furniture.

"Like . . . you know, right? You get it? Like people are gonna see this place and feel like I'm . . . I don't know. Trailer trash. Or whatever."

"I hate that shit," he says. There's enough sudden venom in his voice that I recoil. It's not directed at me; it was just surprising. "I hate it. As though rich bitches aren't dropping a hundred grand on 250-square-foot single-wides, dolling them up, and putting them on Instagram? Like Jesus, dude, tiny houses are just trailers for rich people!"

I sputter out a laugh.

"Okay," I say, "but I'm not staying in one of these places forever. Like I do want to escape this trailer park."

His brow furrows. "I guess?" He stops, then starts again. "I like your house. It doesn't . . . I don't think it feels like . . . like a place to escape."

I stare at the ground.

He says, "I'm not saying you're being crappy or something."

I say, "No, I know. It's just that everyone always says that about . . . about places like where we live. They're somewhere to get out of."

He says, "Yeah."

"I guess I never really thought about . . . I don't know. I mean, I like your house."

He grins. "Same. I like *your* house."

My mouth curves into a smile and I tug him toward me by the belt loop. I kiss him and he leans his forehead against mine.

"Wanna see my room?"

I don't mean it to come out all sultry Marilyn Monroe like, *Wanna see my room, big boy?*

And yet, I fear it does.

To his credit, Oliver doesn't call me out. He just says, "Sure."

I lace my fingers in his and we traverse the hallway. It would maybe embarrass me, if he had any money, that the hall is so skinny we have to walk through it single-file to fit. But he doesn't.

So it doesn't.

I point left, right across from my room, and say, "Bathroom."

He says, "Noted."

Then I open the door to my room. I'm so glad I straightened up earlier.

"Oh, it's so nice in here," he says.

I brighten. He walks in ahead of me and I shut the door.

My room is cheaply decorated, but I think I've done alright. I've got fairy lights strung up behind the old headboard, a corkboard with pictures of me and my friends, this little desk I got off the curb of a neighborhood close to here. Unfortunately that means there's no real walkway when you hit the foot of my bed, but you win some, you lose some.

"Yeah?" I say.

"It's so girly," he says.

I shove him and he laughs, catches my hand against his collarbone. "I like girly."

I take several steps toward him until we're chest to chest. I say into his mouth, "It's not that girly."

"Please," he says, lips touching mine on particularly pronounced consonants, "this whole thing is lavender polka dots."

"Fine," I say, "you win," but I don't make it through "win," before his mouth is really, fully, on mine, deep and demanding, hand sliding down my back. My arms are around his neck and he's walking me backward. Not that we can take too many steps, not that we have the room. My butt hits the bed and he's still kissing me and I'm on *fire*. I don't think anyone has ever made me this absolutely frazzled, this wrecked, just from kissing me.

But I'm shaking. I'm so high on adrenaline and whatever else your body pumps through you when you're being kissed and touched this way that I can hardly think.

We've done more than kiss the past few weeks, little things here and there. But this feels like a step. A leap into something we haven't done together yet. I *hope* it's a step. I'm fucking praying it's a leap.

Oliver nudges me back onto the bed and we stay like that for a long time, him on top of me, just making out, resenting the need to break away for breath.

"Hey," he says, trailing his fingers across my throat, my collarbone. "When you asked me to stay, did you mean . . . what did you mean?"

He's shaking. I can feel it on his skin and hear it in his voice. He locks eyes with mine.

"I meant . . ." It's hard. To say it. But I remember one of the few good things my dad ever taught me was: If you can't say the word *sex* to someone, you're not ready to have it with them. So I shut my eyes tight and draw in a steadying breath and say, "I think I want to have sex with you, Oliver."

"Jesus," he breathes. He's shaking so hard now that his hands are nearly tapping my skin.

"Is that okay?"

"Yeah," he says. He's kind of laughing. I've never seen him this awkward, this nervous, and I'm kind of addicted to it, right off the bat. "I know I want to get this shirt off you."

I bite my lip and raise my arms so he can roll the T-shirt off me, then he does that one-handed guy move where they pull their shirt off over the back of their neck.

I've always found it just stupidly sexy.

He's wearing a black tank top underneath and a compression sports bra. (Binders, I've learned, are a bitch to wear for too long, but this does the job pretty well.)

He's moving over me, skin sliding against skin when his shirt rides up and his stomach brushes over mine.

I can *hear* the way I'm breathing when he moves his leg so it's between mine, draws his thigh up so it hits me right where I'm dying for it to. He makes this noise low in his throat when I gasp, and *that* turns me on, too; god, I'm a mess. I'm an absolute *wreck*.

I reach up and grip the back of his neck, short hair tickling my fingers.

"I need," I say, when I can catch a single breath between the way he's kissing me and the way his thigh is moving, where it's pressing, "I need to know where I can touch you."

He's dragging his mouth down my neck, hand dipping lower and lower until it's resting just under my waistband. "Hmmmm?"

"Where I can touch you. Touch me anywhere—*god*. But I need to know . . . fuck."

The second I gave permission, he slid his hand into my underwear and the contact is absolutely murderous. His thigh is pressing into mine, teeth on my throat, and the way he moves his hands—Oliver West knows what the hell to do with his hands.

"That good for you?"

"Jesus," I say. "Yes."

"This is how you want me to touch you?"

I actually laugh. I can't tell if he's talking dirty or trying to get consent, but I think it's both and it's working.

I'm not laughing for long.

What I come to realize is that it is, in fact, possible for a teenage dude to make a girl come. I will revise my notes.

I pull away, sweating and breathless now, and I turn over on my stomach just to rest my head in the pillow for a minute. To process. To come down. He's tracing lazy circles on my back, until I can get my heart rate under control. Until I can control my breathing enough to say, "Oliver." Then I turn back over and stare up at him.

"Yeah?" he says. The grin is cocky and disarming. "Round two?"

"I want to touch you."

Something vulnerable flashes in his eyes. A little unsure. I don't look away. I just say, "Unless you don't want me to. That's okay; it's okay."

"No," he says, shaking his head, looking at my throat. Easier, maybe, to look at than my eyes. "I want you to. You can. You can—yeah, you can touch me."

"Where?" I say.

His hand stills on my stomach.

"What?" I say. Anxiety creeps in, and I wonder if I've said something wrong.

"Nothing. Just—no one's ever actually asked me that before. I always have to—anyway. I don't, uh, I don't want you to touch my chest." He slides a look from my throat to my eyes. "Is that cool?"

"Of course it's cool."

"But anywhere—anywhere else."

"Okay," I say.

My hand is shaking because I've never done this before and I'm so fucking *nervous*.

"I don't know—" I start. And suddenly I'm embarrassed. Even though, god, I'm seventeen. It's not like I'm supposed to be a sex goddess or something. But I *have* had sex before, and I don't want to brag, but I like to think I'm pretty okay at it, and now I'm back to being like a complete novice when it comes to the mechanics of things, and well. That's it. I'm nervous.

He slides on top of me and brushes my hair back from my face. I'm sure it's a total tangle by now. "You've only ever been with, like, cis guys before. Yeah?"

"Yeah," I say. "I just want you to—I want you to feel good. And I'm nervous because—" I laugh. "Because I don't know what the hell I'm doing."

He scrapes his teeth over his lip, one of a million little gestures that are becoming familiar. "Sure you do," he says, and he takes my hand and guides it to his stomach, down to his thigh. He lets me choose when to slip it up under his basketball shorts and through his boxers. Jesus.

I'm nervous and I'm so turned on and it's so fucking *intimate* and—

He hisses out a breath and then shifts my hand just the slightest bit, and says, "There, yeah?"

I nod and touch him the way I'd touch myself.

It's not quite right, not *exactly* the way he wants it. But I let him move me the way he needs to and he talks me through it and, frankly, I was pretty close to begin with. Close enough not to feel stupid.

Close enough that when I listen, he loses his fucking mind, and when he kisses me, he bites my lip so hard I'm nervous that he's put a hole in it.

He's wrecked, the most vulnerable I've ever seen him, on top of me, and then we stay like that. Kissing each other and trying to breathe, sweat slick and still a little nervous, but when do you decide it ends, if it's not when the guy finishes?

I guess that's kind of a shitty metric to go by anyway, isn't it?

Look at me, becoming more feminist by the second.

I want to keep doing this forever.

He's smiling at me, hands exploring my whole entire body, and I say, "I fear we will never stop this."

He laughs. "Fuck school. Fuck jobs."

"Let me stay in this bed until my grandson gets a golden ticket and wins a tour of a chocolate factory."

"Eh," he says, mouth on my collarbone. "Fuck the chocolate factory."

"You're right," I say, and I'm about ready to go for broke when the front door opens.

CHAPTER TWENTY-FIVE

"OH GOD," I SAY.

Oliver's eyes fly open. "Is that—is that your mom? I thought she was working."

"She is!"

I scramble to find his shirt and run to my closet.

"If that's a robber," he says, "we're dead. My coordination is shit right now."

"One," I say, "not by my measure." He laughs, but it's a little strangled. "Two, it's probably just my sister. Or my brother. But. Ugh. Great."

Oliver's shoulders drop from where they were (by his ears) and he says, "Okay well, at least none of *them* can ground you for forever."

"Yeah."

I'm so nervous, though.

I'm thinking of every possible way to get him out of here without them seeing. Kick him out the tiny window he can't fit through, smuggle him under a blanket through the front door, and say, "Oooooooooh it was a ghooooost!" Anything.

I'm desperate.

And it's not because I'm nervous about them meeting *him*. They're not gonna give a shit that I was having sex with a guy while Mom was out—as if any of them has room to talk. I just—I don't . . . I don't want him meeting *them*.

I don't know what the hell kind of embarrassing stuff my brother might say or what totally inappropriate jokes my sister might make or . . . I just. I can't handle it.

Him seeing my house is enough.

Letting him this far into my life—I just. I can't have it.

I hear voices coming from the living room. It's all of them. Both of my siblings and my brother's girlfriend.

GREAT. FANTASTIC.

"Brynn?" Randi calls.

And that's it. I can't get out of it.

"You okay?" says Oliver. He's looking at me quizzically.

"I'm fine," I say.

"Well, let's go face the music then."

"Yeah," I say. "Yeah." I breathe. "Okay."

I push my door open and Evian says, "Oh hey, babe! You're home!"

Oliver comes out right behind me, hand on the back of his neck, looking a little sheepish, and then Evian gets this big grin on her face and says, "Oh *heyyyyyyy*, babe. You're *home*."

Oh *god*.

Oliver raises his eyebrows and looks at the floor and Randi straight up wolf whistles and Patrick says, "As the man of the house, I believe it is my job to go get and clean the shotgun."

"We don't even have a shotgun!" I say.

Patrick says, "As the man of the house, it is my job to go buy a shotgun, then get it and clean it."

"Jesus," I say. "He doesn't even live here—"

Oliver says, "So hi. Yes. I'm Oliver. We were . . . playing *Monopoly*."

"I bet you were," says Evian. This is what she says when she has no group chats to sext.

Oliver takes this all remarkably in stride. He just slides his arm around my deeply embarrassed shoulder and relaxes there, like it's where he fits.

Because it is.

I lean a little of my weight into him and try to forget that this is all happening. Try not to give into the feeling that I'm going to come apart at the seams, that my skin is going to split right here, and all my organs and nerves and neurons are going to spill out right here on this stained carpet.

"Well," says Evian, "if Patrick's on shotgun-buying duty, one of y'all get me the remote because Randi's hormonal as hell as and if we don't have *The Bachelorette* on in nineteen seconds—"

"Oh, shut *up*," says Randi. "You're the one with the reality TV fetish and we all know it." But she follows it up with, "Seriously, there's like a BIG hot tub scene this week and if I miss it, I'm killing somebody right here, right now, and I'll get immunity. You can't prosecute a pregnant person for murder."

Evian says, "I don't think that's how it—"

But Patrick shuts her up and heads to the kitchen to make snacks for everyone, and that, folks, is how I wind up getting laid and then sitting around for a family viewing of *The Bachelorette*.

Oliver shrugs and curls up on the chair and a half with me, fingers stroking my arm and shoulder.

I say, at one point, between my family loudly making some crass comments about overnight dates and throwing chocolate-covered popcorn at each other, "Seriously, you don't have to stay for this."

He says, "I want to," and kisses my head.

But there's a gentle tension I can feel in his chest. I don't know how to name it.

But it's there.

He heads out when the episode is over.

I can't shake it.

Something, *something* is up.

I got my meds upped, which means that, thankfully, anxiety isn't absolutely taking over my body and brain, and my intrusive thoughts have calmed down, but still. There's something I can't name.

I toss.

I turn.

I consider calling Oliver. Texting him.

But I don't want to come off as this ridiculous, insecure person, so I don't. I just tell myself I'm imagining it. It's hard to trust yourself, is the thing, when you're plagued with anxiety all the time. You never know what's real and what's your brain being a jerk.

Then, at 11:30, my phone buzzes.

I practically leap off the bed to get it.

Oliver: *hey can I ask you a question?*

My stomach drops into my feet.

Me: *ok*
Oliver: *why were you so embarrassed? To have your siblings meet me?*

I just stare at the phone.
Oh no, oh god. I think . . .
I type so fast I screw up half of what I'm trying to say with an army of typos.

Me: *it watsnt you. It wasmy family they canbe alto*
Me: *a lot*
Me: *im nto embarrassed of you or smoething.*
Me: *oh shit. Im sorry*

My phone rings. I'm shaking when I pick up.
"Hello?"
Oliver's voice is smooth when it comes through. Comforting. "Hey," he says. "I'm sorry, I'm sorry. Please don't freak out. I'm not mad. I get it, okay?"
My pulse slows by a few beats, but I'm still riddled with nerves. "Okay."
"I just thought—I don't know, I've had a couple bad experiences, okay? But I get it. You weren't . . . I just need to hear it, and then it's fine. You weren't embarrassed for them to meet me?"
"No," I say. I'm tripping over myself. "I mean, I'm

embarrassed for my siblings to know I'm having sex at all. Like, come on."

He laughs.

I continue, "But I'm not embarrassed that it's with you. I'm just embarrassed for you to meet them. They're just . . . they're loud and crass and, like, I don't know. Trashy."

He's quiet for a minute. Then he says, "I don't know. That's not really the impression I got?"

Everything is so much calmer suddenly. I don't feel like I want to peel my skin off. I just shrug. "Well, you don't live with them."

"Sure," he says. "But like . . . trashy seems a little harsh."

My eyes narrow. "Like I said. You don't live with them."

It's quiet again, and now the tension has morphed into something totally different.

"Are you, like, judging me?" I say.

"No."

"Yes, you are."

"I'm not," he says.

I turn it over, chew on it. Then I say, "Between this and the trailer stuff and like . . . the college conversation? I think—I think you *are*."

"Oh my god," he says. "Are we on the college thing again? I was saying that because I just wanted you to consider something, and I just want you to consider that maybe trailers don't mean trash and maybe—"

"I never said that! I love your family! I love your house!"

He scoffs. "Yeah, well, that's not exactly what it sounds like."

"You're way over the line, Oliver."

"Okay, yeah," he says. "*I'm* over the line."

"Jesus Christ," I hiss.

And now I'm not anxious.

I'm mad.

And it sounds like so is he.

GREAT.

"You're acting like I'm some classist asshole."

He says, "I never said that."

"I'm tired."

I can *hear* the eye roll from here.

"I'm going to bed," I say.

"Fine," he says.

"Goodnight."

"Yeah, goodnight."

I don't know which of us technically ends the call, but I hope it's me.

I'm so mad.

I'm determined to sleep.

I'm so furious, because it's none of his business.

It's none of his business what I think about my house or my family or my college career or . . .

It isn't.

I cling to this, and that's how I get my eyes to close.

The last thing I see in my brain is Mom's note, which she has migrated to just above my desk and underlined in pink: CALL YOUR DAD.

I fall asleep wondering if Oliver isn't right.

About everything.

CHAPTER TWENTY-SIX

TO HIS CREDIT, OLIVER does pick me up for school the next day.

He kisses me and I kiss him, but it's small and hesitant and just entirely unsure. I'm still upset, and he's still obviously upset, and neither of us knows what to do with our hands.

Well. At least he's got the steering wheel to think about. I turn on the radio.

I spend lunch with Alisha.

I haven't been abandoning her to hang out with Oliver; we've done lunches together and I've split my time, but this time, she can sense there's trouble in paradise.

She raises her hand in a cheerful wave, then says, "Uh oh."

"What?"

She gestures to her face and says, "The extreme RBF. Your face is set in like, an eternal strutting Leonardo DiCaprio grin, and the resting bitch face only comes out when you're furious. What's going on?"

We walk out to the courtyard and I sit under a tree, head scratching against the rough bark. I want to lead into this with something a little more tactful. A little more, I don't know, subtle? But what I say is, "Do you think I'm a classist, Lish?"

She blinks. "Well. That's a big question."

"Oh my god." I throw my face into my hands.

"Wait," she says. "That came out wrong."

I mumble, "Oh my *god*, am I?" into my fingers. Oh no. I am! Reddit has decided, and I AM the asshole. Oh no.

"No?" she says.

But then I look up at her and that's not what's on her face.

"I love you, babe," she says. "But like, I don't know. Sometimes, the kind of shit you say about your neighborhood and your house and like . . . your family? It does come out a little shitty."

Tears sting my eyes because I know she's right.

She's right and Oliver's *right* and I hate it.

I wipe my face with the back of my hand because I refuse to cry. I'm just so embarrassed. I'm so mad at myself. I say, "Really?"

She sighs.

"Tell me. I'm not going to get mad."

Alisha shrugs and looks up at the sky. "It's not like it's a problem to want more. Hell, I'm going to college and I'm the first one in my family to do that. But, I don't know. It's like, shit dude, you're from the trailer park and you don't know how to respect anyone who doesn't want to escape it."

Jesus, that stings.

"Like I said, I love you. You've never made me feel like shit for living in that little house on the rez or something. But you are *super* harsh on your family. And I get it, all their shit has made a lot of your high school life hell. Reputation and all that. But, I don't know, man. They're not bad."

"I know," I whisper.

"Do you?"

I take a minute.

To really *think*.

I admit, "Oliver told me, like, all of this stuff last night. Right after we had sex."

She nods sympathetically then does an almost comical double-take. "Wait, HOLD UP. Right after you—you guys had sex? Wait. I need to—"

"Hold on," I say. "We will detail this later. I just . . . you're right. You're probably right and he's probably right and I just . . . god, I need to eat lunch and then I need . . . I need to think."

She slides up next to me on the ground and bumps my shoulder. "I got you, babe."

I lean my head on her shoulder. "I know you do."

The next few days are . . . weird. Quiet. I don't even know what's going on with Oliver and me. He's still giving me rides to school, which I appreciate. But we're not really talking a whole lot. I don't think either of us knows what to say.

I sure as hell don't.

I don't know what to say, I don't even know what I think about what he said. I don't even know if we're broken up or together or what. All I know is that it sucks.

I know that I miss working at the shelter.

I haven't been in a while, because riding places with Oliver is not absolutely mandatory anymore, so neither of us is exactly chomping at the bit to do it. Like I said, it's not like . . . not like we're *fighting*, exactly. It's just wildly uncomfortable.

But today, I decide it's worth it. I call the front desk and ask if they could use an extra hand, knowing that Oliver has basketball today, so he won't be there. I take the bus.

It feels extra lonely.

I pull up to my stop after that two-hour ride I've only just gotten used to not having to make—I've gotten spoiled, I guess, not needing to deal with public transportation. With creepy guys getting too far into my space and people not wearing deodorant and taking a gazillion years to get anywhere and having to walk to the place I need to be, rather than just pulling right up to the door.

But I've done this for years; I can do it again.

Anyway, I walk down the block to Pibbles and Kits and push through the door. "Can I?" I say, tilting my head toward the dog room.

Devika looks up from the donations she's sorting behind the desk and says, "Hey hey. Yeah, go for it. Could use some walks all around if you're up for it."

I nod.

I take a few of the pups out one by one, try not to think, not to sink into melodramatic self-reflection just yet. After

I've gotten enough of them out, I approach Frankie's kennel.

He doesn't growl when he sees me anymore; he wags that little docked tail, his big, scarred face splitting into a huge pittie grin. I crouch, "Hey, my man. You ready to go play?"

If it's possible, his stumpy tail wags even harder, and he jumps up onto the door.

I get the leash around his collar and bring him outside to the fenced in area. Then I let him off-leash and throw him the ball. I throw and throw and throw until my arm is numb.

Until I'm not thinking at all; I'm just working via automation.

Frankie hops on his three legs, gets the ball back, then goes after it again in this perfect rhythm that keeps me from having to think.

Until the exhaustion sets in.

Until it gets cold out, and my muscles start to burn.

And that's when I just sit, right there on the cold, wet grass.

And I start to cry.

Frankie is by me in a second, licking my face and pushing his big, dense body into mine. I'm crying, so it's his job to fix it.

I just can't stop thinking about what Oliver said. The family stuff, yeah—I know I'm hard on them, I always have been. And I'm shitty about where we live because I'm embarrassed and I shouldn't be, but I guess I am. I guess it's something I need to work on.

The thing I really can't get out of my head is what he said about college.

I've always wanted to go to school, always planned on it, at least. Because no one in my family ever has. And, like, being the first to graduate in your family is such a big deal. Someone needs to, right? And that person should be me. Of course.

Who else is it going to be?

I've planned on it for so long that I don't know how to extricate it from my identity.

But Oliver's right.

I don't talk about going to college and doing something for myself. About going for a career. About studying anything I'm interested in. Business. I don't even give a crap about business. I talk about it like there are no other options.

I've fought it off for a long time, but it's just a fact: I'm the happiest when I'm working with my hands.

And I'm *great* at trades. A seventeen-year-old isn't exactly the typical go-to for screwed-up cars or air conditioning systems or broken heaters or whatever, but I always am.

Always.

Because I love it.

Because I'm *good* at it.

Would it make me a failure to give up on school and do . . . something else I love more?

I don't know.

I lay my head on Frankie, and he puts the full weight of his giant shovelhead on me.

And I cry for a little while.

Eventually, it gets really cold.

I go to leave, and I run into Mr. West in the lobby.

"Oh," I say.

He smiles. "So you're still around, huh?"

I shrug. I'm not sure what he's asking—with Oliver, the shelter, what. But I'm here, so I guess I'm around. "Yeah," I say.

"You know it's his last night at the shelter," he says, tipping his chin at Frankie.

A stab of panic cuts through my ribs. "What?"

"My brother," he says. "Adoption's final tomorrow." He grins, and warmth floods my chest. "Always knew he was comin' home with one of us."

"Oh, that's . . ." I take one more look at the big guy and about collapse in happiness. "That's perfect."

"How'd you get here?" he says.

"Bus."

A frown crosses his face. "Hm." Then he takes another stab at conversation, but Mr. West never was a big conversationalist. He says, "Oliver tell you he made it into the finals?"

"Oh," I say. "That's great!" It comes out too bright. "He didn't tell me. But I'm—yeah. That's so great."

He takes a hard look at me, then says, "You want to take a look at something for me?" He knocks on a rattling vent and something in my chest splits open.

I'm so deeply relieved, thoroughly happy to be given something to do with my hands right now, to be given something fix.

"I'll give you a ride home," he offers.

I say, "Of course," and I mean it.

The second I get into the HVAC system, I'm so at ease, so at peace, that I know.

I might not be ready to say it out loud yet.

But I know my answer.

I *know*.

CHAPTER TWENTY-SEVEN

IT'S BEEN A COUPLE days. More than that since Oliver and I descended into this weird half-talking, half-dating, half-everything. But I know what I want, and that's something.

It's something that, right now, in this moment, it doesn't feel like giving up.

I could go to trade school if I wanted the piece of paper, but I don't think that's what I need right now. I've been looking for apprenticeships for after I graduate. I'm not really set on what I want to do exactly, which opens the wide world up to me. Frankly, there's blue collar choices out the wazoo. Jobs are everywhere, and they make you an absolute shit ton once you're past the beginning phases. And the idea of not a dollar in student loans? Actually getting *paid* to learn? That doesn't suck.

I'm excited, for once, because for the first time in forever, I can actually envision my future. I can see what I want to be doing, can feel the callouses on my manicured fingers, the day-in, day-out of working with my muscles. I can't picture the exact setting—whether I want to work in houses, on cars, and if it's houses, where, exactly. The pipes or the wires or what. But I know the avenue I want to travel.

It's liberating.

My mom is home in the evening for once, and she's out of her work uniform and in these yoga pants and a pretty, comfy shirt. She's got her hair up in a messy bun, no makeup, just relaxing on the couch with a glass of wine.

My siblings come bustling through the door without knocking, Patrick already shouting about some recipe he wants to try and Randi mock-weeping about the wine she's not going to be able to have and Evian (lovingly) calling her a slut, and I guess—I don't know. Given everything, I don't feel like I want to leave immediately.

Instead, I slip on my coziest pair of socks, and I slide up next to Mom on the couch.

"We watching *The Bachelorette* tonight?"

She sighs and laughs, and I hear the clear, relaxed joy that she must have reveled in when she was younger. That everyone must have heard all the time before Dad got locked up and she had to support a whole family by herself. I wrap myself up in it.

"Whether or not we want to, I think." She winks.

I wrinkle my nose and laugh.

My laugh sounds a lot like hers.

My siblings come in with popcorn and Evian changes the channel.

We are squeezed into this living room.

I lay my head on Mom's shoulder.

Someone starts making out in the hot tub.

My phone rings.

I try to keep it on silent at home, but I guess I forgot and—yeah. I know this number.

It must show on my face, because Patrick says, "Dad?"

I thin my lips into a line and give him a terse nod, and I shove my phone between the couch cushions.

It's completely silent in the living room, nothing but the hum of the heater and kissing noises coming from the TV.

I try to cut the tension with a, "Dang, if this is how the hot tub goes, what do you think's gonna happen in the fantasy suite?"

But my mom is so wound up beside me and Evian just stands and walks out of the room.

I should ignore it. It's none of their business. I should just roll my eyes and move on and let Evian throw a fit, but—I can't stop thinking about what Oliver said to me. About how I view my family. About what Alisha said. Eight hundred different feelings I try so hard to ignore bubble up all at once and I can't—I can't just sit here.

I jump up and I follow her.

She's in her old room; it looks the same. Peeling wood paneling on the walls, bright yellow comforter. A beanbag shoved in the corner. I almost trip on it.

"Say it!" I say.

Evian whirls around. "What?"

"Just say it. Say whatever the hell it is you wanna say."

My heart is about to crack through my chest because I don't want to hear it, not really. But I have to.

Evian stares at me, crystal blue eyes hard and sad. She says, "Okay. Okay, Brynn. Here it is: you've spent so long running from being a Riley that you've forgotten you *are* one."

That hits me square in the ribcage. I nearly lose my breath.

"Do you know what we do for you? That Patrick and I have pulled extra shift after extra shift and Mom is basically never home so we can pay rent? So you can go enjoy your last year of school and be whatever you want to be?"

"Well, okay, but that's only because Dad—"

"STOP!" she says. I've never heard her raise her voice, not like this. I stop. "Stop blaming Dad for all of our problems! He screwed up, okay? Yes. More than once. And it sucks and we're all tired, but he *loves* you, Brynn. He's sick. And he loves you and I hate him asking after you every time I go to visit him and you aren't there. He loves you, Brynn. And he's not around but he always treated you right. Didn't he?"

I feel so small. Like I want to become a little bug in this carpet. I squeak out a little, "Yes."

And Evian starts crying. "I love you." She can barely talk. "Do you really just—do you really think we're all such *trash* that—"

Something breaks open in me and I let out a sob. They've screwed around, made lives I don't want for myself, and I've resented all the assumptions everyone made about me. But god. I love them. And I never wanted . . . I never wanted them to . . . I rush across the little room and throw my arms around her.

"No," I say. "No, oh my god. I love you. I'm sorry. I'm *sorry*."

We cry together for . . . a long time.

Everyone else has the grace to pretend they didn't hear every bit of it through the thin trailer walls.

When I finally go to bed, it's late.

I look at the note on my desk.

CALL YOUR DAD.

I'm a Riley.

I lie there in the stillness for a half hour. An hour.

I don't even know if it's the right time of night, if they'll let him pick up at all. I've never taken the time to look at policies or procedures for this because it hasn't mattered.

I pick up the phone.

Oliver doesn't see me in the crowd.

I'm sitting here waiting for the final results of the competition.

It's not mine, it never *was* mine, really. And after the first round of judging, my responsibilities had concluded.

I've only kept up with it a little here and there, because, well, somewhere along the line, it stopped mattering to me. I can't even say when. But it was no longer my focus. Because college wasn't my focus and my loss here didn't matter and ... yeah. I never thought I'd say *this* sentence, but I'm kind of glad I got blackmailed. Glad I didn't take this from someone who wanted this and deserved it. I guess—I guess it stopped being a big deal, but it never would have to the rest of them up there. And like I said. It's not mine.

But it's Oliver's.

Snoball is tonight, so I should be doing all the last-minute prep for that. I don't have time to be here.

And Oliver and I had an argument—an argument we haven't resolved yet, but it was an argument. Not, like, a relationship ender, I don't . . . I don't think. I *hope* it wasn't. Even if it was, I'm invested. I care about him. I want him to win.

I want to watch him succeed.

I want to be here in case he fails.

I just . . . want to be here.

So, like I said, I'm sure he doesn't see me in the crowd; I'm in the very back.

But Audra Robbins is on the stage in a blue power suit, and she's beaming. She's been waxing poetic about the honor of sponsoring this grant, the history of what its recipients have done with it, the beauty of the competition this year.

She's running a slide show in the background, of students this year volunteering at Habitat for Humanity, projects at a homeless camp downtown, hanging out at the queer youth center uptown. Oliver's there in flashes.

Frankly, I have no idea how he had the time for all of this. But he made it.

He *wants* this.

I want it for him.

Each of the finalists has a banner on the stage for their organization.

There are four of them left: Oliver, with his housing and work training program for trans kids; Laura Kim, with her community garden program; Alec Price, with a spay and neuter thing; and Shalisa Morena, who's autistic herself and has a really fabulous idea for early intervention program for kids on the spectrum run by humans on the spectrum.

Honestly, the competition is freaking *fierce*.

This year, there are small prizes for those who place at all, whether or not they win, which is nice.

You're gonna walk away with a couple grand to fund your initiative, no matter what.

Still: the places begin to be announced, and I can barely breathe.

In fourth place, winning three grand: Alec Price.

I'm rubbing my hands down my jeans, shedding sweat, gritting my teeth. Honestly, any human up there would be worthy of that prize. Like there is every year, there's a whole host of incredible projects and people on stage. But the name I'm dying to hear in first place is:

"Oliver West."

My pulse skips and my stomach drops at the same time.

They've called his name, but it's two places too early. Oliver takes third.

That's five thousand bucks, so, like, okay. That's not nothing!

And it's something to see a trans kid walk across the big stage in the auditorium and accept thousands of dollars for a *charity* for *trans kids* in *South Carolina*. Come on.

Oliver takes it graciously. He's cool and collected in those freaking red pants, striding across the stage and then shaking Audra's hand. He flashes the crowd a sparkling smile and waits.

Second place goes to Shalisa, who gets ten thousand dollars. I'm not even disappointed, I find, not *really*.

Because like I said, every person up there should win everything. They've worked extremely fucking hard for what they've gotten, and I, like . . . I want all of them to win.

That leaves Laura Kim. Forty thousand bucks to kickstart her community garden; god, for that kind of project, that's huge.

She gets a standing ovation.

She's crying.

There's pictures of her community in the background—Laura is biracial, Black and Korean—and she lives in a heavily Black community around here that's already started some community gardening stuff. Lots of collective initiative and mutual aid—but this is going to make a *massive* difference.

She's speaking when she can, through the fountain of tears on her face. "We're going to start this in my neighborhood. And then it's going to *move*. Thank you. Thank you. Thank you."

Audra is beaming, and she wraps Laura Kim in a huge bear hug.

The whole thing is pretty heavily emotional. It always is.

I'm crying, too, because I just feel like this award is so big.

I didn't get to be a part of the competition, but I got to have a voice in who made it, in who is here, right now, and that makes me so freaking emotionally invested.

This was big.

This means something.

I sit in the back of the auditorium until it clears.

Tonight is Snoball. We've been planning for this for months, and it's a big one. It generates a ton of revenue for the school, and it's one of the most romantic dances of the year, because of the particular logistic challenge of making the gym feel like winter when winter in South Carolina largely looks like fall in South Carolina and we get snow like twice a year. So everything glitters. The lights twinkle and we wear sparkly dresses and everything shimmers. Even the humans in suits usually get into it—an approximation of snowfall. I'm at Alisha's getting ready. She's in gold, this dress that falls just above her knees in the front and dips just below in the back. It drapes over her and shimmers and her hair is down in waves over her back. She's gorgeous. I slip my dress over my head, a crimson and floor length with little threads of silver here and there that almost make it look like a candy cane. But make it fashion.

I'm pulling my hair up into a half-updo when Alisha walks in in a sweat.

"You okay?" I say, making adjustments in the mirror.

"Uh."

I furrow my brow. I hope it's not about Jistu. Swear to god, if they canceled on her after *years* of pining, I will lose my shit. Just because my date situation is in extreme flux doesn't mean I want hers to be.

"What?" I say.

When I turn around, I see that it isn't her she's worried about. She's looking at me with something I hate: pity. "What?" I repeat, this time a little more frantic.

"Don't freak out," she says.

Okay, I guess I'd better freak out.

"It's fine," she says.

So, okay, under no circumstances is it fine.

"Jesus, Lish, *what*?"

"I just . . . okay, remember the guy I splashed in the face with Coke back at the party we do not speak of?"

Something tightens in my chest, and I can't even name what it's doing it. I don't even know what exactly I'm anxious about. What my body is anticipating, preparing to flee. "Ethan O'Hare?"

"Yeah," she says.

"He, okay, so. Okay. So." She takes a deep breath. "Okay. So."

"OKAY SO WHAT?"

She sets her hands on my shoulders. Looks straight into my eyes. "He was at the party, obviously. When you got arrested."

"Yes." Heat floods my body.

"He's been . . . bragging, I guess? For the last couple months. Telling people he hooked up with you."

I roll my eyes. "Okay, that's not even a big deal. I don't know him or his friends, and why would he even be bragging about *me*?"

She shrugs. She doesn't remove her hands. She's not done. "Rileys. Kind of a feather in the cap, you know?"

I groan. "Yeah. Sounds right. Seriously, it's not—"

"People know," says Alisha. "About the arrest. It hadn't gotten beyond the school, but he was mouthing off about hooking up with the littlest Riley and the story got old and so he added in the part about the drinking and the arrest and *his* cousin goes to our school, and *she* was talking about it to a friend of hers, whose niece is actually older than she is and was also there and—"

I cut her off. "And they know. Everyone knows. Everyone."

"Maybe not everyone," says Alisha. "Laura Kim was just texting me and—"

"Oh *god*," I say. Laura Kim isn't even a gossip. If it's gotten so far in the channels that she knows, everyone knows. "FUCK," I scream. "FUUUUUUCK."

I collapse. Just fall right on my butt on the floor and hope a seam doesn't rip and wrap my arms around my knees. I swear a total blue streak into the fabric of my dress and Alisha says, "Breathe. It's okay, babe. Just breathe."

"That's easy for you to say!"

I'm sobbing now. Ruining my makeup.

Not that that matters; there's no way I'm going to this dance now.

I pull my head from my knees and lean it back against the vanity. "Everyone knows, Lish. It's all ruined. Everything I've tried so hard to do, to break free of the freaking *Riley name* and now they all know. Why did I even travel so far to volunteer? What was the point of all that?"

Alisha says, "I—to be honest, Brynn, I was kind of wondering that to begin with. You've been sort of extra about the whole thing, and—"

"You don't know what it's like," I whisper. I can breathe now. It's happened. There's nothing I can do about it, so I might as well prevent a stroke. I say, "To just . . . live in that shadow all the time. To have everyone you ever meet assume things about you before they even talk to you."

She sputters out a laugh. "I'm Native, dude. I'm

Catawbba and bisexual and you think I don't know what that feels like?"

I blink. "No. No, I'm sorry. You're right."

"Doesn't mean it doesn't suck," she says.

"It does not."

Alisha blows out a breath. "What's going to happen, hm? What's the worst thing?"

I breathe. "I don't know."

She leans in very close to my face. She says, "I'll tell you what the worst thing would be."

"What is it?"

"You fucking up this perfect eyeliner job I did on you and making us unfashionably late for Snoball."

The laugh bubbles out of me beyond my control. It's a little watery, and I know I'm being dramatic. And probably, my makeup's already wrecked. I open my mouth to tell her I'm not going to the dance, not now. I can't face everyone, now that I've confirmed everything everyone has been wondering about me for years.

But it's like Lish can smell it on me. She shoots me such a vicious look, one that will under no circumstances allow deviation from the plan, that I wither.

And if I allow myself to breathe, to process, to think . . . I know. I know that this is small. This is a piece of what I am. What's the worst thing? That everyone remembers I'm a Riley?

Okay.

Well.

I am.

I hand Alisha the eyeliner pencil.

I accept my fate.

For what it's worth, the gym looks killer. It looks like a frost-coated *Candyland*. The walls are glittering, the twinkle lights shining like stars. There are bright colors everywhere, gumdrops and lollipops and there's an amazing build-your-own-candy bar that's splashed with color, too. I might have succumbed to a reputation I've spent years trying to hold off, but hey, the dance looks nice.

I try not to look for Oliver. I don't need him to be here, don't need to have a date at all. I don't need to see him looking incredible in a suit, don't need to see him at all. It doesn't matter.

What matters is the look on Jistu's face when they pass through the front doors and sees Alisha looking like *that*. They're a dancer; their whole *thing* is their grace on their feet. And they literally trip. Alisha lights up.

What matters is my friends from student council showing up and crowding around me as I walk into the sweaty gym. And I think, *Shit. Here it comes.* Tanisha elbows me, insanely gorgeous ballgown bumping my calves. She says, "Hey there, rebel." And winks.

Laura Kim's date, Alex, says, "Never thought you had it in you, Miss Extracurricular."

Laura Kim laughs. "It's senior year. Even girls like Brynn Riley get to shake their reputations a little." And they all start to dance.

And suddenly, weight dissipates from my chest. It feathers into the air like smoke. No one here sees me as a screw-up. No one here was just waiting for me to fail. My reputation is . . . is mine. This is not what they expected; it's an anomaly. And it just doesn't matter.

Holy shit.

It doesn't matter.

That's it.

I stand there and blink for a second, just to work through it.

The DJ shifts to playing something by Beyonce and I just . . . dance.

It's half an hour in before I see Oliver. He's so stupid hot in a suit, grinning at something some girl is saying to him, and at once, I'm breathless with want and gripped with sadness.

I don't even know if he's mine.

Anxiety strangles me and I suddenly need air.

I need it *now*.

I see him look up and catch my eye before I flee the gym. I don't stop when I get to the entry hall; I just keep going. And going. Until I'm in an empty hallway upstairs by the science classrooms. I can still hear the bass from the gym thrumming through the building. But it's quiet up here. The lights are only halfway on. I'm alone.

Or I think I am.

Oliver's Converse squeak on the floor. He wears them even in a suit. He says, "Hey, Riley."

His hands are shoved into his pockets.

I jump. "H-hey."

There's that hand. Back of his neck. Teeth on his lip. His bow tie hangs undone around his neck. He stares up at me and does that thing guys do, eyes skating from the top of my head down to my feet and back. It's quick, but he does it, and his lips part. Just a little. Just for an instant.

"Congratulations," I say. "About the contest. I saw."

He turns to glance back in the direction of the staircase that leads down to the auditorium, where it happened. "Yeah. Thanks."

It's quiet, in the almost-dark. "You came," he finally says.

I shrug. "It's not a big deal."

I don't know what to say. I don't even know where we stand—if we're together or not or, or what. If we're even fighting, exactly. I say, "I wanted to see you. I wanted—to see you take it home, you know? I don't mean I was disappointed or something. That you didn't take first. I just mean I—okay, well—"

"Jesus," he says, suddenly laughing. "How's the brain, huh?"

Then *I* laugh. "Weirdly good; I upped my meds. This is me properly medicated."

His smile is so genuine that the skin beside his eyes crinkles. "Welcome to my life."

"Seriously," I say, "I'm glad for you. Five grand isn't nothing."

"Well, it's more than that."

I raise an eyebrow. "Yeah?"

He shrugs. "Some guy caught me after. You know how this shit goes. Anyway, he works with that big queer organization up in Charlotte, and he wants to partner with me to kickstart this. He's got some backers interested. Gonna work on getting some housing stuff going and some job training."

I furrow my brow, because an idea sparks. "You ever think about doing some blue collar stuff for that?"

"Yeah, actually."

"I—well, not that it means much right now. But I might—so I don't know. I didn't tell you. But I don't think I'm going to school."

He frowns. "No?"

"I think I'm going into a trade."

His eyes soften. "Is that what you want?"

I say, and I can hear the truth of it in my own voice, feel the relief in my chest, "Yeah. It is."

It's quiet again, silent but for the background noise of the dance behind the gym doors.

"Maybe I could, like, help out with that. Tutoring and stuff. And later . . . yeah, I don't know."

He nods. "Sure. Let's—let's talk about it."

"Okay."

"Okay."

We hesitate there, in the dark, in the vastness of the empty hallway that makes it feel even more intimate. Makes us seem even more alone. I can feel it right now—the question both of us asks. *Is this it?*

I stare at Oliver, at that sharp jaw and laughing, ornery mouth, the little scar just above his lip that I still don't know the story behind.

And dammit.

I want to.

I need to know that story.

I just . . . I can barely even remember what we were so

mad about, and I'm not done with him yet. And I don't think he's done with me.

"Well . . ." he says. He looks down the hall toward the stairs and the gym but hesitates.

I breathe.

I stare at the floor.

And then I say, "I'm not—I'm not ready to stop this."

"Stop what?" he says.

"This. Us. I'm just not ready and I feel like I'm ten seconds away from losing you and *damn*, I'm just not *done*. We can't be done yet, can we?"

His breathing quickens and he takes a step toward me.

"I haven't even been thoroughly corrupted yet!" I say.

He laughs. Loud and echoing and real. "Well shit," he says, pulling me toward hm by the waist. "Wanna do something trashy and make out against the lockers?"

I smile, relief flooding my chest. "It's not that trashy if there's no one around to offend."

"Alright," he says. He runs his fingers over my waist. Tips his head back toward the gym. "So let's go find some people."

CHAPTER TWENTY-EIGHT

SMOKE RISES UP INTO the air, a white cloud against the black sky over Lake Wylie.

I can't believe I'm here again, after hanging out at a party completely wrecked my life for several months just, well . . . several months ago.

But this time, I'm not here on a mission. I'm not here because I want to get back at my family, at my friends, at everyone who ever judged me for being a Riley and made me feel forced into this perfect little box with perfect little grades and perfect little extracurriculars and a perfect little college plan.

I'm here because I'm happy.

I'm here because I don't have everything figured out, but I have enough.

Everything isn't perfect, with a white picket fence, 1.6 kids, and a dog. But I have a plan. And I have friends I care about and a life I care about and a boyfriend I'm absolutely head over heels for.

I'm here because I want to be here. With Oliver.

Music blares—coordinated speakers from a ton of different cars all working in unison. It's something Top 40 because of course it is. I can feel it in my chest, vibrating, and when I lean against Oliver, I think it's vibrating in his, too.

Absalom of the beard is here, too, along with DeAndre and Trey Gallegos.

Absalom catches us standing at the edge of the bonfire and tips his furry chin up. "Anyone want a beer?"

"ABSOLUTELY NOT," I say, and it garners a few laughs. Oliver about spits out his drink.

It is, in fact, a beer.

If I get an MIP from kissing him, I am going to be *pissed*.

I stick with my Cherry Coke, thank you very much.

"Oh heyyyy, babe," says Alisha to my left. Her hand is tangled in the longest, leanest fingers. I follow them up a toned arm to a broad shoulder and then a face that was probably sculpted by the gods. They've got their long, dark hair thrown up in a bun, eyeliner dark around their eyes. They smile, and it's lit in mischief.

"Hey, Brynn," they say. Their voice is smooth as silk.

Jesus, Jistu is an absolute *nightmare*.

My eyes widen and when Jistu turns to yell something over their shoulder at Absalom, I mouth to Alisha, *CON. GRATS*.

She grins and waggles her eyebrows and says, "Engaging in illegal activity again so soon?"

I hold my can up in a toast. "Cherry Coke all day."

She gives me a little golf clap, and Jistu whispers something in her ear.

I swear I see her go a little pink even from here, even in the dark. She says, "Well, you, uh, have a nice Coke." And they wander off, Jistu's hand trailing like water down her back.

I lean harder into Oliver, shadows dancing on my face.

"Well," I say, turning around.

"Well."

"There any abandoned historical structures in those woods?" I say.

"I'm not sure," he says.

"Wanna go find out?"

His hand frames my chin and he kisses me.

"Yeah," he says. "Yeah, I do."

We walk off, looking for history in the trees.

Or something like that.

The End

ABOUT THE AUTHOR

Photo by Taylor Whitrock

BRIANNA R. SHRUM has been writing since she could scrawl letters. She digs all things bookish, geeky, superhero-y, gamer-y, magical, and strange. You can usually find her writing under her Harry Potter tree, and drinking chai (which she holds as proof of magic in the world). She is also the author of *The Liar's Guide to the Night Sky, Kissing Ezra Holtz (And Other Things I Did for Science), How to Make Out, The Art of French Kissing,* and *Never Never.* She lives in a Charlotte suburb in South Carolina with her favorite people.

MORE FROM BRIANNA R. SHRUM
AND SKY PONY PRESS

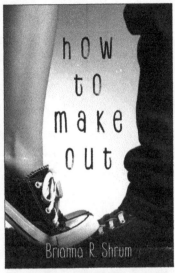

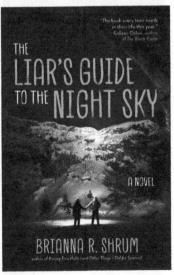